D0457623

THE
HOUSE OF
ONE THOUSAND
EYES

MICHELLE BARKER

annick press
toronto + berkeley

Cover art/design by Emma Dolan
Edited by Lorissa Sengara
Designed by Emma Dolan

A special thank you to Fritz Luehmann for the illustrations of
the Berlin Wall and the maps of Germany and Berlin.

Brief quote from p. 120 from *Stasiland* by Anna Funder. Copyright © 2002 by Anna
Funder. Reprinted by permission of HarperCollins Publishers. (US rights)
Excerpt from *Stasiland* © 2011 by Anna Funder. Published by HarperCollins Publishers
Ltd. All rights reserved. (Canadian rights)

Excerpt from "The Stasi Legacy" from *Berlin Now: The City After the Wall* by Peter
Schneider, translated by Sophie Schlondorff. Translation copyright © 2014 by Sophie
Schlondorff. Reprinted by permission of Farrar, Straus and Giroux.

Annick Press Ltd.

We acknowledge the support of the Canada Council for the Arts and the Ontario Arts Council, and
the participation of the Government of Canada/la participation du gouvernement du Canada for our
publishing activities.

ONTARIO ARTS COUNCIL
CONSEIL DES ARTS DE L'ONTARIO
an Ontario government agency
un organisme du gouvernement de l'Ontario

Cataloging in Publication

Barker, Michelle, 1964-, author
     The house of one thousand eyes / Michelle Barker.

Issued in print and electronic formats.
ISBN 978-1- 77321-071- 1 (hardcover).-- ISBN 978-1- 77321-070- 4
(softcover).-- ISBN 978-1- 77321-072- 8 (PDF).-- ISBN 978-1- 77321-073- 5
(EPUB)
     I. Title.
PS8603.A73557H69 2018   jC813'.6   C2018-901036- 3
                                                     C2018-901037- 1

Published in the U.S.A. by Annick Press (U.S.) Ltd.
Distributed in Canada by University of Toronto Press.
Distributed in the U.S.A. by Publishers Group West.

annickpress.com
michellebarker.ca

Also available as an e-book. Please visit www.annickpress.com/ebooks.html for more details.

For my children
Madeleine, Dallas, Samuel, and Harrison

THE BERLIN WALL

I've been in a place where what was said was not real, and what was real was not allowed, where people disappeared behind doors and were never heard from again, or were smuggled into other realms.

— Anna Funder, *Stasiland*

Where five or six are gathered together, one of them is a Stasi informer.

— Peter Schneider, *Berlin Now: The City After the Wall*

Germany 1983

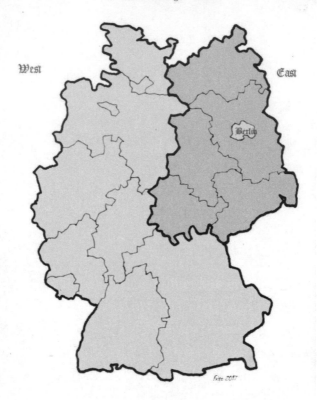

West

East

Berlin

Berlin

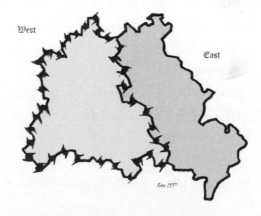

West

East

PREFACE

In 1983, when *The House of One Thousand Eyes* takes place, Germany was divided into two countries: the Federal Republic of Germany, or West Germany, and the German Democratic Republic, also known as the GDR or East Germany. It was the time of the Cold War. After the Second World War, West Germany had become a capitalist democracy, allied with the United States and Western Europe ("the West"); East Germany was a socialist country aligned with the Soviet Union. The city of Berlin was in a unique situation. Although located within the GDR, the city, because of its symbolic importance as the nation's capital, was also divided into eastern and western zones. West Berlin essentially became an island of capitalism in a socialist sea.

While East Germany's formal name was the German *Democratic* Republic, there was no democracy there. The GDR was a totalitarian regime, sometimes a brutal and repressive one, and East Germans tried to leave the country by any means possible. Before 1961, the easiest exit route was within Berlin; from the eastern zone of the city, all you needed to do to enter the West was board a train.

In response, East German authorities built a wall around West Berlin, ostensibly to keep out the "destructive influences" of Western culture and values, but in fact to prevent East Germans from escaping to the West. In the early morning of August 13, 1961, one hundred and sixty kilometers of barbed wire went up in a matter of hours. The Wall grew into an imposing concrete structure complete with watchtowers, dogs, armed guards, and lights so bright they could be seen from space. Families were divided, and people could no longer cross freely between the two zones of the city. East Germans were only permitted to travel to other communist countries.

BERLIN,

GERMAN DEMOCRATIC REPUBLIC

1983

– 1 –

CONTROLLING THE LEAKS

For Lena Altmann, every Sunday felt like the first day of summer vacation after a long, hard year of straight lines and wrong answers. Sunday was the day she made the trip across Berlin to visit her Uncle Erich in the neighborhood of Prenzlauer Berg.

There were many significant Erichs in the Better Germany, but in Lena's life her uncle was the most important one. He was a writer; he knew what it was like to make up places in his head and live in them as if they were real. For the rest of the week, Lena lived with his sister, Sausage Auntie—six days that felt like a year.

Be grateful for Sausage Auntie, Mausi. She gave you a home when you lost yours.

But today was Sunday, and Lena was strolling down an uneven sidewalk with her uncle, trying to control vanilla ice cream on a mid-September afternoon. If she could stay ahead of it, she could keep the runnels of sweet cream from reaching her hands and making them sticky.

Every time Lena visited her uncle's neighborhood, she felt as if she needed a passport. The roads were narrow and full of potholes. The buildings were smaller and older than the ones where she lived, and on the main street where they walked, the walls were only painted to the top of the first story.

"See?" Erich crouched down. "It looks fine from this angle. Volvo level. That's what the dignitaries see from their car windows when they pass in their motorcades." He was frowning.

"It's not true," Lena said. "They just ran out of paint."

"On every building?"

"Your ice cream is melting," she said, and he stuck out his tongue and licked the ice cream right off his hand.

Lena liked his neighborhood because there were trees, and there was something about trees that felt solid and dependable, and a bit wild.

"Have you thought of a name yet for your made-up world?" Erich asked her.

"Yes. The *schrullig* world." Things that were *schrullig* were quirky, strange, outlandish.

Erich's eyes brightened, as if he'd spied a flower coming up through the pavement, or a street sign hanging upside down. Each time the two of them discussed her imaginary world, he would ask questions, and she would think up a new detail. That was how the world grew.

Lena was grateful to talk to her uncle about this. At seventeen, she should have outgrown make-believe—or so said Auntie. There were the doctors at the mental hospital to consider, the ones with pudding voices who used Lena's name over and over when they spoke to her, and gave her "a little something" to calm her down, and told her everything would be all right when it wasn't.

"Tell me about your world," Erich said.

She gave a supervisory lick to the perimeter of her cone. "There's a long row of orange space helmets. Only the important men sit under them, reading their newspapers and waiting for liftoff. But no one has told them which button to press to send them away."

"Into space?" Erich paid such close attention it was as if a pencil in his mind were taking notes.

"Maybe the men go to space," she said. "I don't know. They go away." Space wasn't the important thing. Away was. "And there's an office with big posters of imaginary lands, the kind that belong on a cake." Palm trees, white sand. Impossible places. "If you go into this office and say, 'I want to go to Coconut Island,' the lady will give you a ticket and that's that. You pack your bag and go." That wasn't exactly the truth. The posters were of Rügen Island and Prague, places Germans were allowed to go. Sometimes Lena embellished to make herself feel better.

They arrived at the park, which was busy with couples picnicking, parents chasing little boys who'd just learned to walk and looked like gunslingers from the Wild West, old ladies with stump-ankles dragging small fat dogs behind them. When a couple gave up one of the benches, Erich and Lena sat down.

Erich finished his ice cream and lit a cigarette. "We could travel to the land of icing where the maps are made of chocolate."

"Yes!" Lena loved his imagination. "There's also a bookstore in my world, with the authors you talk about all the time." Her uncle liked to read Günter Grass, Heinrich Böll, Émile Zola—authors whose books were hard to get hold of. "And your books are in there too, Uncle. A row of Erich Altmanns."

"Ah. Nobody buys them." He blew a line of smoke into the air.

"No, silly. They're available, any one you want. I could buy you one of your own books and bring it home."

"Bring it home?" Erich frowned at the scratched wooden bench. "I thought your *schrullig* world was made up."

"It is." But also it wasn't. Lena pushed too hard on the ice cream with her tongue and some of it ran down the side of the cone. That was a mistake. *Things are getting out of control. Your hands will end up sticky.*

She wasn't sure how to explain this aspect of the *schrullig* world to her uncle. She couldn't even explain it to herself without making the wasps in her head come back. *Don't make the wasps come back, Mausi.* If Auntie knew, she'd tell the doctors. No sudden movements. No sharp edges. Auntie said it was important that Lena's life remain tranquil and uncomplicated. If the doctors got involved again, they might not let her out of the hospital.

Auntie saved you. Yes, she did. But the prize was that now she got to live with Auntie so Auntie could straighten her out—for the rest of her life.

"So how do you enter your world, then?" Erich said. "Usually in imaginary worlds there's a portal or a cupboard or something."

"There's a door," Lena said. "But you need to be a member to get in."

"Could I be a member?"

Lena grew serious. "No."

"How about a guest?"

"No," Lena said again. "There are no guests."

"Not even if you accompanied me?"

"Not even then." Lena finally reached the cone. The leaks had been controlled. "There are oranges in my world—all year round, not just at Christmastime, and not the Cuban ones. And there are bananas, as many as you like."

"Now who's being the silly one?" Erich poked her in the arm.

Bananas were a luxury in the Better Germany. In Magdeburg, where Lena had grown up, they'd only been available twice a year. The green Cuban oranges—when they were in stores—were chewy and tough to eat.

"In Narnia there was Turkish delight," Erich said, "but you mustn't eat it because the more you eat, the more you want, and then you can't think of anything except Turkish delight, and you'll never want to leave."

Lena considered that. She wouldn't mind living in her made-up world, but only if she found the button that would send the men and their newspapers away forever. "Have you talked to Auntie yet? About me coming to live with you?"

Erich's cigarette was suddenly the most important thing in the afternoon. He sucked on it. He blew smoke. He studied the orange end burning between his yellowed fingers. "Your aunt Adelheid is very devoted to you."

You're her mission. Auntie believed that Lena was broken and she could fix her. It was another one of those things that was both true and not true at the same time.

Erich always spoke about his sister as if he were handling a sharp knife. "If I push too hard, she won't let you come here on Sundays anymore. She'll think I'm trying to take you away from her."

If only.

They walked, they chatted, and, too quickly, the air grew cooler and it was time to return to Erich's apartment. The afternoon was coming to an end.

Erich lived in one of the old gray buildings that was still pockmarked from the shelling during the Second World War. It wasn't a full-comfort apartment, like Auntie's. There was no central heating, and the bathroom was in the stairwell, used by many other people. Lena climbed the stairs, imagining the building was her home. What would it be like to live there? She would have to share the bathroom with strangers, someone waiting at the door while she tried to poop. *You'd get used to it. You could hum, or bring a magazine. You could make a sign that said "Occupied" so no one would bang on the door.*

Inside, the apartment was cold. The walls were lined with cracks that had blackened over time. There was the houseplant, looking as if it had shrunk since she'd last seen it, one step away from dead. There was Erich's typewriter on a small desk beside the window, because he said writers and windows went together like bratwurst and mustard. Lena sat on a stained armchair and Erich fetched her a Vita Cola. Another Sunday-afternoon treat—Sausage Auntie never bought Vita Cola. Lena took the first sip, letting the bubbles burst inside her mouth and savoring the lemon tang.

She imagined Erich at his desk, a cigarette in one corner of his mouth, eyes squinting at the smoke, dreaming lives out of thin air.

"He's lazy, that's what," Auntie often said about her brother. "Sits around all day in his underclothes and stares out the window."

"He's a writer, Auntie," Lena would reply. "That's what they do."

On the table was a copy of *Der Spiegel* from last year, with a beautiful woman on the cover. Lena stroked the smooth paper as if it were a cat. *Der Spiegel* was a Western magazine. Anyone seen reading it would automatically be suspected of decadence or wrong opinions, and then they might get a card in the mail asking them to meet with the secret police for an instructive chat. The thrill of such disobedience took Lena by surprise. "Who is she? On the cover?"

"That's Marilyn Monroe, an American actress."

Lena opened the magazine, even though part of her worried that Auntie was watching somehow, waiting to take it away from her. She flipped through the pages until she found more pictures of the actress. "She's very glamorous." Such curly hair. Dresses Lena had only seen on Western television, at her friend Danika's house. Red lipstick. Lena was not allowed to wear lipstick because Auntie didn't want anyone to think she worked in a textile factory.

"She's also dead," Erich said. "Suicide—a drug overdose. See?" He flipped back to the magazine cover: *The Immortal Dead.* "It happened over twenty years ago."

Lena stuck her hands into the long front pocket of her sweater to keep them warm. How could it be colder in Erich's apartment than it was outside? Why would a famous actress from America want to kill herself? "Can I keep this?"

"I've already promised it to my next-door neighbor. Anyway, Adelheid would crap her knickers if she caught you with that magazine. Maybe just cut out one picture."

Erich went to fetch scissors, but the blades were so dull they didn't cut.

"*Scheiss Osten,*" Lena muttered. Shitty East. Everyone said that when they couldn't get what they needed or something didn't work the way it was supposed to—everyone except people like Auntie. Lena folded the edges of the picture and licked them. Then she tore, a little at a time.

A loud knock at the door startled her so badly she ripped the picture. Her hands trembled as she shut the magazine and hid it behind her back.

Erich called, "Who is it?" Lena had never heard him sound so cold.

"It's Steffi, for God's sake. Open up."

Steffi was Erich's neighbor from downstairs. Lena tried not to make a face, but she must have, because Erich said, "Don't worry, she won't stay."

He rose to open the door, and Lena prepared herself for a storm of heels and gum-chewing and hands that moved like crazy caged birds. It took a moment before she realized Steffi hadn't crashed into the room in her usual way. Instead, a low and urgent conversation was taking place at the door.

". . . not safe. They're coming. I don't know when."

"I'm not afraid of them," Erich said.

If he's not afraid, why is his voice rising? Why is he rubbing his hands on his pants like they're dirty?

"Then you're a fool." Steffi's voice. "At least protect yourself. We've talked about this."

"Fine, fine. Come in then."

Steffi's angry red boots clipped into the room.

Erich disappeared into his bedroom and Steffi stood there with her short black hair, shorter than Erich's shoulder-length tangles. *No wonder he can't find a respectable job*, Auntie would have said. Steffi looked around until her eyes fixed on Lena and then, "Oh. *You're* here." *Snap snap* went her gum.

Lena forced a smile. She could hear Erich coughing in the other room, a long bout this time, one that would bend him over with a hand to his chest. He had been coughing ever since his work in the mines, though lately it seemed to be worse.

He emerged red-faced and wet-eyed, a stack of brown books in his arms. Lena recognized them as his writing notebooks. Normally he kept them hidden beneath his bed. When he handed them to Steffi, Lena wanted to run over and kick her in the shins.

"What are you doing?" she said to her uncle, but he didn't answer.

Steffi glanced down at her full arms, eyebrows raised in a question.

"Take them to your place," Erich said to her. "But not for long. They'll come looking."

They.

There was only ever one *They*: the State Security Service. That was the Stasi's formal name, but everyone knew them as the secret police. And regardless of what Erich had said at the door, everyone was afraid of them. If you had a subversive thought or wrong opinion, if you made an off-color joke to the wrong person—even something as harmless as saying *Scheiss Osten*—you risked arrest, imprisonment, ruin. The Stasi were experts at destroying lives.

You didn't just think that. Unthink it this instant. Where was the Wall? Not the real Wall—everyone knew where it was. The one in her mind. There, she could see it rising and she hurried to get on the right side. "Everything for the good of the People," as the slogan went. There was an idea at stake, a Better Germany to create.

Naturally, with such a difficult task, there would be casualties.

"I'll leave you," Steffi said. The way she walked in her short red boots made the spindly houseplant lose another leaf. "I'll be back in a *Schni* for the rest of them." She shut the door behind her.

"Take your time," Erich called, winking at Lena—but there was no fun left on his face.

Lena waited for the air to calm. "What if she reads them?" Those notebooks were not meant to be read by anyone. Erich had told her that the one and only time she'd asked.

"She won't," he said.

"She doesn't like me."

"She doesn't like anyone." Erich sat across from her, lit a cigarette, and blew out a stream of smoke. Lena watched his hands. They were strong and square, though the hand holding the cigarette was jittery. He had lost his left pinkie finger in a mining accident. He never spoke of how it had happened, but it must have hurt. She wondered if the missing finger made his typing come out crooked.

"Why is she taking your notebooks?" *Why her, and not me?* "What did she mean by 'not safe'? Are the Stasi coming here? Are you in trouble?"

Erich leaned forward as if to tell Lena something important. She could see him weighing it out, the sides of his face shifting *yes*, *no*, and then he leaned back into *maybe* and said, "I'm just being cautious. I would have given the notebooks to you, but— your job. If anything ever happened and they put pressure on you. You know."

She knew. Lena worked as a night janitor at Stasi headquarters—the place Berliners called the House of One Thousand Eyes.

Working for the Stasi turned real conversations into chitchat about the weather or last year's football results at the World Cup. People didn't treat her the same way once they knew. They acted as if the thousand eyes were pollen, clinging to her hair or dress. Like she was a giant microphone, recording everything and then running back to headquarters with secret information about who was reading the wrong books or receiving packages from Western relatives.

If her parents hadn't died, she would never be working at a job like that. She had dreamed of going on in her education, perhaps to vocational training or extended secondary school. She'd wanted to be a nurse, or to work with children, before things had fallen apart. "I miss Mama and Papa."

"I know you do," Erich said. "I miss them too."

"Nothing's been the same since the accident." The accident at the freight car factory in Magdeburg had killed so many people. The news reporters had given it a name—*tragedy*—but it was like trying to stuff a thunderstorm into a garden shed. There was no word big enough for that kind of sadness. "You want to know a secret?" she said, because all at once she was bursting with it.

"Tell me. Do you have a boyfriend?"

"No, it's nothing like that."

"What about that one you collect bottles with? Didn't he buy you an ice cream once?"

Peter. "He's not my boyfriend." *He wishes he was.* No, he doesn't, Mausi. Stop saying that. "He just lives down the hall." A neighbor, like Steffi, but nicer. "No, it's a secret about my parents."

Erich brushed the hair out of his face, even though it wasn't in his face. His voice changed. "What kind of secret?"

11

"I've always wished they hadn't died in an accident."

"Of course you wish that." Erich let out a long breath. "It's normal."

"That's not what I mean." Lena twisted the bottom of her sweater, embarrassed by what she was about to say. *You've got both feet in the conversation now. You may as well say it out loud.* "I wish it had been someone's fault." A crime with criminals; a mystery with a solution. It made her feel mean to say it, but it would have been so satisfying. Accidents weren't like that. They happened. They were stories that had come to a sudden end for no reason at all, and the people left behind had to find some way to survive.

Erich tapped his cigarette in the already full ashtray, knocking butts onto the table—*Auntie would go wild*—and then rubbing the stump where his pinkie should have been. "Have you told this to anyone else?"

"No. Only you." Lena shifted in her seat. What had she said wrong? Her mind raced, searching for something that might make it better. "Do you remember the *solyanka* Mama used to make whenever you came to visit?" It was Lena's favorite soup.

His shoulders settled. "We used to soak our bread in it until it was mushy."

"It tasted sweet. And sour. Both at the same time. Will I have to live with Auntie forever?" This was the big question. Lena couldn't even look at Erich when she asked it. *I wanted to live with you.*

"One day you'll be old enough to live on your own."

"Auntie says I'm too simple."

"Adelheid doesn't know shit." Erich clapped a hand to his

mouth in pretend horror at the bad word. He took her hands in his. "You're always so cold. See? You couldn't live here with me. We still heat the place with coal and there's never enough."

He stood up and looked out the window as if he were expecting someone. Then sat down. Then stood and drew the curtains. Then sat down. "Did someone tell you to say that? About the accident?"

"No. Why would anyone do that?" Oh. Her job. Not even her uncle trusted her. If only it would wash off. Even having a mechanic's grease-stained fingers would be better than this. Everyone assumed she was a *Spitzel*—an informer. A spy.

The clock in the kitchen measured the moments between them that had somehow become awkward, and there were so few of them left before Lena had to go home for supper. She remembered the magazine behind her back. She pulled it out and finished extracting the photograph, and Erich repaired the rip with sticky tape that didn't stick very well.

"You mustn't show that to your aunt. If she finds out it came from me, she won't let you visit anymore."

"She'll never know." Lena smoothed the picture on her lap, then folded it and tucked it into her front pocket.

Erich glanced at the plant as if it were listening. "Do you still have a set of my keys?"

"Of course."

"Good. My freezer might need defrosting. You never know."

What? Was he going somewhere? Why in the world would he want her to do that? Well. His freezer was a prized possession, probably the most valuable thing in the apartment. Not everyone had a fridge with a freezer; they were expensive, and even if you could afford one, that didn't mean the shops would have any.

Footsteps crunched up the stairs. There was a knock and Steffi said, "It's me again."

Lena reached for her uncle and hugged him goodbye for another week, memorizing his arms and the smell of him— tobacco, vanilla, ink. She held him so tightly she imagined breaking him in half and taking part of him home. And that was it—her daylong summer vacation was over.

Uncle Erich didn't break in half. But the way he waved from the window when she looked up from the street filled her with a strange and terrible feeling. As if she might never see him again.

– 2 –

THE HUMMING-UNDERNEATH SOUND

Lena boarded the S-Bahn and then the U-Bahn, and then she was walking down the much wider, barer streets of the borough of Lichtenberg. Past the partially finished buildings that were forever under construction. Past the hanging-around place, which Auntie said must be avoided, because hooliganism was contagious. Past the first of the huge housing developments that Erich called cardboard mushrooms. "East German concrete is made special," he liked to say. "One-third cement, one-third spit, and one-third microphones."

It was impossible not to feel small on these streets. Someone could reach down and move Toy Lena like a game piece. Finally she came to the cardboard mushroom where she and Auntie lived, and mounted the stairs to the fourth floor.

Two turns of the key and, "How was that layabout brother of mine?" Auntie called from the kitchen.

Though Sausage Auntie came from the same family as Erich and Papa, she was nothing like them. Aunt Adelheid was too much meat stuffed into a tight casing—round sausage legs in tight black stockings, generous bosom straining the black dresses she often wore, her wedding ring that would never come off now, no matter that her husband had been dead for years. The ring must have reminded her of the good old days, which probably meant the time before Lena had come to live with her.

How was Erich? Lena had to be careful how she answered. If he was too fine, Auntie would feel snubbed and jealous, and would fall into one of her tempers, which meant a headache was coming on and Lena would have to stay in her room. If he was not fine enough, there would be comments about his hair (too long), his job (you call that a job?), his friends (subversive), and his clothing (Western, decadent). Everything would be his fault.

"Uncle is good," Lena finally said, lining up her outdoor shoes beneath the *Everything Has Its Place* needlepoint. "We had ice cream in the park." She put on her house shoes and hung up her coat.

Auntie's head popped out of the kitchen. She had short home-permed hair that was always frizzy and made her look like one of the porcelain dogs she liked to collect. "I suppose you're not hungry for supper. The grocer had butter yesterday, so I'm making sandwiches."

Lena glanced to the upper-left-hand corner of the sitting room, above the table that had been dedicated to Auntie's late husband, Helmut. On it was his photograph, a candle, his pipe, and his wedding ring. Helmut had been a high-ranking Party member, which meant Auntie had a good pension and lots of special relationships—including one with the grocer. Any time these relationships came up, Helmut had to be thanked, and so Lena looked up and she looked left.

"I am hungry," she said. "It was only a small ice cream." Even when she wasn't defending Erich, she felt like she was defending him. But also—sandwiches with butter!

Lena entered the kitchen to set the table, and Auntie gave her a businesslike pat on the shoulder. There was no denying she took good care of Lena. Supper at Erich's might have been a bottle of Vita Cola and some pickles, or a trip to the nearby *Kneipe* where he smoked and drank with his friends and they talked about poetry. It would have been exciting, but there was something reassuring about a knife and fork, a glass of milk. Bedtime.

When supper was ready, Auntie switched off the radio and they sat at the table.

"I've decided to involve us in a little project," she said.

"Oh?" No sudden movements. "What sort of project?" And would it be little? Really?

"We're going to beautify the courtyard and win the Golden House Number plaque for our building. Hans made those fine-looking benches, a crying shame if you want my opinion"—as if Lena could say *No, I don't actually want your opinion*. Which she had tried, but only once.

Hans was one of their neighbors, an older man who lived alone and had a talent for carpentry. Auntie always referred to the benches he'd made as a crying shame. At first Lena had thought this was because the courtyard was a swamp and their beauty was wasted. But that was not what Auntie meant. They were a crying shame because Hans did nothing but drink schnapps all day, which meant he wasn't fulfilling his potential. In Auntie's book, not fulfilling your potential was written in big capital letters with the word NO printed next to it in red.

"I'm organizing a work brigade," she added.

Lena didn't have to ask if she was on it.

"You'll start tomorrow, digging a drainage trench. I've already measured it out."

In truth, it would be nice not to have to make her way across the sheets of plywood that had been laid atop stinking mud to get to the other parts of the housing development. It would be nice to have a shady place to sit and read, or chat with Peter and Danika, or play a card game like *Skat* at a table outside. "Can we put tables in the courtyard? And chairs?"

Sausage Auntie gave a meaningful nod. "That's a wonderful idea." She got a pencil and notepad and wrote it down. "We'll drain all the water and set down a path of paving tiles."

Lena didn't dare spoil Auntie's buoyant mood by asking where they might get paving tiles. Usually, getting such materials required putting your name on a waiting list at the building-supply store. Your order might arrive a year or two later, but not necessarily in the style or quantity you'd asked for.

Instead she said, "We should have shrubs. Trees too." Lena loved the trees in Erich's neighborhood, the way they grew in whichever direction they pleased. Trees were subversive.

Auntie wrote down *shrubs and trees.*

"Bird feeders," Lena said.

"A vegetable garden," Auntie added.

Like Mama had had. "So we don't have to eat the mushy turnips from the co-op anymore," Lena said.

Auntie gave her a look and wrote *garden*.

The courtyard idea grew until Lena could imagine trellises and flowers and a great tree in the center that she might climb, where she could balance at the top and gaze down on the rest of the city, the rest of the Better Germany, and then take flight.

But she didn't mention that. *Flight* was a troublesome word.

*

The trick was in going to sleep at night. When you were used to working nights and sleeping days, the sudden switch back to normal on the weekends was almost impossible. It would have been easier not to switch, but staying up all night was not normal, and when there were psychiatrists involved, being normal was of utmost importance.

Besides, there was something the matter with Erich, which meant it was vital for Lena to behave if she wanted to investigate later. She said, "I think I'll go to sleep tonight," and Auntie clapped and said, "Well, well, look who's come to her senses."

Lena washed her face and put on her scratchy gray nightdress.

Auntie gave her a good-night kiss and thanked her for the courtyard ideas. "Tomorrow is Monday," she said. Monday meant there might be better cuts of meat at the butcher's—if Lena went early, if she waited in line with the grandmothers and the men who didn't shave because they were unemployed—*though you never say that, Mausi*, because *unemployed* was not a word. There were several words that weren't words in the Better Germany. If you didn't give something its own word, then it didn't exist.

"I'll get the meat," Lena said. If she stopped at the grocer's afterward, there might be ketchup, or even fruit yogurt. You could never be sure what would be on a grocer's shelves. It was important to be open-minded and always carry a shopping bag.

After Auntie had shut her bedroom door, Lena waited three minutes in case of an emergency re-entry. There wasn't one. Then she sat on her bed so she could look at the pictures on her wall.

Auntie had allowed Lena to put up pictures as long as they were the right sort. Marx, Engels, Lenin—so many beards you could make a nest out of them. Her blue Pioneer neckerchief from the younger youth group was pinned on the wall next to the red one, and next to that was some uplifting art, which meant women playing the accordion and men in big boots with their sleeves rolled up for hard work.

But behind these pictures Lena had pinned others that Sausage Auntie didn't know about. She'd gotten the idea after Erich had described how his novels were always about two things at once.

"There's a surface story," he'd said, "and then another story underneath, humming like a machine." The sort of sound you didn't notice unless someone mentioned it. Even then, it was possible to deny it. "The humming-underneath sound is called subtext," he'd told her. "That's how I can write what I want and still get my novels past the Ministry of Culture."

Behind the picture of Lenin there was a magazine photo of the group of Western musicians named after an insect, the ones that sang the *yeah yeah yeah* music. Hiding under Engels was the Western actor John Travolta, with the *Loch* in his chin like someone had chopped it with an ax. There were her parents: Papa with his salt-and-pepper hair and the funny wide-open-eyes face he liked to make; Mama with her hair cut like a porcupine on top but longer on the bottom, and her almost-mustache, and her swimmer's shoulders. She had nearly gone to the Olympics and had been to a special school for swimming, though she didn't like to talk about it.

The photographs of the Erichs had been Lena's cleverest idea. There were two very important Erichs in the Better Germany. Erich Honecker, the General Secretary in charge of the entire country, with his big square glasses and so many formal titles Lena could put herself to sleep reciting them—that was one. Two was Lena's employer: Comrade General Erich Mielke, head of the Stasi, with his tiny eyes that saw everything. But the photographs of the most important Erich hid behind them both: her uncle. She tapped each of his two photos, good night, good night, remembering how her uncle had held her with strong arms, like Papa's.

"You're my wood nymph," Papa used to say to her. "Green eyes, brown hair, you'd blend right in with the trees." *No, no, don't cry.* She'd cried so much after they had died she didn't think her eyes could produce more tears, yet they always found a way, as if somewhere inside her there was a spring of warm salty water that bubbled up at the worst times.

The accident at the factory had divided her life into before and after. Before, she had lived in Magdeburg with her parents, and had been a good student and was recognized for Enthusiasm in Handicrafts. After, she had fallen apart and been placed in a mental institution. "A nervous breakdown," Auntie had called it. The doctors had other names for it. All she knew was that there were wasps, and they lived in her head.

As Auntie crashed around the apartment in preparation for bed, Lena pulled out her favorite of Erich's books from under the mattress—*Castles Underground*. Auntie refused to buy any of his books and wouldn't allow Lena to read them. She didn't know Erich had given Lena a copy of every single one.

There was his face, looking up at her. And there was that feeling again, like the moment when you know you're going to miss a step going down the stairs. What could be wrong? *It's Steffi, that's all. Who wouldn't be a nervous wreck with her living nearby?* Steffi had panicked about something, and *couldn't you see it, Mausi?* The way she stomped around and chewed her gum, she was probably the type who spent all her time worrying about other people's problems.

The photograph on the book's back cover showed a serious but relaxed man, so handsome. Lena's friends at school—back when there had been school—had always liked coming to Lena's apartment when Uncle Erich was visiting. "The famous writer from Berlin," they called him. He would bring treats, things non-Berliners could never get: hazelnut spread, long-life milk, and a bag of Haribo gummy bears that Lena would share with her friends. They would devour the candy and ask, "What is he writing in that notebook anyway?"

What is he writing in that notebook? At work Lena rarely saw the documents that were locked away in desk drawers, files, and cupboards, but she knew there was paper everywhere, and not just in House 1, the building she cleaned. There were forty-nine houses in the compound, which was a lot of paper, all of it off-limits. Paper could get a person in trouble. When you wrote something down, you gave it life and made it yours. Even if you didn't put your name on it, they could figure it out: the type-writer, your handwriting, where the document was found, who had passed it to whom. A thousand eyes watching was a lot of eyes when a person wanted to do something they weren't supposed to. And that was only the agents. Never mind the informers.

Was Erich in trouble? If he was, it would happen at night, when he was home in bed—caught unaware. That was what he always said.

The apartment was silent. Lena glanced at the clock: nine-thirty. She got up, one noiseless movement at a time. She put on the clothes she'd left folded on a chair: a pair of Shanty jeans Danika wouldn't be caught dead in because they weren't Western, a polyester shirt, and her sweater. *Wait. Wait longer*, because even if Auntie was used to Lena moving around at night, Lena was not under any circumstances supposed to leave the apartment after bedtime by herself—though she often did, to walk.

But she'd promised to go to sleep. Things would be much worse if she was caught lying. Auntie would sit very still and fix Lena with those dark eyes above her reading glasses. "I believe my pig is whistling," she'd say, which meant whatever story Lena had concocted, it hadn't worked.

Lena made herself count to one hundred, then she put on her coat. What was lucky was that her bedroom was the one closer to the front door, so she didn't have to pass Auntie's room on the way out. What was less lucky was the noise of the front door lock when she turned it. Lena turned it slowly—once, twice—opened the door, and stepped out into the hallway.

And there she found something even less lucky than the lock: her neighbor Peter, probably coming home from an amateur radio meeting. Scabby Peter, Danika called him, because he had eczema on his arms. Lena wished she'd thought to take out the kitchen scraps. At least then she'd have a reason for being in the hall. But Auntie would have noticed they were gone. *I felt like taking out the kitchen scraps in the middle of the night* was just the type of story that would start the pig whistling.

"You're sneaking out." At least Peter had the decency to keep his voice down. "Where are you going?"

"Nowhere." Lena thought quickly. "We've run out of milk. I'm going to borrow some."

"At this hour?" Peter was tall, and walked like he was made of the wrong pieces put together at the last minute to meet a deadline. "We might have some at home. Do you want it?"

Lena wasn't sure what to say. If she borrowed the milk, Auntie would ask questions.

"Peter, are you coming?" a man's voice called from down the hall. It was his father.

Lena felt a pang of jealousy. No man except Erich ever used her name anymore. Not even the men in House 1—they called her Fräulein. None of them seemed to know her name, not even Herr Dreck. But the anxious look on Peter's face doused that feeling. "Are you in trouble?" she whispered.

He scratched his arm but didn't answer. With his military father he was liable to be in trouble just for breathing.

She glanced at her door. "Please don't tell your parents you've seen me."

"I won't."

Peter hurried down the hall, his shoulders hunching as he got closer to home. Military Papa with all his medals and the thrown-together son: in a flash Lena knew their suppers were silent, and they did not sit together afterward on the couch discussing man things like football or mathematics, and even though Peter had feet as big as his father's he would never fit into those tight black boots.

Lena tiptoed down the hall into the stairwell and then into the darkness, where the nighttime gathered and settled her. All the hectic daytime sounds were gone, as if darkness were a hood pulled over the world. For a long time, she listened to the sounds inside her body—river of air through her lungs, river of blood pulsing from top to bottom and back again.

Was that how she ended up back in Prenzlauer Berg? By not paying attention? Sometimes feet did that—her feet, anyway. Led her onto trains that took her places before she'd fully thought out the consequences and then, surprise, there was Erich's window and the lights were off. Obviously, because he was still out with his friends; it wasn't even ten-thirty yet.

Lena stood with her back flattened against the building across the street, one hand tracing a shell hole. She looked up. The lights were off, but the curtains were open. The lights were off, but when Lena looked hard, and harder, she could see a shadow moving around inside. And then on the street someone coughed, and she nearly jumped out of her shoes.

That was when she realized the dark street, which had seemed empty and sleeping, was neither. The cough came from a man standing in the doorway of Erich's building. There was a flowershop van parked in front and a man sitting at the wheel as if he planned to make an urgent delivery of roses. Eyes. Everywhere, eyes. Lena made herself small, pressing as hard as she could into the wall and wishing she'd thought to hide herself better.

In Erich's apartment, a window opened, and a man made a

signal, but the man was not Erich. He had a bushy beard, and he had the wrong hair to be one of Erich's friends. The flower-delivery man started the van and drove away.

Another van pulled up, and more men entered the building—where had they gotten the key? The front door was locked every night at ten p.m. Now they were coming out with Erich's things: his typewriter, his books, a suitcase, what was happening, where was Erich, what would he think when he came home and all his important things were missing?

Another suitcase, and then came the notebooks. The men must have found them at Steffi's apartment. Was she in trouble too? Lena wanted to run out and stop them, but she couldn't do that. You didn't get in the way of men like this or you ended up in the blank space on the map. Erich said the blank space was really the Stasi prison, and that terrible things happened there, but how could it be? Weren't spaces left blank on city maps because nothing was there?

What had he done?

All his notebooks. The Stasi men would sit with their cigars and beer steins, and read the notebooks out loud to one another, and laugh. What if they didn't give them back? The men gathered in the doorway of Erich's building, three of them, speaking in voices too low for Lena to overhear. Two got into the van and drove away. One got into a Lada, and didn't. He rolled down the window, lit a cigarette, took out a newspaper, and sat there.

Find Erich and warn him about what's waiting for him when he comes home. That was the most important thing. He must be at the pub. Lena edged away from the man in the Lada. He wouldn't notice her anyway, she was just a girl. No one ever noticed her, which sometimes made her sad, but there were advantages. Except Auntie. Auntie had eyes all over her head when it came to Lena.

The pub was on another street a few blocks away. A dark, run-down place that smelled of beer, tobacco, and underarms, it stayed open until the last people left, which was often Erich and his friends. Lena braced herself before opening the door. There was the barman with his fat face and pinched pretend-smile.

"We don't serve warm milk here, Fräulein," he said. A glance at some of the patrons sitting on tall wooden stools, yes, that was very clever, there were the deep man-chuckles designed to shrink Lena down to mouse-size.

"I'm Erich Altmann's niece." Erich had introduced her once, but Lena knew the barman wouldn't remember her, on purpose. "Is he here?"

"Haven't seen him." The barman wiped a glass with a grimy towel and Lena was grateful she wouldn't be drinking out of it. He pointed into a dark corner. "His friends are back there, if you'd like to go keep an eye on them."

Don't let him bother you, Mausi, but her body didn't listen. Heat rushed to Lena's face as she moved toward the back of the pub, and the chuckles receded. There was dark brown wainscoting halfway up the walls, and plastic flowers on each table, and candles that Erich said were for atmosphere. Four of his friends were gathered around a dimly lit table, a haze of bluish smoke above their heads. *Assis,* Auntie would have called them, anti-socials, the sort who drank in the workplace and brought down morale.

Lena had to stand beside the table for a whole minute listening to them argue about a line of poetry before they spoke to her.

"Do you want something, little girl?" one said. He had layabout hair, like Erich.

One of his friends punched him in the arm. "That's Erich's niece. The one who works at . . ."

Lena gazed at her shoes. She hated that this was the first thing anyone said about her, the only thing they associated her with. Not Lena who loved to swim when the pool wasn't closed for repairs, or Lena who was learning photography. Instead, it was Lena who couldn't be trusted.

"I'm looking for my uncle." She searched each face, and each one closed like a box, first the forehead, then the cheeks, then the chin. "Please. It's important." How much could she say? Yes, these were Erich's friends, but she didn't know them, and she wasn't sure how well Erich knew them either. People could surprise you with their secrets—the ones they kept, and the ones they didn't.

One of them gave a head shake that Lena wasn't supposed to have noticed. "He's not here."

Lena could see that for herself. "Do you know where he is?"

"How about at home. Sleeping." That one had a thin face, like a sparrow.

They don't know. They couldn't know what was happening at Erich's apartment if they thought he was home asleep—if that was what they actually thought. The head shake had meant *Don't tell her anything.* When it came to opinions, there were personal ones, and public ones. Only a fool would say how they really felt about something to strangers.

"I've been to the apartment. He's not there. Could there be somewhere else?" The faces around her were blank. "Please."

They turned back to their conversation as if she had

disappeared. All she could do was leave the pub, but at least she could do it without looking at the barman.

For a while she walked. Walking was the best way to figure out what to do next. She ended up back at Erich's apartment, where the man was still in his car reading his newspaper as if this were the most normal thing to do in the middle of the night. If Lena had done that, Auntie would have called the doctors. The window of Erich's apartment was still dark. The man who'd made the signal had left it open, and one of the curtains blew in and out, waving goodbye.

She wanted to wait a while longer, but her feet had already decided: *Go home, Erich is not coming back tonight.* She wasn't sure how she knew that, but she did. Besides, if she didn't leave soon, she'd miss the last trains home. She would return tomorrow, as soon as she could get away. Erich couldn't hide forever; he'd have to go home eventually. His bed was there, and his favorite plate with the schnauzer on it, and his mountain posters because Erich loved to ramble.

That was it. Maybe he'd gone on a ramble and hadn't told anyone.

She decided to believe in that story as she took the trains home. She believed in it while she walked along the wide street, past the cardboard mushrooms that Erich said would melt if it rained hard enough. She believed in it as she reached Auntie's building and took the stairs up to the fourth floor. Slowly, slowly, she turned the noisy lock once, twice, and let herself in, creeping to her bedroom.

The night had worn down her wide-awake edges and she barely had the energy to put on her nightdress before falling fast asleep, forgetting that Monday was meat day and there was going to be a line-up, and she was supposed to be in it. Before she knew it, there was Auntie, standing at the door saying, "I suppose you've already been to the butcher's then."

"Yes, Auntie." Lena's head felt full of wool.

"And the meat? Did they have pork loin? Is it in the fridge?"

Wake up. Where is the meat? "They ran out."

"What's that sound?"

Lena screwed up her face, trying to listen. "Is it the baby next door?" If there was a sound, it was almost always the baby next door.

"No," Auntie said. "It's a pig. And it's whistling."

− 3 −

A HEADACHE CALLED LENA

Auntie wasn't happy about the lack of meat, and her not being happy was like the brown coal dust that had hung in the air in Magdeburg. It covered everything. Get out of bed was *Why didn't you get the pork loin?* Make sure you tidy up while I'm at work was *You were supposed to get the pork loin.* Get to your photography class on time this afternoon was *Every other girl who gets sent to line up for pork loin comes home with pork loin.*

Let Auntie be angry. It meant she had no idea where Lena had been last night.

Anyway, Lena was choking on her own coal dust. *Warn Erich. Warn Erich.* What if he came home while the man in the Lada was watching? What if he went upstairs and saw they'd taken everything he cared about? The typewriter, those suitcases—Lena didn't even know what had been in them. And wait till Steffi told him what had happened to the notebooks.

If he came home, they would arrest him. Erich and his friends had said terrible things about the interrogations. "Hohenschönhausen," they would whisper—that was the name of the prison. The blank space on the map. The secret police would lead you into a little office and make you sit on a milking stool. One man would yell, and the next would give you coffee and a cigarette and make you think it would all be okay. Meanwhile you hadn't slept in days. Meanwhile you were sweating onto fabric that would be stored in a jar with your name on it, so the dogs could find you if you ran.

"Is there something the matter with the porridge?"

Auntie's question startled Lena. "No, I just forgot about it." She picked up her spoon and forced down a mouthful.

"She forgets her breakfast. I don't know. I really don't."

Straighten up. Normal people didn't forget their breakfast when it was sitting right in front of them. *You don't want Auntie to put that in her progress report.* Anyway, Auntie would leave for work soon, and Lena would have the whole day to herself until she had to go to headquarters that evening. There would be plenty of time to find her uncle and warn him.

"I've arranged for the work brigade in the courtyard today," Auntie said as she peeled an egg. "Peter will be there, and that loafer Hans, and Danika. They'll be expecting you."

Monday was the best day for a work brigade. Peter didn't start work at the automobile factory until late on Mondays, and Danika, through some quirk of her employer, had Mondays off. No one really knew what Hans did; he was always available.

So much for having the whole day to herself. Lena's head was getting that stuffed noisy feeling that came from sleeping at the wrong time—and nowhere near long enough. Erich was stuffed in there too, and Sausage Auntie. If only her parents—

"Can you make *solyanka* for supper?" Lena asked. A bowl of sweet-and-sour soup was almost as good as a blanket.

Auntie gave her one of those looks that stopped the clock from ticking. "Oh, I see. My sister-in-law's dish. This is what comes of visiting your uncle. Do I look like I'm made of meat?"

"Yes." The word was out before Lena realized she'd said it.

Auntie stood up in a clatter, her face blooming red, hands clenched as if she could unzip her body and step right out of it.

"Sorry, Auntie. I didn't mean it."

Sausage hands rested on sausage hips. "I'll give you *solyanka* in the eye if you're not careful." Auntie didn't like it when Lena mentioned her parents because it meant Lena wasn't happy, which meant she wasn't grateful for everything Auntie had done for her.

Lena rose and washed her dishes in the sink, while Auntie finished getting ready for work. "They'll be starting downstairs soon, so you'd best get your work clothes on," she said.

Lena was washing her face when Auntie called her into the sitting room. She wore her navy-blue no-nonsense teaching dress, which was buttoned and belted and stiff. It was the same dress that was in the photograph on the sitting room wall from the day Auntie had become a Party member. In the photograph she stood starched into place with an armful of red carnations and her Party membership book, looking proud and serious and ready to talk about the glorious mining industry or her achievements in the collection of wastepaper.

She pushed her glasses down her nose to study Lena over top of them. When she bent forward like that it showed all her wrinkles and made her look dangerous, like she might ram Lena with her head if Lena said the wrong thing. Wouldn't she be happier with that ring off? It cut so deeply into her finger.

"It's not just your smart mouth, you know." Auntie patted the sofa, which meant there would be confidences and important lessons, and Lena must sit next to her and listen hard. "Your parents' accident happened three years ago. It's time to move on." She put an arm around Lena's shoulders and squeezed. "You can't spend your life asking for extra sausage because you're an orphan."

"No, Auntie, I wouldn't dream of it." *There's never extra. You eat it all.*

"You know how important it is to show improvement, don't you?"

Lena knew. She'd been released from the hospital only because Auntie had promised to give the doctors periodic reports on Lena's progress from one hundred pieces back to one.

"Well, then. Let's overcome our inner pig-dog and start fresh." Auntie leaned forward and squeezed the bridge of her nose, which meant a headache was coming on—a headache called pork loin, or *solyanka*, or *why not make it easy, Mausi*; it was a headache called Lena.

Auntie stood up, gave Lena a military kiss on the cheek, and told her to be good, and not shirk her duty in the courtyard, and not forget the tidying up. *I will, Auntie. I won't, Auntie. I will. I mean, I won't.* And then Auntie left for work.

Lena picked up the telephone, then put it down again. If only she could call Erich and warn him. It was fun to have a telephone, but it would have been even more fun if other people she knew had one as well. Telephones only came to those who waited. Erich didn't have one.

She put on coveralls and boots and a pair of gardening gloves and trudged down to the courtyard. At that hour, the yard was still cool and dark. Once winter set in, the sun would never get high enough to brighten it. You could stand in the middle and it would be building, building, building, rain—and then snow. September had already been wet enough that the plywood path was beginning to sink. The courtyard had that fusty mushroom smell that would only get worse once the autumn rain really started.

Auntie had marked out the place for the trench with sticks and string. Peter was there, pacing: three steps north, three steps south. When he spotted Lena, he paced his way over to her. "Where did you go last night? Did your aunt wake up? Did you get in trouble?"

He handed her a shovel. Lena glanced at his fingernails. Auntie would never have let Lena leave the apartment with such long fingernails; she'd use the fabric scissors if she had to. Hadn't Peter's mother noticed?

"I went out," Lena said.

"Out where?"

Lena put her head down and stuck the shovel into the mud. "Where are we supposed to put all the dirt?"

"Into the wheelbarrow," Peter said. "Out where?" He leaned on his shovel, waiting for an answer.

"I needed some air." It was hard to be mean to Peter. For one thing, he was scabby and he had a father who ordered him around and thought he was a big disappointment, and that made Lena sad. But also, Lena didn't have any true friends besides Erich, and he didn't count because he was her uncle. There was a girl in her photography class, but she didn't know where Lena worked yet. As soon as she found out, it would be Party this and productivity that, a friendship like a train station where everything was predictable and on time.

Peter and Danika were neighbor friends, which was like having cousins. You didn't choose them; you ended up with them. But as things went, Peter and Danika were good neighbor friends. Except lately Peter had been acting strangely: standing too close, looking at her for too long—making cow eyes, Danika called it.

Lena deposited a shovelful of mud into the wheelbarrow. "Sometimes I need to—get some air." Her arms were already tired. "You know."

Peter gave a sad smile that made Lena forget his fingernails. "I do. There's never enough air in our apartment. Father uses it all."

Lena was startled by his candor. Peter had no reason to trust her. She could easily mention his disrespect to Auntie, who would feel obliged as the Guardian of a Difficult Child to report such insubordination to his father. And then what? Lena had a feeling Military Papa was the sort of father who took off his belt, while Frau Military Papa hid in the other room with the radio on.

Peter seemed like he was waiting for Lena to say something. Her neck prickled. *How can you tell him where you went? How do you know you can trust him?*

She didn't know. So she said, "Hi, Danika," because there she was, making her dainty way across the plywood path.

"Here comes the little fashion model," Peter muttered. "How's she going to dig dressed like that?"

Danika looked very chic in her knitwear, and she wore shoes with a heel. Though she was apprenticed to a dressmaker, she dreamed of being a model, despite her short legs and square chin. Whenever Lena came over, Danika would pull out stacks of *Pramo* and *Sibylle* magazines and talk for hours about clothes and makeup.

"Are you going to be our supervisor?" Peter asked her.

"Shut up. My mother made me come. Damned if I know why."

"Maybe because you live here like the rest of us," Peter said, "and walking across this swamp every day will ruin your Western shoes." He ran a hand through his short hair and took a step closer to Lena.

He was doing it again—making himself and Lena into a team. Teams made Lena nervous, even though Auntie said that was antisocial and not good for morale.

"You're on Comrade Mielke's team, aren't you?" Auntie had said once when Lena had expressed her opinion about teamwork.

"What do you mean?" Lena had thought Auntie was talking about Comrade Mielke's football team, the BFC Dynamo. It was considered the Stasi team. The BFC Dynamo won most of their games, because who wanted to be the player to score the winning goal against the secret police?

"You work for him," Auntie had said.

Lena wrinkled her nose. Because she worked at night, she rarely saw Comrade Mielke at headquarters. She wasn't the one who had to prepare his breakfast according to the diagram. His personal secretary, Frau Drasdo, did that. Two eggs, four and a half minutes exactly, placed here. Bread on a separate plate, placed there. Napkin on the left. Knife on the right. Salt just above. Frau Drasdo couldn't have needed the diagram after all these years, but maybe she wanted to check every morning to be sure she didn't get it wrong. Comrade Mielke's temper was legendary when things didn't go according to plan.

"I work with Jutta," she'd said.

"On a team," Auntie said. "You and Jutta are a team, you see?"

"No, we're not. All she does is smoke and talk about being Slavic."

But then Auntie had gotten quiet. "You should report her."

That had been the end of that conversation.

"We're going to dig this trench together." Peter stuck his shovel into the mud. His grunt said the mud was heavier than he'd expected, but he tried to make it into nothing by the way he tossed it into the barrow.

"That's it, Peter!" Hans arrived carrying a mug of coffee—probably mixed with schnapps. His salt-and-pepper hair reminded Lena of her father. But then Hans lost his balance on the plywood and stepped right into the mud with his short black boots. *"Scheisse."*

Lena put her head down and got started. One shovelful. Two. It wasn't a job you could merely pretend to do. Auntie would know at a glance that the courtyard hadn't been beautified. The day stretched out before her, interminable and hard, and she had to work that night. She wasn't sure she would get through it. But then—

The portal was right there. One step, and in her mind she was in the bookstore of the *schrullig* world, where the spines of books were lined up in perfect rows like teeth.

When Erich's first book had been published, he'd told her the book dealers had ordered ten thousand copies for their shops.

"Where will they put them all?"

He had laughed. "They order ten thousand to ensure they'll receive ten."

Thirteen shovelfuls. Fourteen.

In the *schrullig* world, if you ordered ten thousand copies of a book, you would receive ten thousand copies. What Lena liked most about the bookstore was the smell. New books smelled like shoes that hadn't gone anywhere yet. Lena imagined standing in the center of the room and breathing it in, and in, and in. A person could keep inhaling until their lungs were so full they were ready to burst.

"Why are you breathing funny?" Danika's question almost made Lena drop her shovel. "What are you doing?"

Twenty-one shovelfuls. "Nothing."

Books were Erich's favorite thing in the world. Lena longed to take him to the *schrullig* bookstore and let him stand in the middle of the shop with her and breathe. He would fall to his knees and start to cry. *That isn't good, Mausi.* When men cried, it was like the world had put its pants on backward. The silent hiccup of shoulders, the bent head. She'd seen her father do it once when he hadn't known she was watching.

"God, this is boring." Danika set down the shovel and plunked herself on the bench. After digging in her pockets for a nail file—which she never left home without—she began filing her nails. She had explained to Lena that you needed to be ready at all times in case your One True Love walked past. Even if you didn't have a One True Love yet. Especially if you didn't. It could be anybody.

Hans stood on his sheet of plywood as if he were the captain of a sinking ship and lit a cigarette. "My friend suggested we write to the General Secretary. 'Write to Erich,' he said, 'and tell him what's going on in this courtyard. He'll do something for you.'"

Erich Honecker, the leader of the country—as if he had nothing better to do than read letters from disgruntled citizens.

Twenty-five.

In her mind, Lena left the bookstore and wandered over to the orange space helmets. She sat down and tucked her head under the bubble-shaped hair dryer, wondering what would happen next. The men never traveled anywhere when they sat under the orange domes. They just smoked and read their newspapers. But Lena would go somewhere. There were buttons on the chair arms. You had to know which ones to press.

Thirty shovelfuls. Forty.

Hans disappeared.

Fifty.

He returned with sandwiches and beer. They all sat on the crying-shame benches he'd built, though Lena wasn't sure who should be crying. Hans seemed happy to her, if a bit crooked, not at all upset that he was drinking his life away and would not fulfill his potential.

The sandwiches were made with salami and crusty bread. Lena hadn't realized how hungry she was. She took bites that were too big for her mouth and then struggled to chew them without pieces sticking out.

Danika wouldn't eat hers because "I'm watching my figure." She put up one finger to Lena. It was their sign: One True Love. The point being it was harder to get a One True Love if you were lumpy.

"I think we've done enough digging for the day, don't you?" Peter said to the group.

Lena's hopes bobbed, then sank. "Auntie won't think so."

"Hang Adelheid." Hans blew out an aggressive stream of cigarette smoke. "I'll tell her how hard you all worked. Go out and have some fun."

Peter bent toward Lena in a way that meant a suggestion was coming—to go to the cinema, or play with his amateur radio.

Danika said, "*Hits for Fans* is on this afternoon." It was her favorite show on the West Berlin radio station.

Lena mumbled something about being busy. She thrust the shovel at Peter (*ignore his no-more-ice-cream face*), thanked Hans for the sandwich, said goodbye to Danika, and ran upstairs.

Boots off. Gloves. Coveralls. Erich. Jeans on, the ones that were almost Levi's but not quite, because Levi's were the mark of the Western devil and Auntie said the GDR version was far superior. Erich. Sweater on, because the weather was cooling down. Zehas laced up, because running shoes would come in handy in case she had to make a run for it. Erich. *Go. Go!*

Stop.

The lock on the door clicked twice. Auntie was home early from school. She walked in and took off her shoes in a painful way, as if her feet had been stuffed in as tight as possible. Her face had that pasty headache look to it. "Where are you off to?" she asked. "It's not time for your photography class yet, is it?"

"Nowhere," Lena mumbled.

"Nowhere? With your outdoor shoes on in the house? Is this what happens when I leave you in charge?"

"No, Auntie. I was just—" *What were you just? Were you just going to visit Auntie's layabout brother on a Monday afternoon?* He was in trouble. If only Lena could tell Auntie what she'd seen— *in the middle of the night, halfway across the city, when you were supposed to be in bed?* "I was just going to take out the trash." She went to get the trash can. "I'm tidying up, like you asked."

Auntie looked like she wanted to mention the whistling pig but couldn't think how, and then the baby next door started crying, and Auntie winced, and Lena said, "I'll make you some peppermint tea when I get back." *And a cold compress, and a pillow for your feet, because we know where this is headed.* Swollen ankles, an afternoon at home, and no way to let Erich know he was in danger.

- 4 -

HERR DRECK

Lena often wondered what Auntie did on weeknights while she was at work. Maybe something secret and forbidden involving Western game shows, because surely even Auntie broke the rules sometimes; she had to, or she wouldn't be human. *She might not be human.* Anyway, as a teacher she was expected to lead by example and watched only the Better Germany's television shows—which meant two channels, the ones in line with Party policy.

Certain people might have considered Auntie's collection of porcelain dogs to be decadent and rebellious. But there was something wrong with Auntie's dogs. Their eyes were deranged. Meissen reserved its best-quality porcelain for export, and the Better Germany only got the rejects. These dogs looked like they belonged in the mental hospital.

The only thing Lena could be sure of was that after the Monday-evening film, Auntie watched the political propaganda show known as the Black Channel—Karl-Eduard von Schnitzler's big eyes widening behind big glasses as he ripped apart Western television shows. Filth. Junk. Stupidity.

Erich and his friends made fun of Muck-Raker Eddy, as they called him. "I'll be there in a *Schni*," they would say, which meant fast, because *Schni* was exactly how much of Schnitzler's name you would hear before someone changed the channel. Lena was certain if she hadn't worked on Monday nights she would have been required to sit through the Black Channel with Auntie. Auntie's control of the television was total. No *Kojak* or *Bonanza* or *The Love Boat*, like at Danika's place. It was like living in the Valley of the Clueless, the corner of the Better Germany where they couldn't get Western signals.

Auntie's headache had meant no photography class for Lena. Instead, Lena had gone to the pharmacy, and prepared supper, and practiced walking around the apartment without letting her heels slam onto the floor. By the time she was getting ready for work, Auntie's headache was cured. A polka played on the radio while Auntie sat on the sofa doing needlepoint. She liked to make pillows and wall-hangings with important messages on them. *Be Happy and Sing. Learn, Learn, and Learn Again.* Lena said "Goodbye" out loud and *Have fun with Muck-Raker Eddy* in her head, and then she left for work.

The security compound on Normannenstrasse took up one square kilometer and was only a fifteen-minute walk from Auntie's apartment. Lena was lucky to have this job. Sausage Auntie said the Stasi would not have sought Lena out if it hadn't been for her late husband, Helmut (*look up, look left*). Lena should be grateful. Other girls her age worked in textile factories, and bleached their hair, and got pregnant. There were also the mines, for people like her uncle, who had chosen to spend his eighteen months of military service as a construction soldier—which had meant building military structures and then afterward not being able to find a job.

"The mines were supposed to smarten me up," Erich had told Lena, "though, *shhh*, I'm no smarter now than before."

How could Lena smarten up if she was simple? People acted like being simple was the worst thing. But everyone was simple in some way, even though they pretended they weren't, dressing up the simple bits with big words and Western shoes. Only three things were really important, anyway: to keep your head down, keep your mouth shut, and learn to like cabbage.

The sun was setting while Lena walked. It was difficult, moving in the direction of Stasi headquarters when her feet wanted to take her back to her uncle's place. *Be patient.* Not showing up for work would be unthinkable.

Lights had come on in many of the apartments, most of which looked the same: brown and stuffy, fake-wood-paneled and linoleum-floored, with flashes of orange. But the lives going on inside them—anything could be happening. Arguments, marriage proposals. Someone could be falling in love in one of those rooms right now.

"Good morning," the security guard, Ernst, called to her when she arrived at the compound gates. It was their joke: good morning at nighttime. Ernst tipped the end of his rifle toward her and she waved at him. He was tall and skinny and had the longest arms Lena had ever seen. Asparagus Tarzan, Danika would have called him. They must have made his uniform sleeves special so the cuffs would cover his wrists.

Ernst knew her, so he didn't ask for her identity card. She crossed the grounds to House 24, a building in the compound that dealt with things like repairs, and where she and her partner, Jutta, kept their supplies and had coffee. The small coffee room usually smelled like an ashtray; when Lena walked in, Jutta was already sitting at the card table smoking. Jutta wasn't really a partner; she was more like a teammate, the way Auntie envisioned it—except Jutta was the captain and there was only one player on the team: Lena.

Jutta was around the same age as Auntie, though maybe older; it was hard to tell with her bleached hair. She had one hand wrapped around a mug of KaffeeMix and an overflowing ashtray at her side. A copy of *Sibylle* sat beside her, opened to a picture of three fashionable women in winter coats. Lena loved the smooth magazine pages, those smooth clothes, smooth lives.

Jutta looked up. "How was your weekend? Did you visit your uncle yesterday?"

She never failed to ask about Lena's days off and her visit with Uncle Erich. It was nice that she remembered. "Of course I did," Lena said, trying hard to keep the undertow of fear from pulling her down.

"What did you do with him? Anything special?"

"We had ice cream. We went for a walk." *Some men came in the middle of the night and emptied his apartment. I don't know if he knows. I don't know where he is.*

"So? Is he working on anything new?" Jutta asked. "A big bestseller?"

Is he? What was he writing in those notebooks? "I don't know. He didn't tell me."

Jutta looked as if she expected Lena to say more, but Lena

tightened her smile and the room fell silent but for Jutta's sips of pretend-coffee.

"I'm not even German," Jutta said. "Have I told you that?"

Only about ten thousand times. "Really?" Lena hung up her sweater.

"The SS kidnapped me right off my parents' farm when I was a little girl, because of my blond hair and blue eyes. I had the Aryan look. I was a great beauty, you know."

"I know." Lena tried hard to pick out the beautiful bits from Jutta's dishwater eyes and wild hair that was barely contained by a kerchief. It was like trying to pick the last blackberries of the season, the ones hidden at the back of the bush, without getting scratched by thorns.

Jutta stubbed out her cigarette and got to her feet, making it seem like the worst punishment in the world. "All I can say is that we don't really know anyone. And we sure as hell don't know where we come from. None of us." Jutta kept conversations the way other people kept canned beans and peaches, jars and jars of the same thing on the shelf. *I think I'll open a jar of we don't really know where we come from tonight. But Jutta, we had that last night. Yes, but it's so tasty, don't you think?*

"I know exactly where I come from." Lena pulled on her work coveralls. "I'm from Magdeburg." Where everything was brown because of the coal—the sky, the shops, the laundry hanging to dry. "I went to school there. One year I won an award for Enthusiasm in Handicrafts. I had a Western fountain pen." Erich had gotten it for her so she didn't have to struggle with the GDR version. *Scheiss Osten.* Her teacher had frowned at it, but Lena hadn't been the only one with a Western pen.

"I have photographs of my parents," she added. "I know them." Knew. A twinge. She gave her head a shake.

They gathered mops and buckets, their Purimixes, rags, and cleaning solutions, and then walked over to House 1, which was only a minute away.

Auntie had been so proud when Lena told her she used a Purimix at the Stasi headquarters. "Imagine," Auntie had said. "You could grind coffee with it. Or meat. Or chop vegetables." Which was true, if you had the right attachments. But their Purimixes only had the ones for vacuuming and waxing floors.

They crossed the foyer of House 1, with its three red flags— the flag of the Better Germany, the flag of the Labor Movement (*that means you, Mausi, stand proud*), and "the Party is always right" flag of honor. Past the sculptures of *Good morning, Herr Marx, good morning, Herr Dzerzhinsky, you're looking very solid this morning/evening.*

Jutta stepped into one of the elevators, but Lena took the stairs. Even though it would have been infinitely easier, she refused to take the narrow brown elevators. Even though it meant making two trips with all her equipment. She didn't care. The elevators made her feel closed in, the way she'd felt when the principal of the school had called her out of class to tell her about the explosion. Everything grew too dark and cluttered—the way her head got when there was too much noise.

She set down her Purimix at one end of the long stuffy hallway. Jutta had a plan for cleaning the building that Lena had to follow. Hallways were vacuumed every night, as were Comrade Mielke's rooms, and the main foyer was mopped. Individual offices were dusted or vacuumed or swept, depending on the day. Jutta had her floors; Lena had hers. Except for the third floor, Comrade Mielke's, which they cleaned together for security reasons.

Halfway down the hall on Lena's floor, a door was ajar and a sliver of light crossed the corridor. Herr Dreck was working late—again. That wasn't his real name, of course, but Lena preferred it. *Dreck* meant filth.

Everyone who worked at Stasi headquarters had a military title—even Lena, who was a Junior Sergeant—but she refused to call Herr Dreck by his. She felt dirty just thinking about him. Her legs suddenly felt too heavy. She couldn't walk down the hall. She couldn't pass that sliver of light, and yet—there was no choice, even if it seemed like there was.

She started the Purimix and began vacuuming the red carpet. *Such an impractical choice of color*, Jutta was always saying. Red showed every stain and footprint. But red carpets were for dignitaries and special people, and House 1 was where some of the highest-ranking men in the Stasi worked.

She wished the vacuum didn't make so much noise. He would know she was there. But he already did—he was waiting for her.

Sure enough: "Is that you, Fräulein? Come in, come in." He made it sound like the visit was her idea.

It was strictly forbidden for her to enter the bureaucrats' offices while they were working. "You are to be silent. Invisible." Jutta had explained the rules for cleaning House 1 on the first day, and she reminded Lena of them often.

Lena stepped into Herr Dreck's office.

"I have a treat for you." That was how it began every time. "Shut the door." He beckoned Lena to where he sat behind his large wooden desk. Her knees shook beneath her coveralls.

The heavy curtains were drawn. The filing cabinets and drawers were closed. No one could see. No one would tell. Lena barely heard her own footsteps on the carpet, though she realized she had dragged the Purimix into the office and was holding on to it.

The chocolate sat in the middle of the desk, wrapped in gold foil and waiting for her, and Herr Dreck sat behind it like a mountain troll—also waiting. Black hair sprouted from his nose, his ears, his chin. He had a pointed beard like Lenin's. There was even hair on his knuckles, wiry like a pig's.

"Put down the vacuum," he said.

She tried to set the handle of the Purimix carefully against the desk, but it slid away from her and landed on the carpet with a *thunk*.

Herr Dreck scowled and brought a finger to his rubbery lips. "Quiet, now. Quiet as a mouse." One hairy hand grasped her hip, pinning her in case she had the notion that she was free to leave. The other undid her coveralls. First it made its way up her blouse and under her bra. Then it traveled down. *Don't think about it. Don't feel anything.*

Just say no. Wasn't that the slogan the Americans had come up with for their war on drugs? Lena had heard about it on a Western television channel at Danika's apartment. *No* was an American word. You could say it and the sky would still be above your head and the floor would still be beneath your feet. In the Better Germany, *no* was not the end of anything. It was only the beginning.

Herr Dreck undid his belt buckle and unfastened his trousers. He took Lena's hand and guided it inside his undershorts. "That's it," he said in a husky voice while she rubbed him. "That's the way." *It isn't happening. Someone else is doing it, not you.*

He had a handkerchief ready for when he ejaculated, so there would be no mess. Even so, all Lena wanted to do afterward was wash her hand. She would have washed her whole body if she could have, in a solution of lye, to remove the layer of skin he had touched. But the toilets in House 1 were for men only; so few women worked there they didn't need their own bathroom, and rushing back to the toilets near the ashtray room would mean risking a confrontation with Jutta. Lena would have to settle for dousing her hand in cleaning solution at the first opportunity.

Herr Dreck made her eat the chocolate in front of him. Lena ate it quickly, with the clean hand, conscious of the brown smears forming at the edges of her lips and how her mouth stuck together. Had she been alone she would have savored each moment of sweetness, but not with him watching, in that strange hungry way he had. It seemed like he would devour not only the chocolate but also her hand, her arm.

As soon as she finished eating, his large forehead wrinkled with surprise, as if he had no idea what she was doing there. He reached for the key he kept beneath the telephone on his desk and unlocked one of the drawers.

"Out you go." He shooed her the way Auntie did when she was fed up to here. Lena blinked, and the Wall in her mind went up. She had wandered into his office by mistake while he was still in there: *Careless girl, don't you know the rules?* She hurried out with a mumbled apology, dragging the Purimix behind her and turning it on right away to vacuum the corridor and drown out the wasps.

She cleaned her hand.

It wasn't so easy to convince her body to forget the pokes and prods, though. Herr Dreck's fingers left imprints, as if she were dough, which meant the Wall needed to be higher. If she could see over the top, she would remember, and if she remembered, she could not go on. It would make her want to tell someone, and who could she tell? Auntie would say she was crazy: anyone who worked for the betterment of the State must be respectable. "Should I put it in your progress report?" she'd ask. "Would you like to explain it to the doctors?"

Head down, focus on the carpet, make it cleaner. The Wall in her mind grew taller and taller until whatever had happened was on the other side and Lena was safe.

When Herr Dreck passed her in the hallway on his way home, she barely saw him.

He always stayed late. Or rather, he worked as late as it took for Lena to show up. Once she'd tried saving that hallway for last, but no matter the hour, his light was on, his door ajar. Afterward she'd gotten into trouble with Jutta for not doing things in the right order.

"Does he ever call you into his office?" she'd asked Jutta once.

Jutta had frowned and shaken her large square head. "Are you trying to get me into trouble, is that what this is?"

It would have been nice to know Lena wasn't the only one. Plus it would have made her more sure of things. On one side of the Wall it happened every night. On the other side, it had never happened.

Mostly, Lena liked working nights while the rest of the city slept. Night shift meant the world was upside down and she was walking on the ceiling. She was sure it was why so many babies were born at night, and why the eyes of owls were so big. Shadows lengthened; secrets stepped out. It was when people talked about the things that were never to be spoken of: life in the West, the possibility of flight. *Use* unemployment *in a sentence, Mausi. Or* prostitution.

The slow, rhythmic motion of vacuuming settled her and helped her think. *We don't really know anyone.* Lena thought she'd known her uncle. She knew so many things about him—his favorite flavor of ice cream (chocolate), the way his eyes closed when he took the first drag of a cigarette, the pattern of his pajamas (blue stripes). But maybe Erich had a secret, a big one, and it was like being pregnant. At a certain point, you couldn't hide it anymore.

It was quiet in the large building, in the world, in her head. Only her footsteps existed, and the *swish* of the broom on the floor, and the *drip* of the mop in her bucket. At midnight, she and Jutta met to clean Comrade General Mielke's floor, starting at opposite sides of each room and working their way into the middle.

Jutta liked to talk while she worked. Tonight she talked about her previous job, a favorite subject. "The houses aren't so posh, you know, in Wandlitz." Jutta had been a housekeeper in the residential compound where the Politburo members lived before she'd come to work at Normannenstrasse. Wandlitz was another place that apparently wasn't on any city map. The streets didn't even have names. The neighborhood was surrounded by a high wall eight kilometers long, with guard towers. Usually Jutta referred to it as Volvograd because of all the Volvos and the chauffeurs that drove the bigwigs around. "The best thing about the houses, really, is the gardens. Each of them has one. They're huge." Jutta spent all her spring and summer weekends working in her allotment. Gardening was her special thing.

"Mmhmm," Lena said at regular intervals. She preferred silence, or humming. Sometimes while she worked she hummed the songs her mother had sung to her, but she had to be careful with those. Memories had sharp edges. Her head got noisy after those songs.

Most often she liked to hum the Sandman's song, the one he sang on television every night, with his yarn goatee and pointed cap, to send the children to sleep. The Sandman's song reset the day, put it to rights again after books had been knocked off shelves and milk had been spilled. When she hummed that song, she could tell herself nothing was wrong: she would visit her uncle and the Sandman would already have brought back all his notebooks and suitcases, even the typewriter—everything in its place, as before.

After Mielke's rooms were done, Lena returned to her floors. She knocked carefully at each office door before she entered, even though everyone had long since gone home. But she was not to disturb, never to disturb. The men in House 1 made big decisions about complicated issues of security that a girl like Lena could not possibly understand.

When she entered an office, she worked quickly and carefully: dust, sweep or vacuum, mop, get out. She had perfected a method of looking and not looking at the items on any given desk, so that she could tell you how many children Comrade So-and-So had in the family photograph, and whether he had a miniature Lenin bust on his desk (so many of them did), but she could not say which important documents it might be holding in place. *You don't know anything.*

Most of the papers were locked away, and all of the files. There were occasional security checks after hours to make sure none of the drawers or cabinets had been left unlocked. It was silly, really, since so many of the men tucked their keys beneath the Lenin bust. Lena lifted everything to dust. She knew.

Not that it mattered. She was not to touch any top-secret material; Jutta had made that clear. "If they catch you touching things, you will lose this job." And Sausage Auntie couldn't promise her another. Helmut or not, connections and promises were fragile things.

Some of the building's windows were smudged, so she cleaned them with newsprint and vinegar, making squeaking noises that echoed in the night's silence. Thankfully, there weren't a thousand windows in House 1. The ministry compound as a whole, though—the compound was huge. It was a rabbit warren of buildings, with windows like eyes everywhere. She'd never counted, but a thousand sounded right—maybe more. Whenever she crossed the grounds, the eyes watched her, the way cats watched. Pretending not to care, when in fact they were getting ready to pounce.

As the sun rose and agents began to arrive at the Stasi headquarters with their *clip clip* heels and morning smells of hair tonic and tobacco, Lena and Jutta put away their cleaning things. That was when they were granted entry into the *schrullig* world. Lena had described this world to Erich as if it was made up, but in fact it did exist, in the unlikeliest place—inside Stasi headquarters. The entrance was in the basement of House 18, but only people who worked for State Security were allowed in, and they weren't supposed to talk about it with strangers. It was meant to be a reward for service to the State. Lena had been tempted to tell Erich the truth so many times that she'd finally devised her make-believe world as a safe way of saying it out loud.

Nothing in the *schrullig* world was real; everything in it was real. There was no such place, but here was Lena, going inside.

Lena liked to spend time there before she went home. There were so many colors and smells; it was overwhelming. The rich aroma of Western coffee. The extravagance of yellow bananas. Oranges as bright as the sun. Smoked eel, spiced plum jam. Ridiculous items, all of them.

Lena passed the travel office, and a cinema, and a place to get one's hair done, where afterward you could sit under one of the orange domes and pretend you were going into space. Mostly the chairs were occupied by men who'd had their brush cuts done. Often in the morning there would be a row of them sitting under the dryers, reading and smoking. That morning, when Lena walked past the orange space helmets she saw Herr Dreck, but he did not wave at her, or smile, or even raise an eyebrow, because they didn't know each other.

She wandered through the grocery store pretending she needed something and couldn't decide, but in fact she simply liked the kaleidoscope of colors on the shelves. One of the women who worked there scowled at her and asked if there was something she wanted, so she said *yes* and paid for an orange, and sat at a table and ate it.

When she was done, she left through the portal and returned

to the regular rain-gray world, repeating Mausi's instructions to herself: You didn't see anything. *You don't know anything. You don't say anything.* Imagine, such choices in a grocery store—and everything was there every single day, so there was no need to stock up. Imagine, a bookstore filled with books you'd want to read. Erich was right; it was pure silliness. The things in the *schrullig* world did not exist in the Better Germany; that was what made it so exciting to visit.

Lena walked across the compound grounds in the cool morning air until she reached the barricade leading onto Normannen-strasse. She peeked at who was on security that morning. Was it still Ernst? If so, the good morning/good night joke, a wave, a smile—but no, it was that jowly fat fellow whose eyes disappeared beneath his forehead and who was humorless no matter what Lena tried, so *no wave, just show your identity card and keep walking.*

At home there was a boiled egg waiting for her in a chicken-shaped eggcup, a mug of Melange coffee, and some honey for her bread—a luxury, but Auntie was a good citizen, and goodness was rewarded.

Badness, however, got you a one-way ticket to smartening up, which was why Lena had to find a way to get to Erich's apartment without getting caught. He would be sitting at his desk, smoking and staring out the window, staring, staring, and then it would happen in a burst, he would start to type, and he would type and type until all the birds flocked to his window thinking it was a cavalcade of nuts dropping from the trees. Because the typewriter was there. It had always been there. And so was he.

She would sit in the stained armchair drinking her Vita Cola and reading the Western magazine. When he was finished working, she would make him tell her what was really going on.

There was only one problem, and it bothered her more than anything. That Wall she'd built to protect herself—it had grown so high she couldn't be sure she had seen anything.

– 5 –

FRIEDRICH SO-AND-SO

Lena ate breakfast, then slept—but not for long. When her alarm rang in the early afternoon, she pulled on her sweater and laced up her Zehas.

She was convinced the trains were slower, the stops longer; first the short trip on the U-Bahn, then the interminable ride on the S-Bahn. There were announcements to get off on the left, get off on the right. *Erich. Erich.* As usual, the trains were grimy and smelled like sweat. A round-faced woman with a tooth missing stared at Lena with the *why aren't you doing something productive* look on her face. Lena knew that look. Sausage Auntie had invented it and then taught it to all the older women in Berlin.

Finally, she got off the train and walked as quickly as she dared until she reached Erich's corner. She peered around, watching the movement on the street: a young woman pushing a stroller, an old couple walking together as if each was afraid the other might fall. Cars passing, and cars parked. Some of the Trabis had defiant scraps of fabric attached to their antennas. A white scrap meant the person had formally applied to leave the Better Germany, but these pieces were black—which meant the applications had been rejected. If the People's Police saw them, they would make the drivers remove them.

There were also Ladas parked on the road, but from where Lena stood it was impossible to tell if the man with the newspaper was still there.

You don't know there's a man with a newspaper. How could you? You weren't there, remember? She was just a girl coming to visit her uncle on a Tuesday afternoon. *You don't visit Erich on Tuesday afternoons.* But this was a special Tuesday. It was . . . it was almost the Republic's birthday and they had to make plans for attending the parade. There would be banners to paint, flags to organize. When in doubt, mention a national holiday.

Walk naturally. Don't look inside the parked cars. Only nervous people did that. *Find the building. Go inside and ring the bell.* Erich would answer. He was home, because all he'd done on Sunday was spend the night at a friend's. Maybe he had a girlfriend, a One True Love he hadn't mentioned to Lena.

She climbed the stairs to the third floor and rang the bell. The door opened. A man Erich's age stood scowling at her in a stained undershirt, his belly hanging over the top of his pants. "Can I help you?"

Who was this? "I'm looking for my uncle. Is he home?"

"You've got the wrong apartment. There's no one here but me."

How silly she could be. "I'm sorry," she said, and went back downstairs.

This time she counted floors and made absolutely sure she was on the right one when she stood in front of the door. But when she checked the name beside the bell, it wasn't Erich's. It was Friedrich So-and-So.

Was she in the right building? She ran downstairs and went outside to check the address. Yes, this was the right one. Erich was playing a trick on her, that was all. By the time she'd climbed the third flight of stairs, she had the whole story worked out and was laughing to herself at how clever her uncle was. He'd always been a *Spassmacher*, a joker. Mama used to call him a noodle-head. On New Year's Eve when he came to visit and they ate dough-nuts filled with jam, Erich would secretly fill one with mustard and laugh like crazy when the poor person who bit into it made a sour-mustard face.

Lena rang the bell. "Come out, Noodle-Head, I know you're in there. It's Lena."

Footsteps sounded across the floor and then there was the man in the undershirt, Friedrich So-and-So. "You again. What do you want?"

Lena closed her eyes. Opened them. "Where is my uncle?"

"Look, I don't know what you're talking about. Your uncle doesn't live here."

She peered behind him into the apartment. None of the furniture was Erich's. Or almost none—the table by the window was there, but instead of Erich's typewriter there was a radio on it. A small black cat wound itself around the man's legs and mewed. Erich was allergic to cats.

"When did you move in?" she asked. "This morning? Yesterday afternoon?"

"What do you mean? I've lived here for five years."

"That's not possible." She held on to the door frame. Something was welling up from the bottom of her belly. She wasn't sure if it was tears, or panic, or the bowl of soup she'd eaten earlier.

"If you're going to be a nuisance about this," the man said, "I will telephone the police."

Lena wrinkled her forehead. "Erich doesn't have a telephone." How did this man have one? People waited up to twenty-five years for a telephone.

"Who is Erich?" the man said.

"My uncle."

The man let out a huff that smelled like onions. "Fräulein, I'm going to have to ask you to leave."

But—

"I'm closing the door now. If your fingers are in the way, you will get hurt."

But—

"Don't come back. Do you understand? If you come back, I'll call the police."

He shut the door. Lena stood there, staring at it. It was faded, and tired, like her. *You're asleep, Mausi. This is a dream.* She pinched herself on the arm. No, she was definitely awake. It took her a minute to gather herself before she trusted she could make it down the stairs without falling. She went all the way down and sat on the bottom step.

Think. Think what to do.

Sausage Auntie said she wasn't much good at thinking, but that hadn't always been true. Lena had been a good student when she'd lived in Magdeburg, when she'd had parents, and teachers, and homework. "You have a knack for figuring things out," her father used to say. Uncle Erich always said she had a good imagination and could think sideways instead of up and down like everyone else.

Think.

She'd seen the men two nights ago taking Erich's things away. She'd seen the man reading a newspaper in his Lada. Maybe Erich had been arrested. Was that it? *You know it is. You saw a man make signals from the window. You saw a flower-delivery van drive away. Do you think it was only full of flowers?* The typewriter. The notebooks. Steffi! She would know what was going on.

Lena climbed the stairs, rang the bell, and braced herself. Steffi was never happy to see her.

She waited, rang again. But nobody came.

Had there ever been a man with a newspaper?

She went back downstairs to Erich's mailbox. The sticker on it said *Friedrich So-and-So.* She struggled to peel it back, wishing for Peter's long fingernails. Auntie was always saying that Lena should quit biting hers. Erich's name would be there, like the humming-underneath sound, some confirmation that she wasn't losing her mind. But beneath *Friedrich So-and-So* there was only a blank space.

She opened the door to the storage area where Erich kept his bicycle. It wasn't there. Her heart lifted. *He's run away.* Erich had always been so clever. He'd known this was coming—*remember how nervous he was*—and he'd taken his bicycle and was hiding somewhere. He would find a way to contact her. She must be patient.

She decided she'd spent enough time in the entryway of the

building. Auntie would be home soon. Lena would say she'd been to the swimming pool but hadn't gone swimming because it was closed for repairs—which was almost always true. She hauled open the heavy front door, squinting at the sudden light. It took a second for her vision to adjust, and then she saw: the Lada. Right in front of the building. The man with the newspaper was staring straight at her.

She looked away, *make yourself small*, checked her watch, *put your head down, walk. Don't look back. Don't look up. Get to the S-Bahn station and find something to read.* A train schedule, a banner. She hurried past billboards proclaiming, *The state is me . . . is us . . .* She passed the merchants with their goods for sale and took the steps up to the platform two at a time. But everyone in the Better Germany knew how things were organized. If one man was here, another would be there. *Get busy, stay busy.*

There weren't many people at the station. Older folks were giving her the look that said *work-shy. Class enemy*—an enemy of the revolution. She wished she had worn her *Free German Youth* shirt. She wished the punk rockers would arrive; they liked hanging around Erich's neighborhood. Then at least the older people wouldn't stare at her anymore—although everyone was too afraid of the punk rockers to stare at them for long. They had rooster hairdos and wore makeup and safety pins, which they could take out and stick you with if they felt like it. The Transport Police were watching for anyone who stood out. *Don't call attention to yourself.*

Men in suits; there were two of them. One was reading a magazine; the other was checking the train schedule. Both carried briefcases. But it was the man on the bench who made Lena most uneasy. His armband and dark glasses marked him as blind, but the way he looked at things gave Lena the odd feeling he could see. She was certain he was one of them.

You've been listening to too many of Erich's stories. It's making you see things. Up went the Wall in her mind, and she scrambled to be on the right side of it, wishing she could believe that she would have her Sunday visit with Erich and he'd be fine.

When she arrived home, Auntie was preparing goulash, a much fancier supper than usual. The baby next door was crying, but Auntie didn't grumble about it, didn't even bang on the wall, which was usually how she tried to get the baby to stop, although it never worked.

She asked about Lena's afternoon.

"I went to the pool, but it was closed for repairs." *Scheiss Osten,* she added in her head, because it felt good to say it.

"Again," Auntie said. "We should complain, you know."

Complaining was encouraged in the Better Germany. You could complain about the pool being closed, especially if you mentioned that you wanted to remain physically fit to be a good team member, to keep up morale at work. You could complain about the quality of the coffee, or the housing shortage, or that there wasn't any ketchup for sale. You'd form a group of concerned citizens, and bring a petition to the authorities—even to General Secretary Honecker himself—and they would listen and do something about it, if something could be done. One couldn't make ketchup appear out of thin air, after all.

While Lena set the table, Auntie talked. Her new students were so well behaved; the drainage trench was already making a difference; maybe it was time to buy Lena a camera so she could practice taking photographs between classes. So many young people were getting involved with photography these days, she said—and, "Isn't it wonderful for young people to have an appropriate creative outlet?" She flitted from one topic to the next like a bird surrounded by too many flowers.

Lena stared at her, but Auntie didn't seem to notice. They sat at the table and ate their goulash, though it seemed as if Auntie didn't want to look at her. When Lena stood up to clear her dishes, Auntie whisked them out of her hands and told her to go rest up before her long night of work.

What?

Lena went into her room and pulled down a boy-meets-tractor book, as Erich referred to most of the accepted literature in the Better Germany. But she got stuck on one paragraph, seeing the words but not reading them. She took out the small hand mirror from her drawer. Auntie said if she gazed too long in a mirror, hair would sprout from her ears, which was what had happened to Herr Dreck and so many of the other men at House 1. Lena's hair seemed straighter than usual. "We'll straighten you out in no time," Auntie had said when she'd brought Lena home from the mental hospital. And look, even her hair had cooperated. The doctors would be pleased.

It was when she put the mirror back that she realized something was wrong. Her brush and hair clips were not in the right place. Someone had been in here. As soon as the thought formed, she saw evidence of it everywhere. The books were not quite in line, the pictures on the wall not quite straight, the orange quilt on her bed not tucked in the way she'd left it.

Had Auntie been snooping? It was possible, even though she was a firm believer in Lena keeping her own room in order. "Responsibility," she'd say, and, "I don't want you making extra work for me." But if Auntie hadn't been in here, then who had? It couldn't have been the Stasi, could it? That sort of thing happened to other people—layabouts, class enemies, shirkers who spray-painted the word *Freiheit* (*Freedom*) on the outside of buildings.

She changed her clothes, pulling on her Better Germany jeans and buttoning her blouse, though it all felt dreamlike, as if another girl had taken her place in a life that resembled hers but in a mixed-up way. Someone had touched her things, maybe even the clothes she was putting on. It made her feel sticky and short of breath, the way she felt whenever a stranger on the train sat too close.

Before she left the bedroom, she went over to one of the Erich pictures: Honecker, with his brown television-screen glasses. She needed to see her uncle's face behind it, just for reassurance. The important Erich, the one that mattered. But when she lifted Honecker's face, the only thing behind it was flowered wallpaper. She stared at the wall, touched it with her hand. She set Honecker's picture back in its place and raised the other, the one of Erich Mielke. There, too, was wall. Whoever had been here had taken away the photographs of her uncle. Had it been Auntie?

You can't very well ask her. Auntie would be waiting for it. *Aha!* Photos behind photos, these were subversive techniques, they were one step away from Western decadence. Auntie had been married to a high-ranking Party functionary, which explained the telephone and special relationships and needlepointed slogans, but would not explain how she had become the Guardian of a

Difficult Child who was still difficult. No, it just wouldn't do.

Auntie was calling for her to hurry. Quickly Lena lifted the other pictures, just to see. Yes, there were her parents. There was John Travolta and the insect band. Only the photographs of her uncle were missing.

This would be a bad time to cry. Because sooner or later, *sooner, right now, put the Marx picture back in place*—here came Auntie who didn't believe in knocking—and Lena stepped away from the wall.

"What on earth are you doing in here? Off you go—you'll keep Jutta waiting."

There was something nervous about Auntie, as if someone had wound her too tightly and the spring that kept her from flying into ten thousand pieces was about to let go. The way she hurried Lena into her coat. The way she pressed a bun into her hand in case she hadn't had enough supper. The way she bustled behind her, practically shoving her out the door, when every other night it had been Lena's responsibility to arrive on time—"If you don't have the sense to be punctual for our Comrade General, then I can't help you." If Auntie had been younger, Lena might have wondered if she'd invited a man over.

Lena stepped out into the night and onto the wide street leading to Normannenstrasse and the Stasi headquarters. As she walked, she glanced back toward her apartment's lit squares of windows, as if they knew what was going on and could offer her a clue. But they told her nothing.

Twice she heard footsteps behind her. She turned, but no one was there.

*

Lena barely noticed the sky darkening and the stars emerging. She didn't smell the tang of wet autumn leaves, nor did she play her usual game of peering into windows and guessing people's lives. Someone had been in her bedroom. Someone had gone through her things and slipped her uncle into their pocket.

Yes, it happened in the Better Germany, though you had to be careful who you mentioned it to. You couldn't tell who was on your side just by looking. There were many people who believed that the Stasi, and the Party, were doing what they must to create the ideal society. Sometimes that meant weeding out the bad influences. But when the bad influence was a member of your family, what then?

Lena was so preoccupied that when a man said "Good morning" to her, she was taken aback.

"What? Oh." It was the security guard, Ernst. How had she already reached the compound gates? Her feet had done it to her again. "Good morning." She forced a smile.

"Is everything all right, Comrade Lena?"

"Yes, yes." She hurried past him and across the grounds toward House 24, into the tiny, stifling room where she and Jutta were supposed to bond as colleagues over cigarette smoke and burned pretend-coffee. A group of men and women wearing hard hats and operating heavy machinery was the inspirational subject of the one piece of art in the room.

Jutta always arrived before her. She sat at the card table staring at the fashionable magazine women in their winter coats.

"I'd like a winter coat like that." Lena pointed to a dark green coat with fur at the collar.

Jutta looked up. "The world doesn't owe you a winter coat."

"I know. I'm just saying I want one. The magazines always make us want things we didn't even realize we were missing."

Jutta pointed the burned end of her cigarette toward Lena. "What does anyone really want?"

Here we go. This was another one, canned beets, the supper of *we don't know what we really want*—but Lena knew. She wanted to know what had happened to her uncle. She wanted her life back, the before life. Before doctors with pudding voices. Before explosions and *we're so very sorry.* Before an important Stasi man who made Lena feel like a dirty scrap of carpet.

What were they accusing Erich of? And anyway, being arrested didn't explain the men emptying his apartment, or the new man, Friedrich So-and-So, whose name was now on the mailbox, whose cat was in Erich's apartment. Who claimed he had lived there for five years.

"Am I okay in the head?" Lena blurted. "Jutta? Do you think I'm normal?" The doctors didn't think so. Lena felt all right, usually— but wasn't that the first sign? Crazy people never thought they were crazy—it was everyone else.

Jutta gave a phlegmy cough. "What is normal? Is anyone normal?"

Now you see? That was a mistake. Do not ask for Jutta's opinion. You will only get another jar of pickles. Lena took the brooms and mops and Purimixes out of the cupboard, and the two buckets, already packed with the cleaning solutions and rags they would need for the night.

"My job on the farm was to take care of the chickens." Jutta picked up her bucket. "We had a rooster. Damned nuisance.

Nearly took out my eye." She pointed to a thin scar the shape of a comma at the corner of her eye. "They named me Jutta, my new father and mother. I don't even know what my real name is."

How long before Erich would be allowed to contact her? He could use the telephone in prison to call Auntie's place—if that was where he was. Surely there were visiting hours. Would he be skinny and pale? Lena could bring leftover goulash.

". . . came for me when I was only a little girl. I was born in Poland, you know."

They walked together to House 1 and entered through the main doors. Three red flags. Two black statues. One shiny black floor. Jutta got into the elevator; Lena trudged up the stairs. Once. Twice. She decided to start in the offices, rather than the hallway. Maybe Herr Dreck would get tired and go home. Maybe his wife would call.

The graveyard shift. Why did they have to call it that? A building at night was like a cemetery—so silent and empty. Mostly the men were cautious about the documents they worked on; they tidied their desks before they went home, locking everything away, or shredding it. But every so often, like tonight, there were papers left on a desk or a side shelf. Lena didn't look at them, so she didn't see notes, and dates, and times. She didn't see recommendations scribbled in the margins. She didn't notice the words *flight risk* at the bottom of certain pages, which meant the people in question were suspected of wanting to escape. All those things were on the other side of the Wall in her mind, so how could she be expected to see them? She touched one of the pages with two fingers, but didn't pick it up.

Eventually she had to clean the hallway. She dragged her

Purimix out. The door down the hall was ajar; light spilled onto the red carpet. Lena felt like taking Herr Dreck's heavy rough hand and sticking it in the meat grinder attachment, if only she had that one.

Afterward there will be chocolate. But she didn't care about chocolate. There would be his reddened eyes, the stench of his breath, and the way it got huskier as she felt inside his pants. Not again, please. *You are small, Mausi, and he is big.* And he was a Stasi agent, a Lieutenant General, and Lena was only the cleaning girl.

Every night she thought about asking Jutta to come down when Herr Dreck called for her. Or drawing attention to the photographs of his family. Or doing something later, when he had gone home and she was cleaning his office, like unlocking his cabinet and shredding his important documents. But thinking about that didn't make her feel powerful. She couldn't do it without losing her job and getting sent somewhere worse: a textile factory, where the hours were long and the lighting was bad and everyone knew the girls were moral degenerates. Or, much worse even than that—the mental hospital.

"Fräulein, is that you?"

This wasn't about choices. It was the way things were.

– 6 –

NOT THIS TYPE OF *SOLYANKA*

The night stretched and stretched until it seemed as if the sun had changed its mind and Lena would have to stay at work for the rest of her life. Even the chirping birds seemed annoyed by how slowly the time was passing. At last the muffled sound of shoes crossing fancy red carpets told her she could go home.

She'd spent the night deciding what to do about Erich. Even though patience was the hardest thing, she would wait one day, maybe two, and if she hadn't heard anything—then she would do the terrible thing and ask Auntie. It would mean admitting to the secret photographs, and the sneaking off at night, but Auntie knew important people. She would be able to find things out. She would be angry at first; Lena might miss supper. But then she would help, especially if Lena made a point of listing all the important people Auntie knew, and making her feel as if she was the only one in the world who could do something.

"I'm the only one around here who—" was one of Auntie's favorite ways to begin a conversation.

Lena raced over to House 18 and one, two, three, stepped through the portal into the *schrullig* world. There were the orange space helmets, man after man sitting in a row, legs crossed, newspaper in hand. Perhaps later they'd go hunting with the Erichs. The Erichs loved to hunt in a forest north of Berlin. Big business got done while they aimed their guns at deer. Jutta said the General Secretary insisted his Tuesday Politburo meetings end on time so he could hunt afterward, and she would know—she'd worked in Volvograd for years.

Past the hair dryers was the bookstore. Lena walked to the middle of the store and inhaled. In, in, in.

"Are you looking for anything in particular?" a woman said.

"No," Lena said. "I'm just breathing." When she saw the expression on the woman's face, she backed out of the store and went to the grocery. There were all those oranges, rows of tiny suns shining their light on Lena. She touched each one until a woman said, "Do you need help picking one out?"

Again. Everything she did was strange. Lena chose an orange, bought it, and ate it. She thought of bringing one home for Hans. Imagine, an orange in September! Sometimes Lena dreamed of handing them out to Danika and Peter, to Hans and the baby next door. She'd be the hero of the housing development. But Auntie would be furious if she found out. People didn't know about the secret grocery store. Lena had never even mentioned it to Auntie. She didn't want to lose her job over an orange.

She stepped out of the *schrullig* world, *you didn't see anything, you don't know anything, you don't say anything,* and *poof,* it was gone. As she left the compound, she said good night to Ernst, and he tipped his rifle toward her, wrist bones poking out of his uniform cuffs as if his arms had grown overnight.

She was halfway home when she felt someone behind her, like a shadow that gave off heat. She turned. It took her a second to realize—"Steffi!" But when Lena ran back to her, Steffi didn't even break her stride. For a second Lena thought she'd made a mistake. Then came the *snap snap* of Steffi's gum.

"It's me. Lena." The look on her face—like Lena was pointing a gun at her. "What's the matter?" Panic swelled inside her.

Steffi kept walking, turning into one alley, then another. She didn't say a word until: "Who did you talk to?" The question was so quiet Lena wasn't sure she'd heard it. "Who did you tell?"

"What do you mean? Tell what?"

The brick buildings they passed were covered in graffiti: *Our Soviet friends*, the sloppy F for *Freiheit* that could send you directly to the blank space on the map if you were caught painting it. If anyone had been following them on the main street, it seemed they had lost track of them. Lena and Steffi were alone.

Steffi grabbed her by the shoulders. Her dark eyes were a mess of old mascara and not enough sleep, and something denser that Lena thought might be fear. "What did you do? You bitch, I know this is your fault. You said something to someone. It had to be you."

Lena wriggled out of her grasp and backed away. She wasn't sure if Steffi would try to hurt her. Steffi was about six inches taller than Lena, and quite a bit heavier. And there was something damaged about her this morning, like a gate hanging by one hinge.

"I don't understand." Lena spoke carefully. "Where is Erich? What's happened to him? When I went to see him—"

"Who?"

"What do you mean, 'who'? Erich. My uncle. Your neighbor."

Steffi brought her face level to Lena's, too close. Lena could smell the spearmint of her gum.

"You don't have an uncle," Steffi said. "Do you understand?"

What? "What's the matter with you?"

From somewhere behind them came the grinding of a tram. Steffi started walking so fast Lena could hardly keep up. A brown mutt with tangled fur barked and lunged at Steffi's legs, and she kicked it and kept going.

"Listen to me. There is no Erich anymore. They made me say I don't know him. I've never known him. You don't know him either. You better not, or they'll take you in. Don't go looking for him. Don't ask anyone about him, not even that bulldog aunt of yours. You don't have an uncle. You've never had one." She walked faster.

"Wait. I don't understand." Lena broke into a jog beside her.

"Don't follow me. I'm going away. Don't talk to anyone." She crossed the street and disappeared around a corner.

Lena held herself steady against a lamppost. What could she possibly have said to anyone about Uncle Erich? Had he been involved in something subversive? Why did Steffi think she knew anything about it?

Something hurt inside her all over again, even though it was supposed to have gotten stronger. That was what she'd been told after the explosion, when she didn't have parents anymore. "It's like a bone, Lena," the doctors said. "After a broken bone heals, it is stronger." Then why did Lena feel so weak?

How could someone suddenly not exist? It made Lena think of what Danika had done after her One True Love had broken her heart. She'd cut him out of all her photographs using pinking shears that made zigzag patterns, like teeth—as if she'd bitten him out of her life. "He's dead to me," she'd proclaimed to Lena one afternoon when they were walking to youth group.

Lena had never had a One True Love, so she didn't know what that felt like. But she'd had a John Travolta love, and she had a good imagination. Someone you loved, who didn't love you back anymore: you would rather they'd been hit by a tram than know that somewhere in the world your One True Love was eating his porridge and not thinking about you.

You must accept the reality of the loss. That was what the doctors kept saying after the explosion. *Work through the pain, Lena. Find a new reality, Lena. Adjust. Move on.* Their voices were so smooth, and that repetition of her name—it was comforting somehow. No wonder Steffi had run away. Lena had used entirely the wrong tone with her and had only said her name once.

When Lena arrived home, Auntie was waiting for her. Her boiled egg sat on the table in its smiling-chicken eggcup. Pretend animals with their plastic smiles and sweet painted eyes always looked slightly insane, like Auntie's collection of porcelain dogs. You would never want those dogs to come to life.

"Would you believe Peter's mother has a recipe for *solyanka*?" Auntie said. "I'm going to the butcher's right after work today to place an order, see if they can't find us something special. With any luck this apartment will smell sweet and sour by tomorrow afternoon."

"What?" Lena held a piece of egg in her mouth, forgetting for a moment how to swallow.

There was a second of stiffness, then back to this make-believe Auntie with gumdrop eyes and hair made of ice cream. "*Pardon me*, Lena. We say *pardon me*. After we've chewed and swallowed our egg."

Chew. Swallow. "Pardon me?"

"You wanted *solyanka* for supper, didn't you?"

I did. But not this type of solyanka. This *solyanka* meant something was wrong.

"Finish your breakfast and go to bed. I'll have news from the butcher when you wake up."

Finish your breakfast. Go to bed. Everything is fine.

But when Lena went to bed and lifted the Erich pictures to say good night to her uncle, she was reminded all over again that everything was not fine. Behind the Erichs there was no more Erich. She reached under her mattress for one of her uncle's books; maybe the first few pages of *Castles Underground* would comfort her. But the books weren't there. Even when she raised the entire mattress—nothing. No wonder her blankets had been askew yesterday. Under the bed—nothing. In her cupboard, on the shelves next to the boy-meets-tractor books and the copy of *The Catcher in the Rye* Erich had bought for her birthday— nothing, and nothing.

"A full bookcase is the best defense," he always said.

"Against what?" Lena had asked.

"Everything."

Must not ask Auntie. Lena wasn't supposed to have copies of Erich's novels: Auntie thought they were inappropriate reading material, bordering on Western decadence, bad for morale. They would make Lena's hair fall out and turn her toenails yellow.

"Auntie?" she called.

"Yes?"

"I'm missing some books."

Auntie appeared in the doorway. "What books?"

"Uncle's books." Lena sat on the edge of her bed in her gray nightdress, hands clasped in her lap, trying her hardest to look normal.

Sausage Auntie came into the room, sat next to Lena, and took off her reading glasses. *Now you've done it.* Next would come a talk about the dangers of certain books, and why it was so very important to listen to Auntie at all times. It didn't seem like there would be an *or else*, but you never could tell with Auntie. She tossed one in sometimes at the end of a conversation, like a hand grenade.

"Lena." Even worse, she was using Lena's name. "You don't have those books."

Lena sighed. "I know. They're missing."

"There are no books." Auntie stared at the wall across from the bed.

"There were." What was wrong with Auntie? It was like trying to speak to a five-year-old.

"There weren't."

"Auntie, I'm sorry I didn't tell you, but the truth is, Uncle Erich gave me copies of his books and I hid them under my—"

"There is no such person." Now it seemed as if Auntie's neck had stiffened. She faced straight ahead, refusing to turn toward Lena.

"What are you talking about? My uncle. Erich. Your brother."

"I don't have a brother, dear one." At last she turned and looked right into Lena's eyes. Auntie's eyes were strange, watery and hard at the same time, like frozen puddles of steel. "Do you understand me? It's important that you understand."

Don't cry, not in front of her. But Lena couldn't help it. First Steffi, now Auntie. The tears leaked out against her will. "I went to see Erich yesterday, and another man was living in his apartment. He said he'd been living there for five years."

She waited for Auntie to react to the unplanned, unapproved visit, but all she said was, "That's right. Five years." She put her glasses back on. The important things had been said.

"But it's not right. It's wrong."

Auntie stroked Lena's hair. "You're simple, Lena. It's nothing to be ashamed of. You don't understand the big things."

Simple, maybe. Not crazy. She wasn't crazy, was she? "Are you going to put this in my progress report?"

"Of course not. Go to sleep. Things always feel better after a good night's sleep."

Good night. But the morning sun lit the edges of her bedroom curtains.

Uncle Erich. But she didn't have an uncle.

But she did.

You didn't see anything. You don't know anything. You don't say anything. You don't have an uncle. You've never had an uncle.

After Sausage Auntie left the room, Lena lifted the photographs and said good night to her parents. They were still there— even though they weren't. "You come from humble origins,"

Auntie always said with a nod of approval, because Lena's parents had both worked in a factory.

She said good night to Erich number one, General Secretary, Great White Hunter, the man you could write to if you had a complaint. As long as it was the right sort of complaint, Erich used to say. *See?* She could still hear his voice in her head.

"You mustn't complain about our Soviet friends, or about the right of the GDR to exist. You mustn't mention the Wall." He wagged a finger. "Else they'll take you away in a bakery van, or a fishmonger's van."

Or a flower-delivery van.

Lena felt her morning egg come up. She swallowed hard. *Say good night to the other Erich.* Good night, Comrade General, head of the football team that never loses, diagrammer of the breakfast table, wearer of too much hair tonic—it had made a spot on the wall where he leaned back in his desk chair in a way that would have driven Auntie wild, and Lena still hadn't found a cleaning product that would remove it.

And the important Erich? What about him?

Lena lifted the pictures of the two Erichs and touched the wall. *Good night, Uncle, writer of notebooks, teller of stories. I know which pickles are your favorite.* Funny Mausi, there is only one type of pickle. *I know what it feels like when you hug me. I know which face will make you laugh, the one where I pull my eyes down to make Sad Clown.*

All she could think of was how cold it must be in the blank space on the map, and how Erich's cough would get worse, and if he asked for a blanket or a hot cup of tea they wouldn't give it to him. And the way his clothes smelled, that musky forest scent—how easily the dogs would find him if he ran.

But that was if he'd been arrested. No one was saying that.

It wasn't that he'd been arrested. It wasn't that his books had been banned.

It was that he'd never existed in the first place.

*

Asylum. The word meant a safe haven. Protection. But shake it and set it down crooked and it became a place for people who weren't quite right. The ones who didn't have all the cups in their cupboard.

Lena's memory of the hospital was smudged, ghostlike, as if it wasn't her who'd stayed there for a year but rather a cousin who'd told her about it.

She hadn't known about the *schrullig* world back then, or else she would have pretended with all her heart to be there the entire time she was in that hospital. You could survive anything if you could convince yourself that it was only your body that was suffering, not the rest of you. Not the important part.

Down the hall from her there'd been a heroin addict. But heroin addiction was a Western illness. You didn't mention it in the Better Germany. Instead, it was hidden behind the doors of the mental hospital where it was called instability, or an uncertain grip on reality. No one talked about when the heroin addict might get out.

And her? With her fingernail (she'd had long fingernails back then), Lena had made a mark on the wall for each day that passed:

bundles of five, like firewood. They were days that deserved to be burned. But soon she had too many bundles, and the sight of them piled up beside her bed had made her feel so sad she'd stopped keeping track.

MAYBE JUST CUT OUT ONE PICTURE

Solyanka was arranged for Thursday's supper. Lena awoke early that afternoon with the sweet-and-sour soup on her mind, which made her think of her parents, which made her think of Uncle Erich. There was no going back to sleep once the voices in her head started chattering, so she decided to visit the public library and pick up one of her uncle's books. She left Auntie a note. The library was an outing that Auntie always sanctioned, especially if Lena brought home something for her.

But when she got there and looked, none of Erich's books were on the shelves. The librarian checked in all the card catalogs, and even made a telephone call—during which she faced Lena at first and then, halfway through, turned away from her and hunched over, the way people did when a conversation was so secret they tried to hide it with their entire body.

Finally she hung up the phone, turned back around, and

straightened her dress, which was made of such stiff fabric Lena wondered how she could sit down. Lena waited for her to say something. The librarian's mouth moved as if she were chewing imaginary gum, but she didn't speak.

"Erich Altmann?" Lena said again. Maybe the librarian needed reminding. Sometimes even Auntie walked into the kitchen and then couldn't remember why.

The librarian sat down. "There is no such author." She straightened the pens on her desk, gathered stray index cards and placed them into piles. Bits and pieces—scissors, small notes, anything to keep her hands busy. When Lena tried to ask another question about where the books might be, she said, "I suggest you choose something else."

Fine. It sometimes happened that the library didn't have things. Books got lost. The good ones got stolen, because once you had your hands on a good book it was hard to give it back. "Someone stole your books from the library, Uncle," Lena whispered. He would love to hear that. He'd told her once it was the highest compliment for an author, but perhaps it was considered a terrible failure on the part of the librarian—she couldn't control her books and thank goodness she wasn't a zookeeper. Therefore, best for the librarian not to admit it. Best to say the books had never been there in the first place.

Lena selected a collective-farm saga for herself and a book for Auntie on the social realism movement. By the time she walked into the apartment, it smelled sweet—and sour. The *solyanka* bubbled on the stove, and Auntie was humming, and there was a fresh loaf of bread on the table, and two large bowls, and polka music on the radio.

"Don't rush off to the courtyard," she said. "I told Hans you were resting this afternoon."

Lena stared at Auntie, and said nothing. At suppertime she dipped pieces of bread crust into the hot *solyanka*. It wasn't as good as Mama's—she wouldn't let it be—but almost.

Lena went to work, endured Herr Dreck's hairy hands, and Jutta's stories about Volvograd and not being German, *did I ever tell you that?* She dusted, and swept, and polished up the eyes of House 1 until finally it was time to step through the portal at House 18.

Yes, you are granted entry, Comrade Lena Altmann. One. Two. Three.

This time Lena didn't stand in the middle of the bookstore and breathe. She went directly to the shelves. This bookstore had the best selection of books in the city, but there was not a single book in there by Erich Altmann. She approached the woman at the counter, who was watching her as if she were one of those insects that ate paper. A silverfish. They'd been in House 1 once. Lena and Jutta had used a special powder to get rid of them.

"I'm surprised you don't have *Castles Underground*," Lena said. "It's very good."

The bookstore clerk had never heard of it.

"But I've been in here before," Lena said. "I've seen the book. Right there." She pointed to the space next to Hannah Arendt, which was now taken up by a series of books by Stefan Andres. "Erich Altmann, my uncle. Surely you've heard of him," she said, breaking both the *Don't ask anyone about him* rule and the *You don't have an uncle* rule. *They weren't real rules, only bad advice.* Usually a person could disregard bad advice without getting into trouble.

The clerk handed her the first volume of Trotsky's *The History of the Russian Revolution.*

Lena didn't take it. "I already read that in school." When there was school.

"You might want to read it again." The clerk placed the book on the counter with a curt *thump.*

"I don't need to." The proletariat and the peasantry. The Bolsheviks and Lenin. The February Insurrection and the April Days. Just thinking about them made her sleepy.

*

"What did you mean about not really knowing anyone?" Lena asked Jutta that Friday night when she arrived in the ashtray room.

Jutta took a cigarette out of the package and tapped its end on the table several times. She always did this. Lena had no idea why.

"I never said that." She lit her cigarette and sent a long gray stream of smoke into the air.

"Yes, you did, when you were talking about being Polish. I think you meant that people keep secrets. Didn't you?"

"Not me," Jutta said. "I tell you everything."

"You couldn't. I don't tell you everything."

There were things Lena hadn't told anyone except Erich. Her plans for her life. How much she missed her parents. How she wished their deaths hadn't been an accident so she could blame someone, blame them hard, with every part of her body: her ragged fingernails, her spit, her spleen.

"I've always wanted One True Love," Lena said quietly. "And

I have a voice in my head called Mausi, which is sort of me, but sort of not—both sides of me at once, so that I can have a real conversation with myself. Arguments, even. And I never wanted to be a janitor. I hope that doesn't insult you. Auntie says it's a very good job. What I really wanted—"

Jutta stamped out her half-smoked cigarette and put it back into the package. Even tucked away, it would make everything stink. She stood up abruptly, catching Lena off guard. Jutta was never the first to leave the table. She rushed to the cupboard, gathered her cleaning things, and said, "Put on your coveralls, child. We're going to be late."

Lena glanced at her watch. Maybe it had stopped, because it was telling her they were early. Nevertheless, she got ready and they went outside, Jutta walking close to her. For someone who'd been in such a hurry to get ready, she had now decided to dawdle.

"Don't tell me your secrets," she said. "That's not a good idea."

"But then you can know me." There was a half-moon in the sky, which always made Lena think of a winking man—*joke's on you.*

"I don't want to know you. If I know you, that means they can ask me more questions about you. I don't want to have anything to tell them."

"More questions?" Lena stared at her with wide eyes.

"You misheard. I didn't say *more.*"

She didn't say more.

They reached House 1 and split up at the elevators. Jutta rode. Lena walked. She had said *more. More questions.*

No, she didn't. Why would anyone want to know about Lena? She was no one. She cleaned the eyes of House 1 so they could watch other people, not her.

The man in the Lada, reading the newspaper. When she'd come out of Erich's apartment that day. The apartment that now had a cat in it, and Friedrich So-and-So on the mailbox, and the real Friedrich So-and-So in his ugly stained undershirt. That man in the car had looked right at her.

She didn't say more.

Up went the Wall in Lena's head. It was tall, four meters of concrete like the real Wall, and topped by a sewer pipe so that it was impossible to gain any purchase on it if a person ever thought of climbing to the other side. And that was the far Wall, not the one on this side, the *Hinterlandmauer,* which was small and ordinary—*like you*—and neither Wall took any account of what was in the middle.

The middle part was the real thing. It was the part you couldn't see until you got there. Everything important happened in the middle. The signaling fence that set off a silent alarm. The watchtowers. The guns. The dogs. The bed of nails hidden in sand to pierce your feet. Barbed wire. Trip wire. The lights— as bright as daylight. The sirens.

The small, ordinary Wall was only a trick. It made you think you could get away with things. And then, when you had climbed it and gotten yourself stuck in the middle part, and realized you couldn't get away with anything, it was too late. Border guards had orders to shoot on sight.

She didn't say more. *And if you say she did, you are climbing the small, ordinary Wall, and you will get stuck in the middle, and no one gets away.* Not from there.

"Fräulein? Is that you?"

*

The Wall: it was all in how you thought of it. It hadn't been built to stop citizens from leaving the Better Germany; it was there to keep the capitalists and class enemies from getting in. It was a form of protection. It wasn't even called a Wall, not in front of the authorities. It was the Anti-Fascist Protection Rampart.

Life on this side of the Anti-Fascist Protection Rampart was easy. *Repeat after me, Mausi. I wonder what it would be like to have an uncle. What do you mean by hidden notebooks? I've never been to Prenzlauer Berg. Friedrich So-and-So?* Never heard of him.

Lena felt as if she were hanging from a branch by her fingers. One breeze, one crooked thought, one shard of memory—and she would fall.

But you don't have crooked thoughts. That was why her hair was so straight.

She worked. She said good night to Ernst with the long arms and went home. She ate her egg, put on the dishwater nightdress, and repeated all the straightened-out thoughts she now had about not having an uncle, not having had his books, not having had the pictures behind pictures. It was like being a member of a new club. When she'd turned seven and joined the Young Pioneers, she'd had to practice saying the things the Pioneers believed in until she could reach for them without thinking, like bedroom furniture in the dark.

She almost went to sleep. But then she began to think about pockets.

Pockets were good places to keep secrets, as long as the pockets stayed out of the laundry. She'd put something into her sweater pocket not long ago—folded, forgotten, a picture from that Western magazine *Der Spiegel*. The forbidden one that had been in the apartment that now belonged to Friedrich So-and-So, where Lena had never been because it was in Prenzlauer Berg and *you've never been to Prenzlauer Berg, though one day you'd like to go.*

She hoisted one leg over the small Wall. It was easy to climb, if you wanted to.

"That's Marilyn Monroe," he'd said. "An American actress." He? He who?

She had opened the magazine. *No, you didn't.* Yes, she did. There went the other leg over the Wall. *Be careful. There will be capitalists, and men with layabout hair.*

"She's very glamorous." That blond curly hair, those large breasts and beautiful dresses, the red lipstick Lena was not allowed to wear.

"She's also dead," Erich had said. *Not Erich.* "Suicide—a drug overdose." *Don't say* suicide. Suicide was something that only happened in the West.

Lena took her sweater from the cupboard. The people who had erased her uncle had made everything disappear. *Now you've done it. You said* erased. *You said* uncle. Every trace of him was gone: his books in the libraries and bookstores, the photographs she'd hidden, every little thing he might have given her.

She fished inside the pocket, felt the smooth folded page. *If you take that picture out . . .* She remembered the thought she'd had as if it were a chestnut in its prickly burr. She held it so tight it hurt. How could someone who looked like Marilyn Monroe, someone who was famous and lived in America, decide to kill herself?

Western decadence. The class enemy. Too much of too much, like being buried in candy, which would be fun, but only for the first few bites—and then buried was buried, you still needed to breathe.

But the dresses, that lipstick. Seeing Marilyn Monroe had produced a tug-of-war inside Lena. Too much of too much. Not enough of anything.

Lena's chest felt knotted as she held the smooth magazine page. She didn't have to unfold it. She could throw it in the garbage without looking at it. She could take it outside and set fire to it. She could leave it alone.

She pulled it out, unfolded it.

"Maybe just cut out one picture."

He'd given her scissors. They hadn't worked. *Scheiss Osten.* Lena had folded the edges of the picture and licked them so they would rip cleanly. Then Steffi had shown up, and Lena had torn the picture by accident. There was sticky tape on it now.

"You mustn't show that to your aunt," he'd said.

In the commotion of Erich's disappearance, Lena had forgotten about it. But now Marilyn Monroe stared up at her with the kind of smile you practiced in front of a mirror, the kind Lena had practiced when there'd been school, when a smile had mattered. Her fingers tightened around the picture until she forced herself to relax them or she would ruin it.

"What's that?" The bedroom door had opened without warning. There stood Sausage Auntie, encased in the doorway. "I thought you were in bed. I was coming to say good night."

"It's nothing." *Put it away.* But where? *Just down. Lay it down as if you don't care about it.* On the night table? *Just down.* "It's a

92

picture from a magazine." But the red lipstick, the blond hair, the white dress—Marilyn Monroe knew how to glow in the dark.

"Even from here I can see it's unsuitable. Where on earth did you get it?"

If she finds out it came from me, she won't let you—"Erich gave it to me."

Three steps, big ones. Auntie had a good stride when she wanted to get somewhere. She ripped the picture out of Lena's hands, ripped it until it was in shreds.

"No one gave you anything." She cupped the shreds in her hands as if they were snow that was about to melt, then stomped out of the room, pulling the door shut behind her with her foot.

But Lena wasn't crazy. Erich had given it to her, from a magazine he wasn't supposed to have had. Erich. Her uncle. *You do have one.*

"Then why do you keep saying I don't, Mausi?" she whispered. If Auntie heard her talking to herself, she would put it in her progress report under the heading of *No Progress Whatsoever*, and there would be appointments, and *we know where appointments lead.*

She put her sweater back into the cupboard and climbed under the covers. She was still settling into bed when Auntie burst back into the room wearing her time-to-have-a-chat face. "You understand that they've been here."

Lena sat up. *They.* She understood. *They* meant notepads and questions and *Do you mind if we look around?* Everyone minded, but no one ever said so. Lena had had enough of that. "How many of them were here? What else did they take? Did one of them have a newspaper?" And that man with the bushy beard she'd seen at Erich's window, had he been here too? How could Auntie have stood aside while strangers poked around in their private things?

Are you really asking that? Standing aside was what you did. You stayed out of the way, made yourself small, hoped they would forget about you altogether.

Auntie stood in the middle of the room. "Whatever is going on, it's a matter for State Security, not for a seventeen-year-old girl. You go to work, and to youth group meetings. You collect recyclables and have the right opinions. You do not ask questions; otherwise you'll get in trouble and—sit up straight so I know you're paying attention!"

Lena sat straighter. Auntie seemed ready to deliver the lesson of the day in her stiff teacher dress.

"Otherwise you'll get in trouble and so will I, do you see? There will be repercussions for me too. My Party membership. My friends." *Look up, look left.* "They're talking about making you a member, you know, when you turn eighteen. We must start thinking about your application, and what you might do during the probation period to prove yourself. We must start thinking about your future."

Her future: Was that what it would be like?

"When I come home this afternoon, I hope to find a new girl in this bedroom."

"You will, Auntie. I promise."

Auntie left the room and Lena lay down again. A new girl? Well, then she would have to pretend, especially if she wanted to track down her uncle.

She was supposed to be going to sleep, but for the first time since her parents had died, she felt awake. Or something inside her did. It was like a spark, a sudden certainty that sleepwalking through life was not the same as living.

She was awake, and she was determined to stay awake.

- 8 -

WRITE TO ERICH

It wasn't until the following Wednesday that Lena could finally get away for the errand that her newly awakened self had determined was necessary. She used the air raid siren as her alarm. The siren went off every Wednesday at one p.m., a thirty-second test that was impossible to sleep through. Usually it was an annoyance because Lena would struggle to fall back asleep afterward, but today it suited her purpose.

As she made her way to the state registry office in the town hall, she passed a whole row of buildings that had been painted to Volvo level. The registry office smelled yellow and dusty. The women who worked there were also yellow and dusty, and grim-faced to the people waiting in line—"Next?" "Yes?"—as if they were playing the game Lena and Erich used to play when they tried to use the fewest words possible to get what they wanted. Erich had done it with a policeman once and had nearly gotten arrested.

"I'd like to see Erich Altmann's birth record," Lena announced at the counter. "Date of birth: October 14, 1941." *You haven't erased his birthdate too, have you?* But she wouldn't say that, or the one thousand eyes would start watching her more closely. Maybe they already were.

Jutta said *more questions. She didn't.* She did.

The woman who was supposed to be helping Lena took down a big brown book, licked the tip of one finger, and flipped through its pages. A long look, and then, "I'm sorry." She put the book back on its shelf and sat at her desk. "We don't have a record of anyone by that name. Are you certain of the spelling?"

"Yes. Please have another look. He was born here, in Berlin."

She stood up as if she'd become the oldest woman in the world: *For God's sake, you're making me check again?* As she returned to the shelf, she made a joke to one of her friends, something they must have talked about at lunchtime. The two women laughed. Lena tried to smile, even though she had no idea what they were talking about, and the joke made her feel as if the woman wasn't looking very hard for Erich's birth record.

She remembered the state registry joke Erich used to tell her: "A man enters the registry office and says, 'I'd like to change my name. My whole life I've endured the name Erich Shitbucket and I can't stand it any longer.' The clerk says, 'I understand. Who could live with the name Erich?'"

Lena watched the woman's fingers flip through the brown book again, wondering what would happen if she told the Shitbucket joke.

"There's nothing." The woman shut the heavy book with a *thud.* "Like I said."

Nothing? What did that mean? Had they crossed off his name? Taped over it with someone else's? "Maybe you haven't checked carefully enough," Lena said. Being awake was making her too bold. *You don't speak like that to women in dusty registry offices, or they will un-help you.*

And here went the woman, un-helping Lena with a glare and calling for the next one in line. Normally Lena would have accepted the situation and gone home, but today she stood her ground. "It's important." She pleaded with her eyes. "Maybe I could look." But the woman was already may-I-helping the man behind Lena, who had placed his elbows on the counter to claim all the available space, edging Lena into a no-man's-land where there were no line-ups or women behind counters, just worn and warped flooring.

Behind her, a clock ticked. The warm office made her feel sweaty and panicky. She had to get home before Auntie arrived back from work. But she couldn't give up.

"Please," she called to the woman, who was now in a deep conversation with the man with the great wingspan. "I know my uncle was born."

The man turned to her. "She said the records aren't here. Maybe he was born somewhere else and someone didn't tell you the truth, huh?"

The woman behind the counter smiled at him. They were forming a team, becoming friends. Lena stuck her hands into the pocket that now didn't contain Marilyn Monroe and scuffed her way out of the office. She was getting that closed-into-an-elevator sensation where her head got too noisy and her skin went clammy. In the hallway she plunked herself onto a wooden chair and bent toward the floor to keep from fainting.

Must get home before Auntie. Auntie would be upset by Lena's unexplained (and unsanctioned) absence. She would ask questions. But Auntie was part of the problem. Whatever was going on, she was in on it. Erich was her brother. How could she say he didn't exist? Who had told her to say that?

You are small, Mausi, and they are all big. As she walked to the U-Bahn station she'd never felt smaller in her life.

When she entered the apartment, Auntie's coat already hung on its hook, smelling of chalk and classrooms and all the right answers. Her sensible black teacher's shoes were lined up on the mat, laces tucked in. Lena glanced at her watch. Auntie must have come home from work early. Probably it was another headache, which was about to become Lena's fault.

Sure enough, here came Auntie out of the kitchen. She stared at Lena for several long seconds, as if to emphasize that Lena standing in the hallway was very wrong, very wrong indeed.

"I leave you in bed. I come home and the bed's empty. Where have you been? You're going to be late for youth group."

Lena tried to come up with something that would be good for Auntie's morale. "I wanted to go swimming."

She slipped off her shoes. Her stomach was protesting the earlier-than-usual wake-up that afternoon. When she tried to edge past Auntie into the kitchen, Auntie reached for her and brought a handful of hair to her nose. "I don't smell chlorine."

"The pool was still closed for repairs." Lena entered the kitchen, pulled a piece of crispbread out of the box, and took a bite.

"Well. Danika and Peter will be waiting for you."

"I'll stay home and help you with your headache. I don't feel like going to youth group." *Yes, you do. You're a new girl, remember? There will be singing, and they're making plans for a winter excursion. You're on your way to a Party membership. That was what Auntie promised the men who came to hire you for your cleaning job.*

"You swore an oath," Auntie said. "You have to go. I'll be fine here on my own."

Lena stood in the center of the kitchen, dropping crumbs onto the floor. Any minute now Auntie would take up the broom with a loud huff and sweep too hard, making the crumbs fly all over the place, because that sort of sweeping was not designed to pick anything up. Lena could smell the kitchen scraps and remembered it had been her job to empty them. Normally she would have felt bad. She would not have dropped the crumbs, not on purpose. But that spark inside her, foreign and exciting, made her brave. She remembered the man in the registry office who had spread his elbows like wings, and she put her hands on her hips to see what it felt like. Dangerous, that's what. And exhilarating. Like she could fly.

"Where is he?" Lena said. "I know you know where he is. Give me an address at least, so I can write to him."

Auntie's eyebrows went wavy. "Who?"

"Erich."

"That's General Secretary Honecker to you. Do you have a complaint?"

Wait, what? A complaint?

"If you have a complaint, you can write to our General Secretary. He reads all the letters. I know that for a fact."

Lena had believed that when she was younger. She'd also believed Father Christmas read all his mail.

"Is it about the swimming pool?" Auntie continued. "I've half a mind to write to him myself about all the youth who are missing out on important physical activity because the repairs are never completed."

"Auntie, I want to write to Uncle Erich."

Sausage Auntie's eyes went buggy, as if her panty hose had shrunk a full size. She switched on the radio and turned it up loud, then grabbed Lena by both shoulders. "You. Don't. Have. An. Uncle." Shake, shake, shake, to the beat of the Puhdys. "Do you understand?"

There was a loud knock at the door. Both Lena and Auntie froze.

"Lena, are you coming?" It was Peter.

Auntie brought her face so close to Lena's she could see a wiry hair growing out of the mole above her lip. "Stop this foolishness, for your own good. There are things you don't understand, and it will only lead to trouble."

Lena backed away from her and called, "I'll be right there. I just have to change." She went into her bedroom, found the blue shirt with the rising-sun crest on the left sleeve, and pulled it on over her T-shirt.

Stop . . . for your own good. Anytime Auntie said something was for Lena's own good, it was never true. It was for Auntie's good.

I'll write to Erich, then. I do have a complaint. Where's my uncle? What did you do with him?

Lena pulled the door open with more force than she'd intended, startling Peter. Danika stood next to him, studying her long nails, which, today, were painted brown. The sight of her friends calmed

Lena down. She shut the door behind her, relieved that there was solid wood between her and Auntie.

"Mein Gott, take that damned thing off." Danika nodded at Lena's shirt.

Auntie wouldn't hear of Lena walking to youth group without her blue *Freie Deutsche Jugend* shirt on, but Danika refused to be seen in public in hers, and only put it on right before they entered the meeting. Lena pulled the shirt off and stuffed it into her bag.

Peter wasn't wearing his *Free German Youth* shirt either. He had something new on. It was synthetic, with a swirling purple pattern, buttoned right to his neck.

"That's swanky," Lena said.

"It's only okay," Danika said. "Feel it, it's not Western."

"You're not starting that again, are you?" Peter said. Danika had a thing about Western clothes. Nothing Peter or Lena wore was ever good enough because it hadn't come from *Exquisit*— even though Danika could barely afford to shop there herself. The only other way to get Western clothes was to have a relative in the West send you a parcel, but that could cause problems. Auntie's late husband, Helmut, had a brother in the West, but Auntie had no communication with him. Otherwise she wouldn't get her bonus at work, and they would kick her out of the Party.

"What does your father think of that shirt?" Lena suspected Military Papa and swirling purple patterns wouldn't be sitting at the same supper table.

"He hasn't seen it." Peter hunched his shoulders. "He'll say it's homosexual. He'll make me take it off and then I'll have to go to extra meetings of the GST."

The GST was the Society for Sport and Technology, though

which sports and what technology Lena had never been able to figure out. At the GST, boys learned to strip machine guns, throw hand grenades, and shoot at targets.

"I'll wear my youth group shirt home," Peter said. "He'll never know."

Peter had thought ahead. This was subversion. Did it mean Lena could trust him, or was it a trick? She wanted so badly to tell someone about what had happened to her uncle. About the strange meeting with Steffi, and the missing books from libraries and bookstores, and the dusty yellow woman who couldn't find his birth record. But if Peter felt compelled to tell his father—*no, you don't mess with a man like that.*

They arrived at the center where the youth group meetings were held and went inside for roll call. *"The Party, the Party is always right,"* they sang. Lena gave a report on their project of beautifying the courtyard: the trenches they had dug, Auntie's enthusiasm, and how good the whole thing was for the morale of the housing development. Jobs were assigned for planning the winter excursion. Peter talked about the bottles and cans he'd collected. Danika studied her nails.

The center also had a newsstand and a post office. They waited while Danika ran errands for her mother, and then on their way home stopped behind some trees so Peter could take off the purple shirt. Danika waggled her eyebrows at Lena while Peter was undressing. *He likes you*, she mouthed.

"Shut up," Lena said. "He does not."

Peter emerged from the bushes wearing his youth group shirt.

"I don't understand why you bothered with the purple one," Danika said, "if you can't wear it all the time."

"I wanted to see what it felt like," he said.

Danika rolled her eyes, but Lena understood. It was like dropping crumbs of crispbread onto Auntie's clean kitchen floor. Dropping them and not sweeping them up, and feeling that rise in the stomach of *I'm doing it, so there.* Even if you couldn't do it for long, still, you'd done it, and that was something.

*

Dear Herr Honecker, Mr. General Secretary,

I'm looking for my uncle, Erich Altmann. I know that's his name because he's my uncle.

Wait. Do you know? What if Oma and Opa named him something different when he was born? Erich might not be his name at all, or it might be his middle name. What if he was adopted? Remember what Jutta said about not knowing where you come from.

It might not have been his name at birth, Mr. General Secretary, but you and I both know he is the author of many good books, including Castles Underground, if you happen to have read it. Although no one can read it anymore because it has vanished from every bookstore and library.

Perhaps it's not the best idea to mention the books. Remember the men at Erich's apartment? One carried the typewriter like it was an unexploded bomb. They took all the notebooks. They sat in front of his building reading the newspaper for hours and watching the door. Maybe writing is what got him into trouble in the first place. Maybe writing will get you into trouble too.

Dear Herr Honecker, Mr. General Secretary,

Everyone keeps telling me I don't have an uncle, but I do. His name might be Erich Altmann. He might have been born in Berlin. We won't talk about his writing. I think you know where he is.

Oh, Mausi, no. That's too accusatory. You cannot get angry at the General Secretary. He's a hunter. You will become prey.

Dear Herr Honecker, Mr. General Secretary,

I hear you are a very good hunter. Also, I like your glasses. The swimming pool in my neighborhood is always closed for repairs. Do you think you could look into that? I cannot be an effective citizen in my community if I don't get enough physical activity.

From,
Lena Altmann
(Niece of Erich Altmann, who has disappeared off the face of the earth and please can you tell me where he is.)

She ripped up the first letters and threw them into the wastepaper box. The last one she folded and left in her night table drawer. She would have to find an envelope; with any luck there would be some for sale in the stationery shop. Then she would send it, and see if Mr. General Secretary really read all his mail.

– 9 –

THE BEST SECRET EVER

Lena entered the ashtray room and slumped into the brown wooden chair next to Jutta. "What did they want to know about me?" Because this was the sort of question you asked when you were awake.

Jutta glanced up from *Sibylle*, the same issue as before, the women in winter coats looking impossibly chic and whispering secrets to each other that must have been very amusing, judging by their euphoric expressions. Jutta's eyes were hooded and tired. "Good evening to you too. What, did you hit your head and wake up as a savage?"

"I'm sorry. Good evening, Jutta. How are you this evening?"

Jutta blew out a stream of smoke. "Nothing changes. Some might call that boring, but I call it dependable."

Dependable misery? Don't open that jar of pickles. "Jutta?"

Jutta covered the winter women with her large red hands.

"Here we go. What is it this time, child? And don't let's go where I think you're going."

Lena leaned toward her so she could speak softly—which was silly. The ashtray room was the size of a cupboard, and there was no one in it except the two of them. "What did they ask you? Please tell me. It's important."

Jutta glanced at her watch. "Time to get started." She shoved her chair back from the table so hard it made a sharp scraping sound.

Lena didn't move. "We still have fifteen minutes."

But Jutta was already on her feet, bending toward Lena. "I told them you had a plank in front of your head," she said. "That you didn't understand anything and wouldn't go around asking questions that shouldn't be asked."

"But my uncle—"

"You don't have an uncle, you hear me?"

Wait. Every Monday night in the history of Monday nights, Jutta had asked about Lena's weekend. Specifically, she'd asked about Lena's visits with her uncle. Two Mondays ago, she had asked. But this past Monday, she hadn't. Lena hadn't thought anything of it—but now, she wondered: maybe Jutta hadn't asked because she'd already known.

How could Lena have an uncle and not have an uncle? *Things can't be both true and not true.* But they could. She remembered the time she'd asked Erich about *Castles Underground.* "Is it a true story?"

"It's a novel." They were walking on the uneven sidewalk in his neighborhood. You had to keep your eyes down or you risked tripping. Erich was smoking, and his boots made a *clip-clop* sound on the concrete that Lena found comforting. "A novel means fiction," he said. "A made-up story."

"But you worked in the mines." The way he'd written about the castle being underground, the constant sound of dripping water, the walls sparkling with hidden treasure—to her it had sounded just like a mine. She glanced at his left hand, the one missing its pinkie finger.

Erich had nodded. "Writers draw on the truth they know to build an imaginary world that they don't know."

"So all stories are true, then," Lena said.

His smile was like a prize. "Yes, I suppose they are. Also, they're all lies." He'd made a voice like a crazy man and waved his arms in the air. "All lies, damnable lies!" An older couple walking toward them had veered out of Erich's way, as if afraid of the attention he was calling to himself.

All true. All lies. Somewhere in the middle, Lena would have to find a solid place to stand. *Black is white*, she told herself, or it could be if you squinted hard enough. She pulled on her coveralls and gathered bucket, broom, mop, and Purimix. Jutta wouldn't tell her anything, she could see by her face. Someone who had made up their mind to keep *stumm* had an unmistakable expression: *closed for business, do not call again.* Jutta had become so concentrated on getting ready that she didn't even have a moment to look at Lena. And yet there was something in her not-looking that made Lena think she felt bad.

They crossed the compound and entered the foyer of House 1, with its three red flags. They passed the sculptures of serious men with serious beards, and Lena went up the stairs, once, twice.

When Herr Dreck called her into his office and told her to put down the Purimix, she told herself silently, *There is no prostitution in the Better Germany,* because Sausage Auntie had told her that many times. *Prostitution* was not a word. Despite the textile factory girls with their red lipstick and immoral ideas. Despite the chocolate wrapped in gold foil that Lena ate afterward. Despite the dismissive wave of Herr Dreck's hand, because now he could go home to his wife and daughters, and eat his supper with a shiny knife and fork, and smoke his expensive cigar with a little (or big) glass of schnapps, and rest his hands on his Party-size stomach while Lena swept the floors and didn't pee in the cupboard where he kept a pair of shiny shoes.

A metal filing cabinet had been left open, probably by accident, behind the desk in another agent's office. He would have been in huge trouble if there'd been a security check that night. Lena didn't notice the dividers, which were labeled with street names. She didn't think of Erich's street, or the ones that intersected it. She didn't look, really. *You didn't see anything. You don't say anything.*

At the end of her shift she and Jutta went through the portal together and entered the *schrullig* world. If they'd been in a story, they would have held hands as they crossed the threshold, but this wasn't a story—even if Lena had wanted to pretend it was for Erich. She and Jutta walked inside single file, businesslike, and went their separate ways.

Lena wandered over to the place where they made magic keys. A locksmith was always working, grinding keys that would grant a person entry into any place they wanted, even Erich's apartment. *Mausi! These are keys for magical places, not people's homes.* Then how did the men in suits get in? *They knocked*—the way they did. Not a polite knock. A *bang bang bang* designed to bring down the door if necessary. Lena had heard it once, down the hall in her building.

"Do you still have a set of my keys?" Erich had asked. He'd given them to her long ago, after she'd come to visit once and he had been delayed coming home, and she'd had to wait on the stairs for an hour. He had held her, and said he was sorry, and had the keys made for her by a locksmith like these ones. "From now on, if I'm not home, you let yourself in and take a Vita Cola and find something to read while you wait for me," he'd said.

The grinding of the *schrullig* locksmiths set Lena's teeth on edge. She moved along: orange space helmets, shiny shoes, crescent-moon bananas, as many as you wanted—but not in the regular world of the Better Germany. When Lena had lived in Magdeburg, they'd lined up twice a year and gotten one banana per person per household, then sliced them into tiny round full-moons and made them last just long enough that the moons didn't turn brown.

What was the *schrullig* world even doing here, hidden away in House 18? *If you're going to have subversive thoughts, you might as well go home.*

She was on her way out of the compound when it began to pour—a hard, cold autumn rain that would turn the not-yet-beautified courtyard into a swamp. She hadn't thought to bring an umbrella, but she remembered there was one in the ashtray room, folded in the corner behind a chair, dusty and forgotten.

Lena ran back to House 24 and burst into the ashtray room, rainwater dripping off her hair and coat, her shoes squeaking across the floor. The small room was empty and smelled of stale smoke. Jutta's favorite copy of *Sibylle* sat on the table, still open to the women in their winter coats.

Why did Jutta like this magazine so much? Everyone was always saying Lena was the simple one, but from what she saw every person had a weakness—an inner pig-dog to overcome, as Auntie would have said.

Lena flipped backward through the magazine until she reached the cover. She decided she would play a trick on Jutta. She'd put another magazine on the table in place of this one and see what happened. *Where's my* Sibylle? she imagined Jutta barking in her cigarette voice. *Where are my women in winter coats telling each other the best secrets ever?*

When Lena picked up the magazine, she almost missed it—the bump. She wouldn't have noticed anything if her fingers hadn't grazed over it. She stared at the table for a long time. The bump was tucked beneath the vinyl covering that had been glued to the table. An easy way to wipe it down, Jutta had said, although no one ever bothered. The stains on that vinyl had been there for the entire two years Lena had worked at Stasi headquarters. But why a bump? Why beneath? It was almost not there. Almost, but not quite.

Lena bent down and crawled under the table. She didn't want to see what she was looking for. *Then why are you on your knees? Don't look. Just go home.* She looked. There it was: a bird's nest of wiring, rows of batteries. She stared, and looked away. And looked back again.

Black is white. But batteries were batteries, and wiring was wiring. And the bump beneath the vinyl was a listening device.

And Jutta had known.

She couldn't have known. She just likes Sibylle. *She loves* Sibylle. *She loves it so much that she reads the same magazine every single day.*

No, Mausi. She was told not to move the magazine. Because if she moved the magazine, Lena might get the same idea, might pick it up to get a new one, might notice the bump. If Jutta never moved the magazine, Lena would understand that the magazine was not to be moved. Jutta was the older one, a staff sergeant, the one in charge of the two of them, and if she wanted *Sibylle* to stay on the table, then *Sibylle* would stay on the table.

Lena crawled out and stood holding on to the back of a chair. Her legs felt as if they were made of cardboard. She picked up the copy of *Sibylle* and placed it carefully where it had been, opening it to the women in their winter coats. What was the best secret ever? *They're listening. They're listening to you.*

She walked backward out of the ashtray room, as if turning her back on the device would put her in even more danger. Then she went out into the rain, having completely forgotten about the umbrella until she was halfway home and too soaked to care.

"Look what the cat dragged in," Sausage Auntie said when she arrived. "You're late. Your egg is cold."

"I'm sorry," Lena mumbled, and sat down. Next to her egg was a piece of paper. Lena recognized the handwriting. It was the last of the letters she'd written to Erich Honecker, the one she'd been thinking of sending.

Auntie didn't sit down. "Would you like to tell me about that?"

"No." Lena banged the top of the egg on the table and peeled away the shell, wishing yet again for Peter's or Danika's fingernails.

"There's nothing wrong with writing to our General Secretary, you understand. He wants to hear from his people. And writing to him about the swimming pool is laudable. Do you know what *laudable* means?"

Lena knew, but she said *no*, because she also knew Auntie cherished every opportunity to teach her something. If she was going to be a new girl, she had better be teachable.

"It means it's a fine idea. But we're going to cut the bottom of the letter off. It's unsuitable. It makes you sound unstable."

Lena chewed on a mouthful of egg. She had to swallow hard to make it go down.

Auntie sat next to her. "You know, Lena, I saw your school records in Magdeburg."

Uh-oh. She's using your name. Will she take off her reading glasses? If she takes them off, you'd better stop eating that egg.

She took off her reading glasses. Lena folded her hands in her lap and braced herself.

"You were a good student. The doctors did everything they could to help you after your parents' accident."

Lena remembered school, the notebooks filled with her careful handwriting, the common sense of numbers and equations. In the early grades, whenever she'd done good work, the teachers would stamp a buzzing bee on her assignments. Never a wasp. She used to be so proud to show those bees to her parents.

She hadn't liked the doctors at the mental hospital, though.

"They're not trying to help you," Uncle Erich used to whisper when he came to visit. Lena didn't think so either. She had wanted to remember her parents. They were trying to make her forget.

"If you ever want to get out of here," Erich had said, "you'd better submit. Tell them what they want to hear."

It had meant shutting a part of herself down, putting it to sleep. And that part had slept so well it had forgotten to wake up—until last week.

"It was Uncle Erich who helped me," Lena said now. "Not the doctors."

"Is that so?" Auntie puffed up like an angry goose. "Let me tell you something about that layabout brother of mine."

Lena clenched her fists. "So now I have an uncle?"

Auntie glared at her and turned the radio on loud. It was a song by October Club called "Tell Me Your Standpoint." Lena hated it, and so did the baby next door. He would start to howl in three, two, one, go.

"Do you understand how you got the job at headquarters?" Auntie asked. "Not because of Erich, I'll tell you that much. Because of me. And Helmut's Party connections, which I have taken great care to maintain."

Look up. Look left.

"Otherwise you might have ended up in a textile factory, or they would have kept you in the hospital. I got you out. Me. I'm the only one who can get anything done around here. You don't apply for a job at headquarters, you understand? They come to you. Well, they came to me."

"Because of Helmut," Lena said.

"That's right. I had to show them your school records, hospital records. I assured them you wouldn't be a nuisance. And then"—*smack* went her meaty hands onto the table— "when they asked around for character testimonials, what did they discover? She's the niece of the celebrated author Erich Altmann. Well."

"What's wrong with that? Everyone loves his books." Loved. When his books had existed.

"He chose to serve as a construction soldier in the People's Army." Auntie's voice dropped. "Then he was work-shy. When he finally got a job in the mines, he caused trouble. Grew his hair long, listened to Western music. The men from State Security didn't trust him. I even offered to put an end to your Sunday visits—"

"What?" Lena leaped to her feet, rattling her spoon on the table and almost overturning her egg.

Auntie motioned for her to sit. "The men from the Stasi were generous. They said no, a simple girl should get to spend time with her uncle once a week."

"But you said I wasn't simple." *Not simple.* Two words. They fit funny, like a beautiful new pair of shoes that hadn't yet formed to her feet; shoes she wanted so badly but wasn't yet convinced she deserved.

"Don't you see? *Simple* is why they've left you alone. Please, Lena, you must listen to me." Auntie's voice softened, and Lena began to panic. "I told them you were simple; it's what I've been telling them all along. You must let this business of my brother go. Show gradual improvement in the progress reports, and move forward."

Auntie poured Lena a glass of apple juice. "Finish your breakfast and go to bed. I need to get ready for work." She shut off the radio.

"Are you going to have a headache today?" Lena asked.

Auntie glared at her. "I have one already." She left the kitchen to get dressed, and Lena sat at the table alone. The baby's crying had become rhythmic, wave upon wave of howls that showed no signs of stopping.

Simple *is why they've left you alone.* But the bump under the vinyl in the ashtray room meant they hadn't. And she had asked Jutta about Erich—and they had heard every word.

How long had the bump been there? *Well, how many Mondays—without fail—has Jutta asked about your weekend? The visits with your uncle.* Lena couldn't quite remember, but it was possible Jutta had known about those visits before Lena had ever mentioned them.

You're not simple. She'd read every book Erich had ever given her, many of them twice. In class, she used to raise her hand often, not the limp-noodle arm of a student who wasn't sure of the answer, but a ruler-straight, I-know arm.

Then came the accident. The principal had called her into his office in the middle of Geometry—all the straight lines running crooked, all the balanced equations slipping off the table and piling up on the floor. There was that closed-in feeling, like the room was too small to hold what he was telling her. Then came the way her head had grown noisy with wasps. First a few, sensing a sugary drink, then the call to families, friends, distant cousins in flower beds and trash cans to come, come quickly, there's something big to sting.

A nervous breakdown, that was what it was. Then when it wouldn't go away, they called it other things: severe depression, prolonged traumatic stress.

The doctors had advised against continuing with her schooling. They'd said it would be too hard on her. She was fragile; she might break. They'd kept her in the hospital for a year, had warned

Auntie if there was no improvement they would consider surgery. The accident at the freight car factory had happened right before the end of eighth grade. Lena had missed her *Jugendweihe*—the ceremony when all the young people, all her friends, had become adults, had their first glass of wine. There'd been speeches, new dresses, vows to recite—but not for Lena. She had never been recognized as a young adult.

She took her dishes to the sink to wash them.

Maybe they're afraid of you.

Of her? Lena Altmann, who counted Erichs every night, and had a voice called Mausi inside her, and liked the sweet and sour of Vita Cola and *solyanka*, and (shh) the *yeah yeah yeah* music? Who could be afraid of her?

If they weren't afraid, why had they bugged the ashtray room?

But if they were afraid, why was she still working at Stasi head-quarters? Maybe Auntie's relationships were very special indeed. Or had Herr Dreck insisted? Did he think she had a special relationship with him? That left Lena with a sick feeling in her stomach.

No, that's not it at all. They'd come to Auntie. They'd hired Lena, even though they had known about Erich. They had allowed the visits to continue. Jutta asked about them every Monday, in the ashtray room that was bugged.

When it finally clicked into place, Lena was so stunned she dropped the soapy mug she'd been holding and it landed in the sink with a *thud*.

She was an informer. She'd been one all along and hadn't even known it. It was the thing Erich's friends had warned him about; the reason Steffi didn't like her.

She set her dishes to dry on the counter. She went into her bedroom, got undressed, and pulled the gray nightdress over her head. *You have the advantage. You know about the bug. They don't know that you know.* It meant she'd have to be careful how she spoke, what she said. Not another word about Erich in the ashtray room, and no more questions about being crazy. If she sounded unbalanced, they would send her back to that hospital. And if she got sent back a second time, not even Auntie would be able to get her out.

– 10 –

HOT OFF THE PRESS

It was noon on Thursday, and Auntie was at work. Lena should have been sleeping, but instead she sat on the sofa and stared at the audience of porcelain dogs. Whatever Erich had done, it must have been serious to make the authorities react in the way they had. She remembered when the news had spread that a Lutheran minister in her neighborhood had syphilis, which later turned out not to be true. And it had all been because he and his family had applied to leave the country. *You're allowed to leave the Better Germany.* All you needed to do was apply. Then wait. Then watch your life, and the lives of your family members, be destroyed.

You said destroyed. Where was the Wall in her mind? *Destroyed* needed to be on the other side. But Lena was on the other side now too. It was too late for that. *Think.* The Stasi hadn't erased the Lutheran minister, so that wasn't what this was about.

Writing is trouble. Erich used to say that. "Unless you're writing Party Chinese"—the language of the newspapers. Then it was just boring. Had he written something that was trouble? If so, he would have hidden it. *If you were Erich and you wanted to hide something*—well, Erich was clever. The regular hiding places— under the bed, between the sofa cushions—would have been too ordinary for him. *Remember all those notebooks you saw under his bed?* Yes, but he'd moved them. He'd known that hiding spot was no good.

If you were him, if it was writing, where would you put it?

In the lining of a coat. But she had a feeling if she checked in Erich's closet she would only find the larger clothes that stretched over Friedrich So-and-So's fat belly. All of Erich's clothes would be gone. *Because he's on vacation.*

Stop that. You didn't take everything you'd ever owned when you went on vacation. You weren't erased when you went on vacation. Your birth record didn't disappear.

A picture popped into Lena's head of the men carrying armloads of notebooks out the front door. There'd been three or four of them combing through the place. They would have taken everything. Once, though—

Wind back. Think.

Erich often gave her things to read that he had written, but one time it had been different. "Hot off the press," he had said with a laugh. The page had been cold—so cold it had made Lena's fingertips feel funny. So cold, she realized, that he must have kept it in the freezer. Of course! Who would ever think to look for his papers in there?

"My freezer might need defrosting." It was almost the last

thing he'd said to her. His beloved freezer, now in the hands of Friedrich So-and-So.

Lena leaped up. She had to go back to his apartment and find out. She dressed in comfortable clothes, and wore her Zehas in case she had to make a run for it. Barring another headache, she had several hours before Auntie might be home. And Auntie had gotten into trouble for her frequent headaches at work. They were bad for morale. Lena was quite sure she was safe.

Erich's keys were hidden at the back of a kitchen drawer full of odds and ends. They seemed like junk, something from long ago that had been forgotten. If Sausage Auntie had known what they were, she would have confiscated them. Lena put them in her pocket.

What do you plan to do in Friedrich So-and-So's apartment? Don't you think you're going too far? No. Going too far was making someone vanish. Going too far was erasing an entire life as if it had never happened.

Lena took the U-Bahn, then the S-Bahn, and then she was in Prenzlauer Berg, on Erich's street. There were no men parked in Ladas anymore, or at least Lena didn't see any. She stood in a doorway across the street and watched her uncle's window. It was dark. Friedrich's cat sat perched on the sill, looking angry at anything that could fly.

It didn't seem like Friedrich was home, but he'd been home in the middle of the day last time, and in his undershirt. If he didn't bother with a proper shirt to answer the door, he might not bother with lights either. No job. A layabout. He must have been a huge disappointment to the Stasi men who'd given him the prize of Erich's apartment.

Ring the bell. See if he answers.

And if he did? *Run away.* He might call the police, but she was wearing her Zehas; the police would never catch her.

The front door of the building was left unlocked during the day, so she let herself in. She had to pass the mailboxes, which made her hate the new name beside her uncle's box all over again. She climbed the stairs and rang the bell. No one answered.

What if he was in the bath? That was why he couldn't hear the bell. Right now, he was lying there naked, his hairy stomach making a round squishy island in the warm water. *Erich doesn't have a bathtub.* What if he was in that stinky shared bathroom in the stairwell? She went over and pushed on the bathroom door. A putrid smell rushed to meet her. No one was in there.

She returned to the apartment and knocked. Waited. Knocked again. She wasn't really going to let herself into Friedrich So-and-So's apartment, but somehow her hand was fitting the key into the keyhole. She turned once, twice, and pushed the door open.

"Hello?" she called, just to be sure, before she entered. Because now, *now, Mausi,* what she was doing was against the law.

Something moved in the corner of the room. It was the cat, slinking toward her. It meowed and sat on its haunches, staring at her as if it was waiting for something. She shut the door, so it wouldn't escape.

"I don't have to show you my identity card, kitty," she whispered.

If Friedrich So-and-So comes home while you're here, you understand you will be trapped, and both of your speedy-fast Zehas will be standing in the biggest bowl of grease you've ever seen. Therefore, she'd better move quickly.

She went straight to the kitchen and opened the freezer. There was half a plum cake wrapped in plastic, which would take about two years to defrost. Something was wrapped in newspaper; Lena didn't even want to know what it was. There was *Ketwurst*—the Better Germany's answer to the American hot dog—and there were a few white rolls. Mostly the freezer was full of ice. *I could have told you this would happen*, Auntie would have said. *How many years has it been since he's defrosted it?* and, *That layabout hair of his—anyone with long hair, you know they won't defrost their freezer.*

But there, poking out of the ice, was a corner of plastic, as if the ice had known its job and had grown around it. There was no time for defrosting. Lena fished in the drawers for a knife. She took out the plum cake, *Ketwurst*, rolls, and unidentified remains, and set them on the counter. Then, with the tip of the knife, she picked away at the solid wall of ice.

No, no, no! You must never chip the ice out of a freezer. You'll ruin it.

Lena murmured an apology to Erich, even if it was Friedrich So-and-So's freezer now. But soon something emerged from the ice: paper, covered in plastic to protect it. She had to be careful not to poke right through it with the knife.

She forgot about the noise she was making. She forgot about the time that was passing. She even forgot about the cat, who sat on the counter watching her. All Lena's attention was focused on the plastic-covered page that she couldn't free by pulling on it. It was stuck.

Hurry.

She hacked more fiercely. Almost. Almost. Yes! She pulled out the plastic-wrapped paper, put down the knife—and the door to the apartment opened. There stood Friedrich So-and-So, not in his undershirt. He was wearing an overcoat and galoshes, and he held a mesh bag full of groceries.

"What in hell's name—? What are you doing in here?"

Go, Mausi. Go.

But Friedrich So-and-So took up all the available doorway space, blocking it so Lena couldn't get out.

I told you you'd step in the grease. Now what?

Lena glanced at the open freezer and the food on the countertop. "I was hungry." The secret paper was still in her hand. She stuffed it into her coat pocket, then glanced around for something, anything, to distract him. All she could think of was the cat. Grabbing it under one arm, she rushed toward Friedrich and rammed into him, tossing the cat toward him at the same time. There was a loud squeal from the cat, and "Jesus!" from Friedrich as he dropped his groceries. Lena pushed past him. She was almost out the door when something caught her sleeve. That something was Friedrich So-and-So's fleshy hand.

"You're not going anywhere," he said.

That's what you think. She twisted and pulled, and then she got free, and at that very moment the best thing possible happened: the cat got out.

Don't let the cat out, Danika was always saying when Lena came over. Letting the cat out was the worst thing ever, because then you'd have to chase it, and cats were experts at making humans look like fools. Plus, all they ever really wanted was to be outside.

Lena flew down the stairs, past the cat who seemed both thrilled and terrified by this sudden turn of events. She expected to hear a scuffle behind her, some gentle tongue-clicking and a promise of fish if the cat would just cooperate for God's sake. Instead she heard lumbering footsteps and the wheezing of a man unused to running. Cat be damned, he was chasing Lena.

She pushed open the heavy front door and took off down the street, hoping to get around the corner before Friedrich So-and-So made it outside. With any luck, he'd have no idea where she'd gone. But who else was watching? There may not have been any men sitting in Ladas, but what about the older lady walking with a cane? Or the younger one in her pretty leather shoes that matched her purse? Or the shopkeeper sweeping outside his shop? Any one of them could point and tell Friedrich So-and-So *She went that way.*

Lena flew around one corner, and another, and then she forced herself to walk. Running made her look guilty. She needed to get away from here. He could be coming around any corner, even this one.

Lena's heart raced. What if Friedrich called the police? Her speedy Zehas wanted to run, fast, away, but her head was full of noise, a thousand voices at once, every clock in a clock store ticking at a different speed, every television set on in her building. On the next street there was a VoPo, a member of the People's Police, wearing his long gray-green coat and fancy hat and speaking into a handheld radio.

Erich used to make fun of how dumb the Volkspolizei were. He said they had to use transparent lunch boxes so they would remember whether they were going to work or coming home. *Are their dogs dumb too?* Lena didn't like those big German shepherds, with their deep-woof barks that sounded like an approaching storm. She needed to get off the street.

You should go home.

But now the voices in her head were screaming. Even the clouds were closing in on her, the way the walls had in the school principal's office—"There's been a terrible accident"—coming closer—"Both of your parents"—the ceiling, the floors—"are dead."

She wanted to sit down, catch her breath. *You should get off the street.* Her ears were buzzing—*oh no*—and when she looked up, the tram lines sagged closer to her head. She would attract attention soon, the kind where they called a doctor with a soft voice who asked if you knew your own name and then reminded you of it over and over.

Down the next street was Erich's favorite *Kneipe*, the one with the piggy-faced barman. Still, the pub was better than the curb. It would be warm in there, and dark, and she could sit and clear her head. *You understand that if Friedrich comes into the pub, you'll be cornered.* But why would he? He didn't know Erich; he'd said so himself. The Stasi wouldn't have told him any more than he needed to know about his new apartment: *congratulations, here are the keys.*

She pulled open the door and was struck by the sudden darkness and the intense smells of beer, and sausage, and smoke. It took a moment for her senses to adjust, and then there was the barman, smiling his I-have-the-right-to-deny-you-service smile. *It might be the only power he has in his life. Maybe he has a terrible wife who orders him around at home.*

"You again," he said. "No milk today, Fräulein."

"I would just like a glass of water." But maybe you weren't allowed to drink water in the pub if you didn't buy something to eat. Only now she realized she was ridiculously hungry. *Auntie doesn't want you spending money in restaurants.* "I'll go look for my uncle."

He shook his head. "He isn't here. I haven't seen him in a while." The expression on his face told Lena he must have liked Erich.

She steadied herself on a bar stool, its seat worn smooth. "I haven't seen him either."

They held the moment between them as if it were made of glass.

"Are you all right?" he asked, but he must have realized she wasn't. He reached for a mug, filled it with water, and said, "Here. Sit for a while."

Lena took the water to the one empty booth, near the back. *He probably didn't mean a booth.* But she would only stay for a few minutes. Friedrich would give up, wouldn't he? He seemed like the giving-up type. There'd been a can of smoked eel in his grocery bag, rare and expensive; Lena had seen it through the mesh. How long would you chase someone if you knew that was waiting for you? Anyway, she had to get back before Auntie finished work. Perhaps she shouldn't have stopped at the pub. But it felt good to be sitting there in the dark. She felt hidden, and safe.

As she sipped the water, a waitress came over with a piece of buttered bread on a plate and set it on the table. Lena took large hungry bites, grateful that no one could see the butter smeared around her mouth.

She was wiping it with the back of her hand and wondering what terrible thing Erich had taken such pains to hide in his freezer when light flooded into the pub from the front door. Two members of the Volkspolizei strode in.

– 11 –

BARLEY. SURE.

The policemen were all business and no beer. "Good afternoon, Citizen," one of them said to the barman. "We're looking for a girl."

Already? Lena pressed herself into the darkest corner of the cracked leather booth and hoped the men were still blinded by the change from daylight to the bar's gloom.

"A girl, huh? Aren't we all?" the barman said with a laugh.

Three young men entered the pub behind the police. They hovered near the door, glancing uncertainly at the policemen's expensive-looking coats.

"Citizen, this is police business," one of the VoPos said to the barman. "Did a girl come in recently?"

The young men were turning to leave when the barman said, "Look, you're chasing my customers away." He called to the men. "Come in. Take a booth. First round's on me."

But Lena had sat in the only free booth. She slid down until she was under the table, taking her plate and mug of water with her. Legs and boots appeared, and the young men hustled themselves into her booth and scooted around, one of them stepping on her hand. She let out a tiny cry and a face appeared beneath the table. Eyes wide, she said nothing. The young man lifted his legs so she could hide beneath them, then set his boots onto the floor with care.

"No," the barman said to the police. "No girl."

"You won't mind if we have a look around?" one of the policemen asked. Everyone knew it was not a question.

"Be my guest."

As the policemen wandered from one table to the next, the pub grew quiet. Lena waited to see trouser legs; they would be coming soon, and then there they were. Creased. Stiff. Would the men peek beneath the table?

Panty-hosed waitress legs appeared. "Your beers, boys. On the house." She seemed to linger there, arranging coasters, glasses, napkins.

"*Prost*," one of the young men said to her, and the trouser legs moved on.

"Thank you for your cooperation, Citizen," the police said to the barman. "If a girl does come in—"

"I'll make sure to contact you." The barman finished the sentence in the expected way.

Light shone in from the front door again, and then the room returned to darkness.

The young man who had been hiding Lena raised his legs so she could climb out, but she waited a full minute before pulling herself awkwardly back up to the table, the mug of water in her hand. She'd left the plate on the floor.

"Thank you." She couldn't look any of them in the eye. "You didn't have to do that." There was no need to say more; they all knew if the police had found her under the table the entire group of boys would have joined her at the station.

She stood up to leave, but the one who'd hidden her placed his hand on her arm. "Stay here with us awhile. They'll have put a man outside."

Lena forced herself to face him. He was only a few years older than she was, and his short blond hair stood up in a cowlick at his forehead. There was something intense about the way he looked at her, but also something earnest, like he hoped she would tell him the rest of a very good story.

"Don't mind the conscription haircut," he said. "I just finished service."

"Now he gets to mess around on the stage with us monkeys," said one of the others. He had an excessively large nose.

"I'm Max," said the one who'd helped her.

The others introduced themselves—Bem with the big nose, and Dieter—and said they were actors at the local theater.

Lena glanced at her watch. "I'll have to find some way out of here. My aunt will be home soon and I have to work tonight."

"Where do you work?" Max asked.

There it was, the question that killed everything. "Stasi head-quarters," she said, and stared into her mug of water.

"And the police are after you?" said the one named Dieter. He had a face that hung a bit at the edges, as if it was tired of holding on to his head. "*Scheisse.* What did you do?"

She should be able to trust them. They'd helped her, after all. But the what-ifs crowded into her head and started ordering drinks. What if the police stopped everyone on their way out of the pub to ask them questions? What if an officer made one of these three young men an irresistible offer—a phone, a Trabi, a better job—if he agreed to talk? Who wouldn't talk if you could get a cardboard car out of it? People waited ten years for a Trabi, sometimes longer. And even though the cars broke down and you had to fix them yourself, and they had no gas gauge, having your own Trabi was a form of freedom.

Already she'd said too much by telling these men where she worked. Now they would think what everyone else thought: if she worked at Stasi headquarters, she must be Stasi herself. Sure enough, the conversation turned to the weather, the football scores, the next youth group meeting.

"I really do have to go," Lena said. Fifteen minutes had passed. How long would those VoPos watch the door? "Thanks for everything. I'm sorry to have inconvenienced you."

She stood up, putting some money on the table to pay for her bread. Bem slid out of the booth to let her pass. To her surprise, Max followed her.

"Where are you going, man?" said Dieter. He didn't move.

"They're looking for a girl," Max said. "If she's seen alone on the streets, someone is bound to stop her." He turned to Lena. "Is it okay? We'll pretend to be together. I'll set you on your way home. You'll be safer that way."

The waitress appeared and gave an almost imperceptible follow-me nod.

"You're as dumb as a bean straw," said Bem. "Don't be late for rehearsal."

"I won't," Max said.

They followed the waitress through the kitchen and out the back of the pub, which opened onto a sour-smelling road. It was empty. Lena wanted to thank her, but the woman's face was a closed door, *say nothing*, so Lena only nodded, and the woman pressed her lips together in understanding and went back inside.

"Where do you live?" Max said.

"Lichtenberg."

"Seriously? What are you doing all the way over here?"

Lena's mouth went strange, as if Erich's name had grown to the size of a bird.

"Don't tell me," Max said. "It's better if you don't. I'll take you to the S-Bahn station."

Lena hesitated. "Would you mind if we walked a bit?"

"Like to the next station, you mean?"

She couldn't help but smile.

"I don't mind at all. I've been cooped up with those two clowns all day. I could use the fresh air." He studied her in a way that made her feel self-conscious. What would he see besides a skinny girl with straight brown hair and crooked teeth? "It would help if you were carrying something. Groceries, you know? A reason for being out here."

She took a mesh shopping bag out of her pocket. Everyone traveled with one, in case something special showed up in one of the shops. It happened without warning—a delivery of honey, or toilet paper, or licorice sticks (*don't tell Auntie*).

They turned onto a main street and saw that people were lined up for something at the co-op. Lena wanted to know what, but she didn't dare draw attention to herself by asking.

"Choose anything," Max said once they were inside. "How about a small bag of barley?"

"My aunt will think I've lost my senses if I come home with barley." *She might put it in the progress report.* But Lena was getting swept away by the whispers in her ear. Max had leaned so close to her she could smell the soap he used—something lemony. She wasn't losing her senses. It was as if the volume had been turned up on every sense in her body. "Barley," she said. "Sure." Then, realizing she'd contradicted herself, she said, "I'll tell my aunt it was a new delivery." Special barley. Everyone was buying it.

It felt strange to wander the aisles of a grocery store with a man beside her who wasn't Erich, to pretend at being one of those many-legged creatures she'd only ever observed from a distance: a couple. *Don't get carried away. It's only pretend.* And yet. He was tall, and he moved like someone who'd recently been in service— not stiffly, but with precision. His forearms were muscular, and still tanned from summer. On one arm he wore a woven bracelet that Erich would have loved and Danika would have made him take off at once. "It looks like his grandmother's sewing," she would have said.

"How long did you serve?" Lena asked him after she'd paid for the barley.

"Just the eighteen months. Got stinking drunk the night before my medical and they still deemed me fit for service." He laughed. "Anyway, my father said it was the wise thing to do. Serve the minimum and get out, then they'll leave you alone."

Lena thought of Erich, who had refused to carry a weapon. He'd told her about the bullying he'd suffered as he dug trenches for the military posts along the borders. And then—no job, except in the mines. He wouldn't talk about the missing finger, not truly. "The fairies chopped it off in payment for a bottle of whiskey," he'd say. Or, "I sold it to an old man who promised to make me rich."

She waited until she and Max were alone on the street. "I know someone who was a construction soldier," she said. "He had trouble finding work afterward." *Careful. Just because this young man is helping you home doesn't mean—* But he'd hidden her under the table. He'd taken a huge risk before he'd even met her. On principle. *So what? Keep him awake for thirty-six hours in interrogation and see what happens to his principles.*

"The People's Theater of Prenzlauer Berg was happy to hire me when I finished my term," he said with a grin.

See? He's being cautious, and so should you. "Are you acting in a play?" Lena asked.

Two policemen appeared up ahead. Lena stiffened, and Max draped his arm around her.

"We're going to walk right past them as a couple," he said softly. "You need to relax." Then louder, for the benefit of the officers, he said, "We're doing a play called *Factory: A Love Story.* It opens tomorrow."

She nodded awkwardly, as if her head was mounted on a stick.

"Bem and Dieter are in it too," he chattered. "It's an original new work by—" As soon as they were out of earshot of the police he said, "Keep walking. They didn't even notice us. You're doing fine."

But she felt as if her body was about to fall apart on the sidewalk.

"You should come see it," he said.

"I work nights."

"At Stasi headquarters." The muscles in his arm tensed.

"It's not what you think. I only do the cleaning there."

He gave her a withering look. *They offered you a job.* A person only got a job at Stasi headquarters if they were the right sort; if they went to all the right meetings, knew the right people, and had the right relatives. *Or the wrong ones.* Lena wanted to glance up to the left-hand corner of the sky to thank Helmut, but stopped herself. She knew now that she'd gotten her job with the Stasi because of Erich. *They used you to spy on your uncle.*

When Lena and Max rounded the next corner he took his arm away. So—it really had been pretend.

"I'm not sure how much longer I'll be working at headquarters after this." *You didn't say that out loud, did you?*

"They didn't catch you," Max said. "Whatever you did, they won't know it was you."

But Friedrich So-and-So did know it was her and he would tell the police: *That Erich fellow's niece came back. She broke into my apartment and emptied my freezer. She took something, some paper; I don't know what it was.* What did it matter which S-Bahn station she went to? They'd be waiting for her at home, or at work. She'd be called down to the police station or ushered into the backseat of a car. Or picked up in a van that pretended to sell fish. *Or flowers.* Sausage Auntie would say she was the most ungrateful girl ever, and they'd contact the nearest textile factory—or worse, the mental hospital—and that would be the end of that.

"I can make it home from here."

He stopped. "But we're nowhere near the next station. You shouldn't walk alone. Please. I don't mind taking you."

She moved away from him. "You've done enough. Thank you, and good luck with your play." She glanced at her watch and realized she would just make it home before Auntie, if she didn't miss the train.

"Please come to see it," he called.

She didn't answer, just turned to walk away. *It's unforgivable what you did, letting yourself into Erich's apartment—impossible to fix, or excuse. You'll lose your job. They'll put you in prison. No more* solyanka, *or pictures on the walls, or beautifying the courtyard with Peter and Danika, or talking to Jutta.* All of it suddenly seemed like the best life ever. How had she not known how good she'd had it? After her parents had died, she hadn't been sent to an orphanage, or made to live with strangers. *No, they put you in an institution.* And now she had her own bedroom, and a plumbing unit right in the apartment, and enough food, and an adjustable multifunction table in the sitting room.

Why wasn't it possible to redo a bad decision? She thrust her hands into her coat pockets and there was the plastic-covered paper she'd discovered in the freezer—a clue to Erich's whereabouts, maybe. She hadn't had a chance to read it, but she wasn't going to do so now.

When she reached the S-Bahn station, she pretended to be interested in the homemade handicrafts for sale near the entrance. There was the blind man she was convinced wasn't blind. There was a man in a suit, adjusting his watch. *He's just a man in a suit.* Sometimes a man in a suit was just a man in a suit. He glanced up at her once, and again, then went back to his wristwatch.

A pair of Transport Police sauntered past, on the lookout for teenagers with good-for-nothing hairstyles and obvious Western clothing. Lena was thankful she'd worn her GDR jeans. Pretend-

Levi's, Danika called them. She was thankful also for her shopping bag with barley in it. She was a girl with a purpose.

The train arrived. She got on, sat down, and stared at the dirty floor. She didn't dare make eye contact with anyone. What if one of those people were following her? When she switched trains, she kept herself alert for that back-of-the-neck feeling, but it didn't come.

Maybe Friedrich So-and-So didn't call the police. Not possible. She'd let herself into his apartment—Erich's apartment. She'd left a large knife sitting on the kitchen counter, along with the entire contents of his freezer. She'd thrown his cat at him. The police had shown up at the pub. He had called them for sure. *Then where are they?*

Maybe they were waiting at Auntie's place. But when she arrived, they weren't there; nor was Auntie. Lena ripped off her clothes and tossed them into the cupboard, pulled on the gray nightdress and climbed into bed. Within minutes, Auntie bustled in and started crashing pots and pans in the kitchen, which meant it was time to wake up, so Lena did.

"Oh. You're up."

As if all that noise had been an accident. The baby next door started to cry.

"How was your day?" Lena asked. *Too polite. You never ask her that. If the police had called her at school, don't you think she'd mention it?*

Auntie let out one of those sighs that meant the entire world was stepping on her toes. "These new trainees they've sent us are not working out. They have too many opinions—and not the right ones. You look exhausted."

The afternoon's stress forced Lena to sit down. She wanted to tell Auntie everything, warn her that trouble was coming, or even beg—*please tell them I'm too simple to be any bother.* It had worked once. That was why they'd hired her at headquarters. She was simple. But not too simple. Too simple would mean slippers, and a gown, and sedation.

No, Mausi. They hired you because they needed you to spy on Erich, and they believed you'd be too dumb to figure it out.

"Go back to bed," Auntie said. "I'll call you when supper is ready."

Lena lay down and prayed to God, and to Helmut—someone who knew how to get things done. In the meantime, the sky felt heavy, the ceiling seemed lower, and the walls crept closer together.

– 12 –

A WESTERN SOMETHING

Supper was sandwiches and a discussion about discipline at school. A boy in Auntie's class still hadn't learned that crying was not acceptable behavior in the Better Germany.

When Auntie settled in to watch the news, Lena shut the door to her bedroom and took out the plastic-covered paper, which now seemed so warm it might burst into flames. One glance told her it was a letter. *Dear Erich.* There was no letterhead. Lena's eyes leaped to the bottom of the page. It was signed *Günter Schulmann.* Who was that? He must have known Erich well to use his first name.

She was only beginning to read the letter when serious footsteps sounded down the hall. Auntie-who-doesn't-knock might just have been marching to the bathroom, but no, she wasn't stopping, *put it away,* the marching drew closer, *under your pillow— quickly.* Under the pillow it went, just as Auntie walked in.

"Aren't you ready for work?"

"Almost." Lena reached for her sweater.

"Well, come on, then." Auntie waited, arms crossed, for Lena to turn off the lights and close the door—with the letter still under her pillow. Someone had already been through the room once while she'd been at work. *You can't leave it there.*

Auntie followed her down the hall. "Get your shoes on."

You have to go back and get it.

Lena put on one shoe—*do it now*—dropped the other, said "Oh!" and ran to her bedroom. She grabbed the plastic-covered letter and shoved it into her long sweater pocket, where Marilyn Monroe had been safe before Auntie had shredded her. *Imagine what she'd do to this.* Whatever it contained must be awful and incriminating. Why else would Erich have hidden it in the freezer?

"I forgot something," she explained to Auntie's befuddled face. She slipped on the other shoe, *out, go,* and said "Bye" before Auntie could ask what she'd forgotten.

On the walk to work she kept waiting for it. Someone would follow her, say her full name—or call her Citizen, or Comrade. A car would pull up, or a van. But nothing happened.

Jutta sat in the ashtray room reading the same copy of *Sibylle* as always. Lena studied her weathered face. She didn't want to believe Jutta had known about the listening device, but she must have. Some men would have approached her, spoken to her privately. "Ask the girl about that dropout uncle she visits every Sunday. Get her to talk." Jutta had worked in Wandlitz, the highest-security neighborhood in the Better Germany. They trusted her.

Jutta looked up from the magazine. "I'm not even German, did

I tell you that? Do you see my high cheekbones and strong chin? Slavs were considered warriors, you know. I was very attractive when I was younger."

This isn't a real conversation. She's making noise. Lena sat and smoothed the stained vinyl with her hands. "Does anyone ever wipe this table?"

Jutta shrugged. "It's rare for Slavs to have protruding ears, did you know that?"

"I'm going to give it a wipe. I can't stand it anymore."

Jutta leaned on the magazine with both elbows. "Since when did you become Miss Tidy Pants?" She bent her head forward so Lena could see the gray roots of her bleached-blond hair.

Let's see how far you can push her. "It is why we're here, isn't it?"

"*Pfft.* Not to clean this little outhouse. We're off the clock right now. I only work when I'm paid."

"Anyway." Lena went to the cupboard where they stored their cleaning supplies and found a rag. She opened the disinfectant they used in House 1—everywhere except in the Comrade General's private rooms, because he'd complained that it smelled like turpentine—and splashed some onto the rag. Immediately the small room was doused in the overpowering smell.

"Ach, you're not using that shit in here," Jutta cried. "It will disintegrate the vinyl."

"We eat and drink at this table." Lena began to scrub the stains off. "It's disgusting."

Jutta made her elbows into a proclamation. "You'll clean around me. I'm reading my magazine."

"Aren't you tired of that page?"

"As a matter of fact, I am." She turned to the next page, a

woman trying to look demure in an orange furry hat. "You'll be wanting one of these too, I expect."

"That magazine is stupid."

"What do you know? Waltzing around in dirty Zehas and that ratty old sweater. How do you ever expect to find a boyfriend dressed like that?"

Her too? Was everyone obsessed with having a One True Love? "I don't want a boyfriend." Lena scrubbed so hard she shook the table. She imagined a man in another room with headphones on, wincing at the terrible sounds, and smiled. There was no moving Jutta, though, and that was all the answer Lena needed. Jutta knew; she'd known all along.

What had they given her as a reward? Maybe nothing. Maybe they'd threatened her with a humiliating rumor: pornographic magazines arriving at her apartment, or a history of shoplifting. *Don't judge her. You don't know what you'd agree to under that sort of pressure. No one knows, until they're in it.* But she and Jutta were friends. Well, not friends, exactly. Co-workers. On the same team. It should have counted for something.

Lena dressed in her coveralls, gathered their supplies, handed Jutta her bucket, and they set off into the cool night for House 1.

Would it be Herr Dreck? Would he be the one to use her full name and tell her she was under arrest? *He doesn't even know your name.* But when he called her into his office, he didn't mention Friedrich So-and-So. He had other things on his mind.

Lena ate her chocolate, and swept and dusted. She was dying to read the letter from Erich's freezer, but she didn't like the idea of not knowing where Jutta was and when she might show up. She needed to time it just right.

By the middle of the night, she and Jutta were the only ones left in House 1. It was almost time to clean the Comrade General's floor. And by then Lena had an idea. She arrived on the third floor ahead of schedule and dragged the Purimix into Mielke's office. One thing she knew: Jutta never arrived early to clean these rooms.

The first room was where meetings were conducted. There was a long table at one end, and a smaller one surrounded by comfortable chairs. All of Mielke's telephones were arranged on the desk. The gifts he'd received from other socialist states—decorative plates, busts, photographs—lined the shelves. On the walls were photographs of him wearing all his medals—so many, he must have clinked whenever he moved.

Lena went through to the next room, which was Mielke's personal area. She pulled the heavy drapes closed and eyed his dark blue recliner. How nice it would be to sit, just for a few minutes. But no, he would know. The angle would be wrong, or the cushions out of alignment.

Quickly, now. She pulled out the letter. *Dear Erich.* It seemed her uncle had written a manuscript, something important. The letter writer, Günter Schulmann, was excited about it. He could definitely find a Western publisher for this. Was Erich certain about the facts? When would it be ready? How would he send it? *You realize this will be huge. Call if you need anything—here is my number at home.*

There was also an address. Günter Schulmann lived in the Other Berlin, the space beyond the border that was missing on maps in the Better Germany. In that Berlin, everyone was unemployed, didn't have proper health care, and was in danger of becoming homeless at any moment. All the teachers and news programs said so.

What did he mean, a Western publisher? Erich had always published his novels in the East. But Herr Schulmann had mentioned facts—so maybe this wasn't a novel. Whatever it was, it couldn't be published in the Better Germany because it was too subversive. You couldn't pull off the humming-underneath sound in a book with facts. The authorities would declare a sudden paper shortage and that would be the end of publication.

Lena glanced up from the page. The zigzag pattern on the drapes made her eyes feel funny. What had Erich been writing about? There was one way to find out, but it would mean a telephone call to the West. She couldn't make that call from Auntie's telephone, and Hans was always saying that the public phones on the street were bugged.

She folded the letter back into her pocket, returned to the meeting room, and plugged in her Purimix. *You could call from here.* But that was dangerous too. Who was Günter Schulmann? A Western writer? He was a Western something, anyway. Lena knew the Stasi monitored international phone calls. She didn't think they would listen in on the conversations of their own high-ranking agents, but surely they would know if such a call had been made. Anyone who called a Western something from House 1 in the middle of the night risked getting into huge trouble. *Huge trouble, you say? Well. That might be one way of thanking Herr Dreck for his attention.*

It was late, and this was the man's private number. Lena would be waking him up. *So what? It's important. This man will want to know what's happened to Erich.*

She left her Purimix where it was, took a rag and some detergent, and went down to Herr Dreck's office. The lights were off. The room was already clean; now it would be cleaner. *I forgot to do the corners, Jutta. Herr Dreck is particular about his corners.*

There was the photograph of the hairy man with his pretty pink wife and fresh pink daughters. One hand, with wiry hair growing out of the knuckles, was wrapped around his wife's shoulder. There was his leather armchair with the patches worn away by his sweaty body. There was the spot on his desk where he placed the wrapped chocolate before calling Lena into his office. She didn't have even a moment of remorse when she picked up the telephone and asked for an outside line.

She dialed the call-if-you-need-anything number. It rang. It rang for so long she was ready to hang up. She had to hurry; Jutta would be arriving on the third floor at any moment and there would be Lena's Purimix, and Lena's bucket and mop, but no Lena—and then a man answered in a voice foggy with sleep.

"I'm sorry to wake you," Lena said softly. "I'm Erich Altmann's niece. I found the letter you sent him, about something he wrote."

"What? Who is this?"

She explained again: a letter, the facts, the Western publisher. And then she told him how Erich had been erased.

"He never sent me that manuscript," the man said. "We had an arrangement, and I never heard from him." But the man refused to tell her anything more. "I don't know who you are."

"I told you—I'm his niece."

"And I'm the man in the moon. Sorry, but I can't help you unless I know for sure you're not one of them. Even then—"

She hung up, wiped down Herr Dreck's black telephone with

the detergent, and walked out of the office—straight into Jutta.

"What are you doing down here? I was waiting for you. I thought you'd gone to the toilet."

"No, I—"

"Are you messing with the order of offices again? Why is your Purimix upstairs? I come down to the third floor expecting to find you ready to work, but you're still on the second floor. Haven't you finished here yet?"

"Yes, I was just—I'd forgotten to do the corners." The alibi had sounded so much better in her head. "You know how the Lieutenant General gets about his corners."

"No," Jutta said. "I don't. Come upstairs at once and help me with the Comrade General's floor." She stood in the hallway with her hands on her solid hips and watched Lena climb the stairs to the next floor before getting on the elevator. *I bet she's an older sister.* Jutta liked being the senior one, the one who got to check up on things and approve or disapprove. She loved yelling at Lena if something was wrong, even though on her own floors Jutta spent half her time smoking and staring out the window.

In Comrade Mielke's rooms Lena straightened up and swept and wiped, trying her hardest not to feel dejected. The man on the phone hadn't believed her. It was her last chance to find out more about Erich and she had failed.

After their shift ended, Jutta said, "You know I'm supposed to report any unusual behavior from a colleague. Was it unusual, you being on the second floor?"

"Of course not," Lena said. "I was being thorough." *Control the jiggle in your voice.* "Why don't you come with me to House 18 and we can eat *Schokoküsse* for breakfast." Chocolate-covered meringues on a wafer. *Auntie will be upset if you're not hungry for your egg.*

Jutta smiled. "You go. Have one for me. This old horse needs to get home to bed."

Lena took off her coveralls and said goodbye to Jutta. At House 18, she went through the portal. *It's a door, just a regular door,* and the *schrullig* world wasn't a world. It wasn't like the one where the lion was in charge, even though there was all that Turkish delight. And yet this place was so different from anything she knew in the Better Germany that it felt like another world.

She bought some *Schokoküsse* and ate them standing in front of the travel office, studying the photographs of Rügen. You weren't allowed to swim there at night—no night boating or diving either. Rügen was too close to Denmark, and the border guards weren't blockheads, not like the People's Police. Rügen was a vacation without the promise of freedom. Just seeing it made Lena want to tear down the poster and stomp on it.

– 13 –

BLINDSIDED

When Lena finally left the compound that morning, there were the usual guards on the sidewalks preventing curious bystanders from wandering too close to the gates—or worse, taking photographs. Photography was an acceptable creative outlet for young people, as long as they took the right photographs. Trees, yes. Dogs, sure. The perimeter of Stasi headquarters? *No, Mausi, that was not allowed.*

Beyond the guards there were mothers pushing strollers, people carrying lunch boxes, children shouldering book bags. And there was a young man on the corner, pacing to keep warm, his hands gathered behind his back. Pace, pace, pace, and then he looked up—and it was Max. Heat rushed to Lena's skin. Jutta was right—she should have worn something nicer, *you should have washed your face.* But cold realization came next.

"What are you doing here?" she asked when she reached him. "How did you find me?"

He kicked at some wet leaves. "It wasn't that hard. There are only so many ways in and out of that place."

But why? What does he want? Unless—"You've spoken to the police." She hurried away.

"What? No, slow down. Why would I do that?"

Why did anyone do it? "Because they threatened you. They saw you with me. They gave you an 'or else.'" An instructive chat and a visit to one of their cells. Or they'd made him an offer he couldn't refuse: a university education, maybe. You couldn't just apply to university and expect to get in because you had good grades. You also needed the right family background, the right political opinions, and solid attendance at Free German Youth meetings. But the authorities had ways of getting around all that.

Max was wearing blue jeans and a dark green coat. His hair stood up in the front, making him look like he'd just gotten out of bed—which he probably had. He smiled, and a dimple formed in his left cheek. That was all it took to make Lena slow down.

Are you out of your mind? He'd spent eighteen months in the People's Army. Eighteen months with his head stuck in one of those weird gumdrop helmets, wearing a stone-gray uniform that would harden anyone's heart. He knew how to march in formation and shoot a gun—and he hadn't been back for long. He still had the haircut. Eighteen months of training didn't wash off in the rain.

"I brought you a ticket to the play," he said. "I'd really like you to come. It opens tonight." He tried to press the ticket into Lena's hand but she wouldn't take it.

"I work tonight. And anyway, my aunt wouldn't approve of my going alone." They passed an empty construction zone, the machines sitting there like they'd been forgotten. People would start liberating them if the construction workers didn't come back.

"Wait. I have another ticket." He fished inside his pocket. "Bring her along. The tickets are good for any night."

"God, no."

"Then a friend. Someone. A brother or sister."

"I'm an only child."

"How about an uncle?"

"I don't have an uncle." She put a hand to her mouth. *How could you?* But to try to explain to this young man who'd tracked her down and waited for her? *You hardly know him.* He'd hidden her in the pub, at great risk to himself.

"Please, take the tickets. That way you can think about it and come when it suits you. You will come, won't you?"

She took the tickets. "Maybe. I don't know." *Maybe? Who will you take? Danika?* She'd be filing her nails within five minutes and complaining about how boring it was.

"Do you go to sleep now?" Max asked. "During the day?" The sky was already light, the rest of Berlin eating their breakfast and brushing their teeth.

"Yes, I live upside down. Night is day, and day is night." *Stop talking. Just stop. You sound like a baby.*

He slowed his pace. Between the large housing blocks there were areas that Lena thought of as *Surprise!* Not exactly parking lots, although there were scores of Trabis parked there. But there were also bicycles, lines of washing, the odd shop, and people her age hanging around as if they weren't quite sure what to do next. "Hooligans," Auntie said. Lena wasn't allowed to stop at those places on her way home.

"It must be nice to work while everyone is asleep," Max said. "Peaceful. Strange."

"It is." Lena tried to walk slowly, matching his pace, even though Auntie's face was in her mind, her no-nonsense eyebrows knotting at the thought of Lena's egg going cold.

"What do you do in the afternoons when you wake up?"

"Depends. My aunt wants to win the Golden House Number plaque for our building, so we're working on beautifying the courtyard. It's a bit of a swamp." *Please don't ask to meet her.* One meeting with Auntie would kill even the sturdiest houseplant.

"Do you live in one of those newer developments?"

"Yes." The Series 70 buildings, Auntie would have chimed in, with their own plumbing units, an entire wall of cupboards and shelving, and an adjustable multifunction table. "I'm very lucky," Lena said. "My aunt's late husband—" But it wasn't proper to mention how high up Helmut had been in the Party.

"Where are your parents?"

So he was bold. That might be a good quality. *Also a dangerous one.* "They were killed in an accident when I was fourteen." *You're not supposed to say* accident. *It's bad for morale.* Workplace accidents didn't happen in the Better Germany. The workers were well-trained and never drunk. The machinery was modern, and the working conditions top-notch. But Lena was never sure how else to describe the explosion. The news reporters had called it an *incident*, but that word made her angry, as if the end of her parents' lives had been some minor occurrence.

Max sputtered an apology and looked as if he wanted to bolt to the nearest U-Bahn station, which wasn't the worst idea.

"I don't want my aunt to see you walking me home. She'll ask questions. She won't let it go." Lena realized she was crumpling the tickets in her hand. "Who are you?"

His forehead creased in confusion.

"In the play. What character are you?"

"Oh. I play the cook in the canteen."

"I'll think about it, all right? I promise."

Suddenly it seemed as if the screws had dropped out of his knees and elbows. He gave an awkward half wave, crossed the street without looking, and was nearly hit by a car. As if—*no, don't think it*; but it was too late, she'd already thought it—as if he liked her.

Why? What? What could he possibly see in her? She was plain, and small. She climbed the stairs to her floor, feeling wide awake and giggly, and entered the apartment with the smile tucked away like money in her purse. She wished she could go to the play that night, every night, for the rest of her life.

"I've rewritten your petition for the swimming pool," Auntie was saying when Lena sat down to breakfast. She'd given herself another home perm and her short hair looked woolly and sprung, like the fur of one of her porcelain dogs. "I added in a paragraph explaining your commitment to beautify—"

His lips. They were full. He had big teeth, but not too big, not like Auntie's.

"Lena! Did you hear a word I said?"

"The swimming pool. The petition."

"I've told them this is not only for your sake but for the good of the community, and ultimately for—"

His forehead. It was serious. Lena decided that was good.

Auntie went on about all the people she planned to bring on board. They would form a committee and devote themselves to these swimming-pool repairs. They would *blah, blah, blah.* When Max was onstage, Lena would be allowed to stare at him. She could watch his every move.

"For God's sake, girl, where is your head this morning?"

"I'm tired, that's all. It was a long night."

"I hope that Jutta woman is picking up her work ethic. I still think you should report her."

Jutta didn't need a work ethic. She just needed to protect her corner of the vinyl and keep an eye on Lena. *Wait, what did you say?* Was that what Jutta was doing? *Might be. Only might, you don't know for sure.* The way she had appeared at Herr Dreck's door, it was as if she'd been checking up on Lena. Had she heard Lena on the phone? If anyone found out about that call—but if they did, they would blame Herr Dreck. He might not even be at work tonight. Lena might have found the perfect way to get rid of him.

"There's no talking to you today, it seems," Auntie said. "I'll get ready for work. What do you think of my hair?"

She left the room before Lena could say "Curly." Lena ate her breakfast without tasting it. Imagine: Herr Dreck gone. Imagine: seeing Max act in a play. She would go tomorrow. She'd think up a story to tell Auntie.

*

On Friday afternoons, Lena was expected to practice her embroidery skills. Auntie knew all about the handicraft award she had won as a student in Magdeburg, and she was a big believer in the value of such work. "Attention to detail," she'd say. "Coordination. Manual dexterity. Do you know what dexterity means?" Handicrafts could solve the housing crisis. They could put a man in space. Plus they were beautifying, and anything that beautified their living quarters became heroic in Auntie's eyes.

Lena was embroidering small orange flowers onto a tablecloth for their sitting room table. It was tedious work that gave her a headache, and all she wanted to do was think about Max and how she might find a way to see his play on Saturday night.

You are a terrible person. Your uncle has been erased, and you're daydreaming about a boy. But no boy had ever taken an interest in her except Peter, and she wasn't sure he was interested—even if Danika thought he was. They just happened to live on the same floor.

Lena ate her supper, all the while thinking. She could tell Auntie she was going to the cinema with Danika. But then she'd have to ask Danika to lie for her, and that was dangerous. There was a part of Danika that liked watching other people get in trouble. *Next time throw her cat out the door.* Then she'd think twice about messing with Lena.

By the time she was leaving for work, she still hadn't hit on a solution. She said goodbye to Auntie, who was sitting in front of the television with her feet on a cushion because her ankles were swelling up again. When she opened the door she found Peter sweeping the hallway. There was something in the way he glanced up—pretend-casual, like, *hey, what are you doing here?*—that made Lena think he'd been waiting for her.

"Where are you off to?" He leaned on his broom, making weird cow eyes at her. *Oh no. Maybe Danika was right.*

"You know I'm going to work."

"I got Sweden on my radio before supper. I couldn't understand a word they were saying, but it was first class. Listen, I was wondering—"

Lena glanced at her watch. "I'm going to be late."

He hunched his shoulders. "Are you busy tomorrow night?"

"As a matter of fact, I have tickets to a play." *Which play? The one my boyfriend is in. Boyfriend.* That was a word. *Use it in a sentence with* my. It practically danced in her mouth. *You're getting carried away. He is not your boyfriend. He hid you. That's all.*

Peter set the broom against the wall and it slid sideways and clattered onto the floor. "That's fabulous. I was thinking of the cinema, but I love going to live theater."

"No, I meant—"

"Lena?" Auntie poked her head out the door.

"I thought your ankles were swollen."

"Why haven't you left for work yet?" Auntie asked.

"Can Lena and I go to a play together tomorrow night, Frau Keller?"

"No, that's not what I—" But no one was listening to Lena.

"What play?" Auntie asked.

"What play?" Peter asked.

Lena sighed. "*Factory: A Love Story.*"

"An excellent choice," Auntie said. "It sounds like a romance between ordinary working-class folk. Lots of powerful emotion. I heartily approve." She turned to Lena. "Off you go, now. You mustn't be late for work."

"I'll see you tomorrow." Peter picked up the broom and hoisted it in a goodbye. Solidarity to the cleaning folk.

Lena trudged down the stairs, the play tickets still in her pocket. She felt like ripping them up. How had that just happened? She was going to show up at the play with Peter? What would Max think? Peter was the last person she wanted to go with. And the way he had looked at her in the hallway, that shirt he'd worn to youth group last week—*God, it was for you*. How had she not realized? Why hadn't he been called up for conscription yet? What if he tried to hold her hand? Perhaps she could ask him to trim his nails before they went.

Max would look for her in the audience. He would see her with Peter. She couldn't even say Peter was her brother because she'd already told Max she didn't have one. Her cousin. The boy who lived down the hall. *Auntie arranged it, I had nothing to do with it.* She was so caught up in thinking about how she might explain things that she barely spoke to Jutta in the ashtray room.

She took her cleaning supplies across the compound to House 1. Hello, three red flags. Good evening, stone Dzerzhinsky, stone Marx. *You could pretend to be sick.* Peter didn't know the tickets were good for any night. *You could go to the play on Sunday.* But that meant she wouldn't get to see Max tomorrow. She lugged her Purimix up the stairs and plugged it in to start on the hallways. What if they didn't perform on Sundays? And how long was the play running for, anyway? Maybe the People's Theater of Prenzlauer Berg was a tiny group with no money. One weekend, a budget version. *Factory: A Brief Infatuation*, and then it was over.

Light shone out from one of the offices. *You could stop in at the theater in the afternoon, to explain.* Yes, that was it. She could tell Max her aunt was forcing her to come with the neighbor boy. It was the only way she'd be allowed to go. The boy might wear a spiffy purple shirt, but it didn't mean anything. Surely Max would be at the theater in the afternoon, rehearsing. Wasn't that what actors did?

"Fräulein? Is that you?"

The husky voice cut through the noise of the Purimix. It cut through her thoughts and made a hole right in the middle of her stomach. What was he doing here? Didn't the people in House 1 know that one of their devoted officials was a reactionary who made midnight phone calls to Western writers—or editors, or whoever the fellow was in Erich's letter? Hadn't the call from his office registered anywhere, with anyone?

Lena unplugged the Purimix and went in.

"Shut the door." Herr Dreck's hands rested on his desk, fingertips pressed against the wooden surface as if he had a button beneath each of them and was preparing to blow everything up.

Lena wished she'd brought her broom, something she might use as a weapon. *Right. You want to spend the rest of your life in a prison cell?*

"I was called in to the Comrade General's office today." Herr Dreck flattened his hands. "Like a schoolboy, to be reprimanded. Except this is my career."

"I'm sorry to hear that, sir." A thousand sparrows had been set loose inside Lena's rib cage. She held on to the back of a chair to steady herself. *You don't know what he's talking about, remember? You weren't here.* Her lip began to tremble, and she bit it to keep it still.

"You telephoned a Western book editor from my office last

night." His face grew redder and meaner with every word.

"Me? Why would I do that?"

"Don't piss on my shoe and then tell me it's raining. The call was made in the middle of the night. I was home with my wife and children. You think I'm a moron?"

"No."

"So—who else could have done it?"

Jutta. But Lena didn't say that; she never would. No matter that Jutta knew about the listening device. No matter that she'd been asking about Erich ever since Lena had started working there. No matter that she sat in the ashtray room with her elbows spread across that stupid fashion magazine every single night.

"Well, then. Tell me: Who was this person you called, and what did you say to him?"

"It was a mistake." Lena felt like she was on roller skates, something she'd only tried once, with Danika, after which she had concluded that human beings didn't have wheels on their feet for a reason.

"A mistake. Again you treat me like a moron. You had a telephone number. You must have gotten it from somewhere."

You're simple, Mausi. Everyone thinks so. "I found it."

The Lieutenant General got to his feet. He was a big man, much bigger than Lena. "You understand I can have you sent to a place where they'll make you talk. Some people believe subversion runs in families. It's genetic, like brown eyes. I'm inclined to agree."

They weren't sparrows in her rib cage anymore. They were more like crows. Spots appeared in her vision. Her head grew crowded with a loud buzzing noise. She heard herself saying something about her uncle.

"You don't have an uncle." He moved around the desk to Lena's side. "Now listen. I covered for you with the Comrade General, said I'd made the call to get intelligence on one of our reactionary writers. Called in the middle of the night to catch him off guard. I was completely blindsided, you understand. I had to think on my feet."

Lena wasn't sure what to say. Was this unusual behavior for him? Was she supposed to congratulate him? "Thank you" was what she settled on, edging toward the door.

"That's the idea." He smiled in a way she did not like at all. "You will thank me. I'm letting you keep your job, and your life. The moment you stop thanking me, you will lose both." He unfastened his belt and unzipped his pants. "Come here."

Make yourself small. Smaller. She stood in front of him, and he pushed her to her knees.

– 14 –

WE

There was no chocolate.

When it was done, Herr Dreck shoved her out of his office. "Get back to work."

Lena searched for the Wall in her head, but there was no way to tell herself nothing had happened when her legs were shaking so badly she could barely stand. Her eyes were wet. He'd made her swallow it—his semen. She was going to be sick.

In a panic she looked around for a toilet, but all the toilets in House 1 were for men. She had to get outside. She ran down the stairs, gripping the handrail to keep from losing her footing, but she didn't make it any farther than the foyer before she was on her knees again. Out came her supper, right in front of Marx and Dzerzhinsky. All over the beautiful black floor which, thank goodness, she hadn't mopped yet.

She sat there shaking and crying. Behind her the elevator

rattled. *Not Herr Dreck, please not him.* She didn't want to give him the satisfaction of seeing her broken like this.

It was Jutta. *"Mein Gott,* child. What happened?"

When Lena opened her mouth to speak, the words wouldn't come. She stared at the splatter of vomit. "I'm sorry. I'll clean it up."

"Na, na, we'll do it together. At least you had the good sense to vomit on your half of the building." Jutta pulled out a handkerchief and wiped Lena's eyes, then around her mouth. "Let's get you something to drink." When she put her arm out and helped Lena to her feet, Lena sank into her as if she were a warm blanket.

Jutta took her to House 1's coffee room for a glass of water. This was one of the agents' special rooms, and Jutta and Lena were not supposed to use it, but Jutta didn't seem to care. She made Lena sit down and waited until she'd taken a few sips.

"Are you all right? You look like you've seen *der Butzemann.*" The bogeyman that hid in closets and under beds, waiting to carry children away.

Say something. And not the truth, or he'll do what he threatened, you know he will. "Must be a stomach bug," she mumbled. "I'm sorry about—"

Jutta's no-nonsense hand stopped her. "We'll take care of the mess. And then I'm sending you home for some rest. Imagine if you'd done this on the carpet."

Imagine if you'd done it all over Herr Dreck's pants. Let him explain that to his wife. *You'll have to work on your timing.* Timing? Would this happen again?

"How will you finish the whole building by yourself?" Lena asked.

Jutta patted her arm. "I'll manage. I might miss a few spots."

Lena felt a bit better, though when they returned to the foyer the stench of the vomit nearly made her throw up again. She was dizzy, her jaw hurt, and there was a putrid taste in her mouth. Jutta went upstairs to fetch Lena's supplies. Together they wiped up the mess and Jutta mopped the floor.

"Off you go. Tell your aunt to keep you in bed this weekend. You'll be tip-top by Monday."

The play! "I'm all right now, Jutta, really. I don't need to go home."

"This is not a democracy. I don't want puddles in the Comrade General's office or it will mean both our jobs."

Lena gathered her things and took them back to House 24. She took off her coveralls, pulled on her coat, and plodded home in the dark.

The fresh air invigorated her. She didn't feel sick anymore, just angry. Herr Dreck would use this telephone call against her—but for how long? How long would she have to go on thanking him? *Well, what do you think?* She wished there was some way to contact his wife, humiliate him. *You think his wife would believe you? An orphan cleaning girl from Magdeburg?* It was all supposed to be honorable in the Better Germany, her job, her circumstances.

The swish of her footsteps in the fallen leaves kept her company, along with her breath. Lights were on in some of the apartments. Brown, brown, brown. But the lives inside them—there were thousands of people with heads as busy as hers.

Was there some way to salvage the play on Saturday night? Probably not. She'd have to wait till next weekend or the weekend after, and then Max would think she didn't want to see him. She trudged up the stairs to her apartment, put the key into the lock, opened the door expecting silence—and heard voices. At first she thought it was the television. Auntie, with her swollen ankles, probably hadn't moved. Then she heard Auntie laughing, but not in a familiar way. It was a girlish laugh, the kind you'd practice.

A man's voice came from Auntie's bedroom.

Go to your room, don't call out. Maybe she should leave. They hadn't heard her. *Auntie has a man in here.* So? Helmut had been dead for years. Why shouldn't she have a man over? No wonder she'd re-permed her hair.

Lena stood in the hallway, not really listening, still stunned by the realization that even in her own home she had no idea what was going on. *Jutta was right when she said we don't really know anyone.* Was this man Auntie's One True Love? Why had she never mentioned him?

Auntie's bedroom door opened and the man came out, as naked as if they were on a beach on Rügen. It was the bricklayer who lived on the second floor. Erich used to say he had a plastic bubble for a head, only Lena found it hard to focus on his head when the rest of him was—but she wasn't supposed to look there. When he saw her, he let out a cry and ran back into the bedroom, slamming the door. Lena went to her room. *Now you'll be in for it.* Wait, if he was naked, that meant Auntie—that meant Auntie—

A moment later, Auntie appeared in her housecoat and slippers, swollen ankles miraculously deflated. She and Lena had the what-are-you-doing-home conversation while Lena sat on the edge of the bed and stared at the floor. They had the no-play-for-you-tomorrow-night discussion, not if you're sick, though it was too one-sided to be properly called a discussion. They did not have the man-in-my-bedroom conversation, because Auntie acted as if it had never happened. Even though the entire time her face remained bright pink and she wouldn't stop talking, as if there were only a set number of words and as long as she used them all up before she got to the man-in-my-bedroom situation then they wouldn't have to talk about him.

If she knew what you'd done tonight . . . Lena wished she could tell her, but there lay Herr Dreck's power. She couldn't tell anyone without incriminating herself. She had made that phone call, after all. Even if she lied about her part in it and Auntie went straight to Herr Dreck's office—which she wouldn't do; she would write a formal letter listing everything she'd ever done for the community—he would deny everything. But an accusation like that would mean the end of Lena's job, the end of any job, except maybe the textile factory, or the uranium mines in the Erzgebirge.

After Auntie left her room, Lena put on her gray nightdress and lay in bed. Despite the ordeal of the night, she was wide awake. This was her daytime. She heard the bricklayer leave. She heard Auntie go to bed. The apartment went silent, which was all her head needed to go party-level noisy. Everyone was invited.

Does Max really like you? arrived wearing an ugly hand-me-down coat that all the One True Love thoughts had worn at some time or other.

You need to call the Western editor again. Yes, that thought was there too, trying so hard to seem nonchalant that everyone could tell it was subversive.

Maybe you're being followed stood in a corner with a drink, wearing sunglasses.

And *where is Erich? Will you ever see him again?* These thoughts were the ones with the lampshades on their heads. They were the center of attention at all times.

*

Lena hoped that by doing her Saturday chores while Auntie was teaching, she might prove herself fit enough to attend the theater that night. *With Peter? Are you sure this is a good idea?* But she wanted to go, and she knew it would be with Peter or not at all. She dusted and polished and swept the apartment, singing the most purposeful Party songs she knew, as if they might build a bulwark against Auntie's giant NO.

She went door to door with Peter to collect recyclables, though he was acting different. When the box grew heavy, he insisted on carrying it himself to the collection point. And he kept saying *we*. "We need to get there early so we can find good seats." "We should try the ice cream at that new *Eiscafé*. We like the same flavors, don't we?" It was such a small word. With Peter it felt like a lead weight around Lena's ankles.

When Auntie came home, she made a heroic effort to use up all of Saturday's words in one conversation. "We've got a big day today in the courtyard," she began. Then came the details. Hans had a friend who had liberated a truckload of sand and another of paving tiles from his workplace. That afternoon they would make a path. Here was what it would look like. *Whatever you do, don't mention bricks, or laying, or laying with bricks, or*—that's enough.

In the courtyard, Peter followed Lena around like an excited duckling. "I've already hidden my new shirt in my coat if you don't mind maybe I'll find a place to change before we get on the U-Bahn do you know how to get to the theater where is it what time does the play start I've never seen *Factory: A Love Story* Danika have you heard me and Lena are going to the theater tonight and—"

Auntie stepped in like a storm cloud. "Lena won't be going anywhere. She's sick."

Lena looked her in the eye. "I'm much better now."

Auntie turned away. *She's afraid of you.* Because Lena knew her secret. It wasn't such a terrible secret, but Auntie seemed to think it was.

"She's much better now," Peter echoed, though when he said it Auntie glared at him and pushed a shovel into his hands. Auntie was armed with several shovels and a variety of small unmatched woolens. It looked like she'd raided the lost and found that morning at her school. Her rolled-up sleeves told Lena that this afternoon would not be a pony ride.

"Aren't you two the cute couple," Danika said.

"We're not a couple," Lena said quickly.

Peter's face turned red and splotchy and he went to find something to dig up.

"Now you've done it," Danika said.

"Shut up." Lena wouldn't look in his direction. She felt terrible.

"Today's the day, everyone." Hans had a way of filling up the air around him even when they were outside. It was his friend who was coming to save the courtyard, therefore Hans was saving the courtyard, therefore he was the one who owned the afternoon. He wore a corduroy cap, and work pants, and proper boots, and he wasn't drunk—at least not yet.

Peter and Hans had already removed all the planks of plywood except one. That had been the only way across the mud swamp. Danika stood on the remaining plank as if it were a life raft. "Is this actually going to work?" she asked.

"You mustn't talk like that," Auntie said. "It's bad for morale."

The rumble of a truck sounded nearby.

"Here comes the Sandman, children," Hans said. "Everyone get ready for bed."

"Thank God," Danika said in her most sarcastic voice. "Nothing bad can happen now."

Auntie looked like she wanted to stab them both. "Listen up, all of you. I've told the fellow to dump the sand in the northern corner of the courtyard."

No one knew which was the northern corner.

"That one, for crying out loud." She pointed. "And when he does, we're going to spread it in a nice thick layer across the mud."

Lena began to feel excited. Up to now, Auntie's plan to beautify the courtyard had seemed pointless. Not only were they never going to win the Golden House Number plaque, but their battle against the mud had become depressing. Every time it rained, the mud won, and autumn had just started.

But now the drainage trench had been dug, with a layer of crushed rock on the bottom and larger flat stones on the sides. The trench led to a vacant lot next door that would be a mud bath by the end of winter, but, as Hans said, that would be someone else's problem.

The truck squealed to a halt and the driver backed in, Auntie waving her arms to guide him. He tilted the truck bed back and Lena waited for an avalanche of sand. A mountain of sand. But the man had only liberated an anthill's worth.

Auntie looked as if someone had stepped on her birthday cake. She rapped on the driver's door while everyone gathered behind her, boots sinking in the muck.

"Is there another delivery coming?" she asked.

"Maybe next week," he said. "If I can organize more sand. I can't take too much, see, or they'll notice and I'll be in trouble. Come grab the tiles, Hansy."

Hans trudged around to the passenger side and took out two paving tiles. "We're grateful." He tried to sound convincing, but even he acted like someone had knocked over his stein of beer. "One step at a time, right, people?"

"Right," everyone said.

Hans's friend said he would do his best to come back next Saturday, and that was that. Peter spread the sand. "Thickly," Auntie ordered, "or it won't do any good." But it wouldn't do much good anyway. Peter and Hans set down the two tiles, and there they had it, two footsteps—out of the eighty or so they had hoped for.

What if you met with that Western editor and showed him the letter? Met him? How? How would Lena even contact him again to arrange the meeting?

Peter walked back and forth from one tile to the other. "It's a beginning."

"It's stupid." Danika stood on the single sheet of plywood with her arms crossed.

"Come on, man," Hans said to Peter. "Let's put the rest of the plywood back or no one will be able to cross."

Say you could find a way to call him again. Wouldn't the letter be proof enough? Nothing would be proof enough. No matter what Lena said or did, the man could still assume she worked for the Stasi. She *did* work for the Stasi. *Not like that.* Really? All those Monday-evening conversations with Jutta—and Jutta asking her question after question: What was Erich working on now? Did he have any big new ideas? What did you two talk about? All the while, someone in another room had been wearing a bulky headset and taking notes.

Two sad tiles, a path to nowhere. That was as far as she'd gotten in finding Erich. Two huge risks she'd taken—for nothing.

"What time should I pick you up?" Peter asked.

Right. That too. "Seven, I guess," Lena said.

Peter put a hand on her arm. He had trimmed his fingernails. This was serious. "I'm looking forward to it." His voice seized up on *forward* and he turned away.

She wanted to say, *We're not going as boyfriend and girlfriend, you know.* She wanted to say, *There's this boy, he's the cook in the play.* She would explain about Max's hair, how it curled in the front even though it was conscription-short. "And there's a dimple involved." She would apologize in advance for hurting Peter's feelings. But she said none of these things.

Auntie would be out for the rest of the day. The afternoon was unexpectedly free. Lena would go to the theater, find Max, and warn him.

– 15 –

YOU DON'T REALLY KNOW ANYONE

Someone was watching her on the S-Bahn—a pinched man wearing wire-rim glasses and a black beret. He looked like the type who might work in a library, or in a building underground with lots of yellow lighting. Every time she glanced over, he turned away.

Erich always said she was pretty when she smiled, but this fellow wasn't trying to catch her eye. He was trying to avoid it, pretending to read his book. *What if he's from the People's Police? What if Friedrich So-and-So—* Maybe they were just waiting for her to return to Prenzlauer Berg. This was a mistake. Or maybe it was all in her head. *For sure it's in your head. There are lots of things in there that no one would believe.*

She considered getting off at a different stop, but what good would that do? If he was following her, he would get off too. Her stop was approaching. She waited until the last possible moment and hurried to the door. Out of the corner of her eye she saw him leap up. But she didn't see if he got off after her. When she looked back through the train windows, he wasn't there. Beside her was a crowd of passengers, maybe with him in it.

She set off for the theater, doing her best not to check over her shoulder. That in itself would attract the wrong kind of attention. She had the address, and she knew the neighborhood well enough to take a circuitous route. *Yes, Auntie, we know what circuitous means.* If the man really was following her, it would be obvious soon enough.

She stayed on the busier main street, repeating the slogans on the billboards she passed to keep calm, then turned abruptly onto a smaller road. *Don't run. Be purposeful. Not like the house is on fire, more like you're determined to buy a decent pair of shoes.*

Soon there were footsteps behind her. *Don't turn around.* She turned. The man in the beret made no attempt to hide. She braced herself for a loud *Halt* or a subtler *You're coming with me.*

Instead he said, "Wait." And then, "Please."

Lena allowed him to catch up to her. "Who are you? Why have you been following me?"

"I'm sorry, I had no choice." He lowered his voice. "I've been watching you all day. I had to make sure it was safe to talk to you. You telephoned me about your uncle. I'm Günter Schulmann."

Günter Schulmann—the man from Erich's letter. Lena stared at him. "That's not possible."

"I assure you, it's true." He showed her his identification, and offered his hand for her to shake.

"But—" She lowered her voice. "You live in West Berlin. I thought visas took weeks to be approved."

"I don't have to apply in advance for a visa if it's only a day trip," Herr Schulmann said. "I just have to exchange some of our good Western currency for your Eastern nonsense—at a terrible rate. I come across whenever I like, as a tourist."

A tourist! How uncomplicated it was for Westerners. Once, Lena had asked her parents if they could make a trip to the West, just to see it. "If you know of a family member over there who's dying, maybe," Papa had said. "Even then, they'd never let us go all together." There was always the possibility that they wouldn't return. Oma and Opa had gone a few times, because they were senior citizens. The government didn't care if they came back. Otherwise, for Easterners, it was forbidden.

"Did you ever meet my uncle?" Lena asked.

"A few times," Herr Schulmann said, "but meeting writers in the GDR is tricky. The Stasi keep a close watch on that sort of thing."

Günter Schulmann's coat looked soft. Lena wanted to touch it. Then something occurred to her. "You didn't tell the border guards you were coming to see me, did you?" There would be questions, possible repercussions at work.

"Of course not," he said. "And I don't believe I was followed." The sound of someone shouting on the road startled them both. "Is there somewhere we can talk?"

Lena took him to Erich's favorite pub. The barman nodded to her as she entered and didn't make a single comment about milk. The waitress who had helped her before gave her a look of *are you okay?* Lena smiled and found a wobbly table in the corner.

"How did you know to contact me?" Herr Schulmann asked once they were seated. "And where did you get my private number?"

Lena told him about the letter hidden in the freezer.

"Your uncle talked about you. He worried your employers might force you to inform on him."

Force? No, not force. They had tricked her into it. "Sir, I—"

"Günter."

But he was a stranger. She couldn't use his first name. "Herr Schulmann, people are saying I don't have an uncle. I went to the state registry office to see his birth record and they said he didn't exist. His novels are gone. He is gone. And I found a listening device in the coffee room at work. Please tell me what he was doing. No one will answer my questions. They keep telling me to stop asking them."

The waitress brought two small glasses of beer and a plate of meat and bread that Herr Schulmann had ordered. Auntie never let Lena drink beer. Herr Schulmann clinked his glass against hers and said, "*Prost.*"

She took a sip and cringed. "It's bitter."

He laughed. "You get used to it." He set his glass down on the table. "I'll tell you what I know, which isn't much. That's probably a good thing. The more you know, the more danger you'll be in." He paused, weighing his next words. "Whoever advised you to stop making inquiries is giving you good counsel. Every time you ask a question, you risk giving the Stasi more information about your uncle."

"I never thought of that." *Oh, Uncle.* She was afraid she might cry.

"Contacting me—I mean, I'm glad you let me know what's happened, because I might be able to help. But if they hadn't known about me before, well—they certainly know now. I expect they'll leave you alone in the hope that you'll give them what they need." He pushed the plate of food toward Lena. "Please, eat. I ordered this for you."

Lena made herself a sandwich to be polite, though she wasn't sure she'd be able to eat much. "Do you have any idea where my uncle is?"

"Probably in a cell in Hohenschönhausen. I suspect they're questioning him and, considering you're still working at Stasi headquarters, he must not be talking." Herr Schulmann took a long drink of beer. "I'm surprised they've taken such drastic measures. Lately they've been very concerned with their image. They want their Western neighbors to think they're respectable. Not that I'd put anything past them. It wouldn't be the first time." He rested his head on one hand. "God, you should get out of this damned country. This is no life for a young girl."

"Get out?" Lena's body went so heavy she wasn't sure she could get out of her chair, never mind the country. Did this man have any idea what he was saying? Fleeing the Republic carried a prison sentence of up to eight years. As a bonus, if Lena succeeded in leaving, Auntie's life would be ruined. She'd lose her job, possibly also the apartment. Rumors would circulate: an addiction to alcohol, or pornography. She would become a social outcast. Lena would never be able to live with herself.

And what would she do in the West? Who did she know? No one. Her life was here, and her life—before Erich had disappeared—was not so bad. She had a job, a place to live. Visits to the doctor whenever she needed them, child care for the children she would have one day, a State-sponsored holiday once a year. There was hardly any crime. The State took care of her.

MICHELLE BARKER

"Everything for the good of the People," as the slogan went.

"Was that what my uncle was planning?" she asked. "To go to the West?"

"No, his business was on this side of the Wall. He was investigating something that was making your security people nervous. Something to do with your parents getting killed in that munitions factory."

Munitions factory? Lena almost choked on her mouthful of food. *Swallow it. Auntie will take away all your privileges if she finds out you spoke with your mouth full in a public place.* She swallowed hard. "My parents didn't work in a munitions factory."

"Actually, they did."

"Herr Schulmann, you have been misinformed. My parents worked in a freight car factory in Magdeburg. I lived there with them. I know what they did."

"You think you know."

Here we go. It's Jutta's jar of pickles all over again. You don't really know anyone. But these were Lena's parents. This had been their place of employment. "Who told you that?"

"Your uncle. He had proof. There was no question, it was ammunition your parents were making."

Ammunition? "Our country believes in peace." All the songs said so. All the slogans, and the promises Lena and other young people had made when they'd joined the Free German Youth. *That's why in sports practice you learn both football and hand grenade-throwing.* Quiet, Mausi. The soldiers at the border were protecting the citizens. *And the Wall was built to keep bad people out.*

"Your country believes in propaganda," Herr Schulmann said.

176

What was that buzzing sound? *Do you really need to ask?* The pub was dark, the air close. Too many people were smoking. Lena's clothes were too tight. How could— "When my parents came home at night they talked about freight cars, and what they did on the line."

"I'm sure they did." Herr Schulmann picked up a slice of salami and stuffed the whole thing into his mouth. Auntie would have sent him away from the table. "They would have been coached."

"The accident—an explosion. No wonder."

"An explosion, yes." He took another slice of salami. "Whether or not it was an accident—that was one of the things your uncle was investigating."

Not an accident. This had been Lena's secret hope: *I wish it had been someone's fault.* A crime with criminals. No wonder Uncle's reaction had been so strange—asking her who else she'd told, or if someone had made her say that. It made sense if he'd been afraid she might be forced to become an informer. *Thank goodness you never mentioned that to Jutta.*

Maybe it *had* been someone's fault.

"You said that was one of the things." Lena was almost afraid to ask. "What else was he investigating?" How much trouble had he gotten himself into?

Günter Schulmann placed both hands on the table. His fingers were long and skinny, and the tips were greasy from the salami. "Think about this. East Germany—"

Lena winced. "We don't call it that. It's bad manners."

"Right. Excuse me. The German Democratic Republic has a People's Army. It's got the Society for Sport and Technology, which is paramilitary. You learn how to shoot in your youth groups, don't you? They even give the children toy weapons in day care. Militarization is no secret in this country."

"It's defensive," Lena said.

"Please." Herr Schulmann gave her a look. "The Soviets have nuclear weapons stationed in your country. The Americans have their missiles in mine. Both sides expect a war to erupt at any moment. None of this is hidden. And yet your parents were instructed to tell everyone—even their own family members—that they worked in a freight car factory."

That did seem odd. "Why?" Lena asked.

Herr Schulmann steepled his hands and smiled. "If you find the answer to that question, I suspect you'll know why they made your uncle disappear."

"He found out."

"He told me he'd found something big, and he was frightened. That was the last I heard."

Lena couldn't eat any more, and she certainly wasn't touching that fizzy bitter beer. She needed to get outside. Herr Schulmann paid the bill and they left, taking a quiet side street.

"I'm sorry to have given you so much to mull over," he said.

She shook her head as if the things he'd told her might fall out. "What am I supposed to do now?"

"If you want to be safe? Nothing." He buttoned his coat. "Keep *stumm*." Silent. "Go back to your life. Anytime you ask questions, you risk putting your uncle in danger."

"Could I at least visit him in jail?" She could bring soup, and warm clothes. She'd go every day.

"They would never admit that he was there. Not after the trouble they've taken to make him vanish." Herr Schulmann looked sad, regretful, the way a person looked when they realized they'd squashed a small animal with their car.

"Listen," he said. "I work with several important writers in the West. Prominent names, lots of publicity. If we can find proof of what's going on, we could blow the whistle on it from our end. Embarrass your authorities. Maybe force them to release Erich."

"They wouldn't release him after this," Lena said.

"Not back to you, no. But they might ship him over to us, for a fee."

"To the West? I'd never see him again." She couldn't bear that. She almost lost her balance, and had to steady herself on a nearby wire fence.

Herr Schulmann took her gently by both shoulders. His face was thin and his blue eyes were faded, as if they'd been laundered too often. "I'm sorry to say this, but you may never see him again anyway. At least if he gets sent to the West he'll be alive. Free to write whatever he wants."

It will be a life without you in it. No, she had to stop thinking of herself. Think of him. This was the biggest gift she could give him.

"So you want me to find out why that factory was making ammunition in secret."

"I would never ask you to do that," Herr Schulmann said. "And anyone would understand if you decided not to. You would be risking everything. But—" He opened his hands as if to catch something that was falling from the sky. "You work at Stasi head-quarters, don't you?"

She nodded.

"You have access to their offices, their files, material that no one else in this country could ever get their hands on. If the secret is as big as Erich suspected, the files will be there, maybe even in Mielke's office."

"They lock up their documents at night. I'm not supposed to touch them." Lena pictured Jutta's big angry face, her nonprotruding Slavic ears going red.

Herr Schulmann cocked his head like a robin waiting for a worm. "I don't suppose you know where they keep the keys."

She smiled. She wasn't supposed to know. But after two years of dusting the offices, she knew all the agents' hiding places.

"You'd have to be careful," Herr Schulmann said. "Put things back exactly as you found them. You mustn't get caught. It could mean death for your uncle. Certainly you'd end up in prison."

Lena bit her nails as a flock of starlings burst out of a tree. *What are you getting yourself into? You don't even know this man.* But Erich was in trouble and there was no one else, no one in the world, who was in a better position to help him. *Help him how? Help him get to the West so you can never see him again?* The Stasi had erased him. He did not exist in the Better Germany anymore. They'd made it easy for themselves. No need for a death certificate if he'd never been born.

"What if there are cameras in the offices?" she asked. Hidden cameras in House 1? Why not? These were the top functionaries in the Stasi. They had the most incriminating secrets at their fingertips and they were above the law. But they weren't above Comrade Mielke.

Then she thought of Herr Dreck. "Never mind." There couldn't be cameras. He would not do what he did to her if he thought someone was watching. And the phone call to Herr Schulmann—

they would have known she was the one who'd made it; they would have seen her. But it was him they'd questioned. They'd known the call had been made; they just hadn't known who had made it.

"We'll have to keep in touch somehow," Herr Schulmann said.

"You can find me if you need me," Lena said. "But how will I get hold of you? If I discover something? We can't use the phones, or the mail." Department M monitored the mail. They would intercept their letters and steam them open. They had special machines; Lena had seen them once when she'd taken some cleaning solution over to House 46.

Herr Schulmann looked to the left-hand side of the sky, because it wasn't only dead Helmut that hung around up there. The best thoughts tended to float left. "Do you know anyone who's familiar with radio?" he said. "Amateur radio, where you can talk."

"Yes. My neighbor Peter has a ham radio in his bedroom." He'd only told her about it a thousand times. He called his bedroom his ham shack.

"I'll talk to some friends and see what we can organize." Herr Schulmann leaned toward her. "I'll arrange for them to leave a note with the details in your mailbox. We'll have to choose a frequency to make contact, and we'll need a harmless phrase that your neighbor won't pick up on. That will be the sign that you want to speak to me, and then we can meet in this pub."

"If your friends are going to leave a note," Lena said, "tell them to do it late in the evening. That way I'll be the first to get it in the morning." It was only too easy to imagine Auntie bustling down to check the mail after work and finding an envelope without any stamps on it, then storming back into the apartment and waving it at Lena so hard it made wind.

Her stomach tightened at the idea of all this adventure, but it was also rather exciting. *Don't be a fool. Do you think prison is an adventure? How about dogs?*

"We'll do what we can to get your uncle out of this mess, all right?" Herr Schulmann said. "But you—you must be careful, at all times. No more questions about Erich. No offhand comments. No friends with dangerous leanings. You don't want to give the Stasi any reason to bring you in."

An autumn wind rattled the remaining leaves on the trees. Lena felt suddenly chilled. "I think they're watching me," she said.

"I'm sure they are," Herr Schulmann said. "They're hunters, Lena. They know how to watch and wait, and they know big game when they see it. Don't trust anyone. Don't get caught." He shook her hand. "You're a brave young woman. Your uncle is lucky to have someone who loves him this much. We'll be in touch."

Lena headed back to the S-Bahn station, lost in a memory of Erich. When she was younger and they'd lived in Magdeburg, her parents were often so tired on the weekends after a full week's work—and still rushing off to committee meetings and Party school, all incredibly dull, according to Papa—that Erich would sometimes come from Berlin for the weekend to look after Lena. He'd take her to the cinema, or the *Eiscafé*, or the park. Sometimes he'd bring her a new book, something guaranteed to keep her sitting quietly while he wrote in his notebook for hours.

Afterward he'd tell her stories. It took a while before Lena realized what he was really doing—working out his stories by describing them to her. This happened, and then that happened.

"But why, Uncle?" she would ask. "That doesn't make sense."

He'd clap himself on the forehead and say, "By God, you're right." He would ask what she thought should happen next, and they'd discuss it. And he would listen as if the advice of a nine-year-old girl was the most important thing; as if she mattered to him.

One Christmas she and her parents had gone to Berlin, and Erich had taken her to the Christmas market. There'd been a Ferris wheel, a train, even a merry-go-round. There were games and lights, roasted almonds and hot chocolate. Erich bought a cup of warm, sweet glühwein and gave Lena a sip while they listened to the choir. It had been her first ever taste of mulled wine.

She hated the thought of him in a cell, forced to stay awake for days. Ten days, he had said once; ten days was all it took before someone broke. *Has it been that long?* Lena counted backward. Yes, it had been longer. What if they weren't feeding him? The cells would be cold. He would be cold—or worse. There was worse. Absolute darkness, or constant bright light. Isolation. Cells where people lost their minds, or their lives.

That's why you're going to do this. You'll do it, and you won't get caught.

It wasn't until she was walking home from the U-Bahn station that she realized she'd forgotten to see Max.

– 16 –

FACTORY: A LOVE STORY

Lena turned away while Peter changed into his swanky purple shirt behind some bushes. The last thing she wanted was to see him half-naked. He'd be skinny, maybe with eczema on his chest. *Don't be unkind.* She couldn't help it. He had been scratching at his coat sleeves from the moment he'd appeared at her door. It seemed worse now that his nails were short.

"No dawdling after the theater," Auntie had warned. "You bring her straight home, Peter."

How Auntie had fussed at the door, adjusting Lena's hair, her scarf, while Peter stood there watching and scratching. "Your first date." She patted Lena on the cheek, looking as if she might cry.

Lena had been embarrassed, and surprised. *She cares about you. She just forgets sometimes.* But Lena had also been horrified. *It's not a date*, she wanted to say, *just two friends going out. So you can see another boy, the one you really like.* How had this happened?

She would have preferred to be honest with Peter—but there was a problem, and the problem was the radio. Peter was the only person she knew who had one. There was no possibility of gaining access to one herself. The Society for Sport and Technology was one place to learn amateur radio—while you were also learning how to clean a machine gun. But to join it, you had to be a boy. Even if you became a member of a ham radio society, you still had to get a radio license, and that took months. Peter had told Lena many club members were restricted to listening only. "We're all supervised by the government," he said. Military Papa must have had something to do with Peter getting his own radio. If Lena upset him, that would be the end of her plan to help Erich.

You're going to use him. Yes, Mausi, that was what she was going to do. *You are a despicable human being.*

While she waited in the dark for Peter to come out of the bushes, she considered that human beings were truly capable of anything—good, or bad. There was no way to exempt yourself from a particular category, to say *I would never do that.* Given the right (or wrong) circumstances, you might not have a choice.

It would be slightly less horrible if she could tell Peter why she needed to use the radio. But Herr Schulmann had been adamant: no one was to know about this. And there was Military Papa to consider—if he found out. . . .

Peter had buttoned the shirt right up to his neck. Erich would have said he looked like a *Sitzpinkler*—a man who peed sitting down. Even so, Lena said, "The shirt looks good on you," and Peter smiled. *Despicable.*

They rode the trains sitting side by side like packages bound with twine—elbows tucked in, no chance of a leg or shoulder

touching. Eyes forward, no talking. The closer they drew to Prenzlauer Berg, the worse an idea the whole thing seemed.

The train clack-clacked along, then stopped, and someone
came on eating a *Fetzer* bar. The Better Germany did many things
better than the Other Germany, but chocolate bars weren't one of
them. No one knew the exact cocoa content of the chocolate they
used in bars like *Fetzer*. Erich said they were only brown because
of the addition of lentils.

By the time they reached their stop, it had begun to drizzle. It
made Lena walk faster, even though she didn't want to get to the
theater—ever. Except she did, because of Max.

"Have you heard anything interesting on your radio lately?"
she asked.

"Australians." Enthusiasm made Peter's voice crack. "Do you
believe that? I mean, I didn't talk to them, I just listened. Father
doesn't want me talking to Westerners. I have to follow the rules,
or he'll take the radio away."

Lena kept her hands firmly in her pockets so there was no way
Peter could try to hold one. "Is it hard, using the radio?"

"Not at all. It just takes patience. There's a lot of chirp and AC
hum to deal with, but that's because my radio is a homebrew. And
there's the damned Woodpecker."

Bewilderment must have pinched her face, because Peter
started laughing.

"Right, I forgot, you're not a ham. Chirp and AC hum are just
radio noises. A homebrew means I built it myself. And the Woodpecker is this terrible tapping sound, some kind of Soviet radar
that no one can get rid of. It's very annoying."

"How long did it take you to learn all that?"

186

Peter seemed both embarrassed and pleased by the attention. "I guess I've always been interested in radio, so I don't know."

"Could you teach me?"

His cheeks went raspberry red. "Of course. I mean. Your aunt. You think—?" It sounded like he was talking in Morse code.

"She wouldn't mind." As long as a parent was home and the bedroom door was left ajar. *Not that she follows those rules—not with the bricklayer.*

Up ahead was the theater. There was a line-up of patrons and, as Peter and Lena drew closer, a drone of conversation. What would Max be doing right now? Dressing in his costume, probably. Practicing his lines. Would he look for her in the audience? She and Peter joined the line, showed their tickets, and went inside.

The theater felt damp. People had brought the odor of their suppers with them on their coats, onions and black pudding mixing with tobacco and sweat. Many of the theatergoers mingled in the foyer, but Lena didn't like mingling. Her attempts at conversation with strangers always led the other person to complain about something: their car if they had one, or if they didn't, the food at the canteen at work, a physical ailment, the poor cuts of meat at the butcher shop, the telephone they were still waiting for.

"Let's find seats," Lena said. If they got in early, they could choose a place near the back and Max would never see her.

"I like to sit close." Scratch, scratch. "So I can feel like I'm part of the action."

The stage was set up in the middle of the theater with seating all around. If an actor tripped, he would land in someone's lap. Max would see her for sure. "I don't think—"

"Oh yes, you must sit close," said a man with a bushy white mustache. He led Peter and Lena down the stairs to the front. Did he work at the theater? Was he an overbearing stranger? Auntie would have pulled people down the stairs too, if she thought it was good for morale.

On one side of the stage there was an assembly line; on the other, a canteen table. Who was going to fall in love in *Factory: A Love Story?* Would it be Max? What if he kissed a girl onstage?

Lena sat there with stiff legs and read her program so many times she had it memorized. Every time she glanced at Peter he was staring straight ahead, seeming unsure of what to do with his arms. Finally the lights dimmed, and the play began.

It turned out no one was going to fall in love in *Factory: A Love Story*, at least not the kind of love Lena had imagined. Everyone fell in love—with the factory. It was the best place ever to work. The machinery was modern and never broke down. No one showed up to work drunk. The lighting was superior, the air quality first class; even the food at the canteen was excellent. It was one of the dumbest things Lena had ever seen. Erich would have walked out. Auntie would have taken Lena to see it a second time.

Lena stopped listening and her mind wandered. Had the accident at the munitions factory been caused by a malfunction in the machines? Was that how her parents had died? *Scheiss Osten.* But that was hardly news. Everyone knew the truth about the working conditions in factories, no matter how many slogans General Secretary Honecker made them learn.

But whether or not it was an accident—that was what Herr Schulmann had wondered. Which meant Erich suspected it wasn't. Had someone blown up the factory on purpose?

The lights went on in the canteen corner of the stage. A man with a beard and a large round belly came on wearing a big white chef's hat. It was Max. Lena didn't recognize him at first. He was dressed in a dirty apron and he danced around the kitchen holding oversize knives and spoons, talking about how to make a good borscht.

Don't look at me. Don't look at me.

But he was staring straight at her. He gave a tiny smile. Then he must have spotted Peter beside her, with the purple shirt that screamed *first date* buttoned to the neck. On her other side sat an older couple who clearly didn't belong to her. The smile disappeared. When Max stumbled on his lines, Lena wanted to run right out of the theater.

"Cabbage and beets, beets and cabbage," Max kept saying. He was the cook. He was supposed to know what went into a borscht.

"Onions," Lena wanted to call out. "Carrots. Potatoes." *He'll never speak to you again.*

Peter reached over and held Lena's arm.

Lena went rigid. "What are you doing?"

"Quiet!" The older woman sitting next to her swatted her with a program. "Show some respect."

Max started banging on the pot with his soup spoon. The factory workers got a this-wasn't-in-the-script look on their faces, until big-nosed Bem said, "Come on, Comrades, let's take lunch early. The boss doesn't mind, he knows how hard we work." And then, pointedly to Max, "The cook will serve us some borscht *right now.*"

Max seemed to snap back into what he was supposed to be doing. He ladled out the soup and everyone commented on how good it was, and the play dragged on for another hour. The moment it was over, Lena shot out of her seat.

"What's the hurry?" Peter said. "If we hang around, maybe we'll get to meet the actors."

"No." *You're being too aggressive. Calm down.* "I mean, Auntie was very clear. We're to come home as soon as it's over."

"All right."

Lena pushed past the others making their way up the stairs. She had ruined the performance for Max. She had ruined her chances of ever seeing him again. *And if you don't start being nicer to Peter, you will lose the only chance you have of saving Erich.*

"I'm sorry," she said when they were out in the cold night air. "I'm really hungry. You want to stop somewhere on the way home for a *Ketwurst*?"

"Sure," Peter said. "I know a good place not far from our building."

*

Auntie wanted all the details: the lighting, the story line, where they sat. "Did he hold your hand?" As Lena lay in bed that night, all she could think of was that tomorrow was Sunday, the day she had always reserved for her uncle, and she would not see him.

Go to the theater tomorrow. Find Max. Explain. Explain what? That she was using Peter to communicate with a Western book editor to help save her uncle who had been erased? Which part of that could she tell him?

She thought back to her life in Magdeburg. In the Better Germany's schools, classes were matched up with factories, and every two weeks students were sent to work there so they could get a taste of that life. Probably no one had ever been assigned to work in the freight car factory.

On Sunday, after their roast lunch, Auntie went to visit a neighbor. Lena had intended to see Danika and listen to Western music, but it never happened. Her feet were to blame. They were contrary, walking her onto a train instead of up the stairs to Danika's apartment.

She made it all the way to the theater without thinking about what she was doing. The front doors were locked, but the actors must have been rehearsing. After last night's performance, they would have to make sure Max knew how to make borscht.

Circling the building, she found a worn brown door. It too was locked, but she knocked just in case. No one answered. She turned around, and there was Max, across the alley.

"What are you doing here?"

Lena's head grew crowded with noise. She took a deep breath. "I came to apologize. I'd meant to warn you yesterday afternoon, but—"

He took a few steps toward her. "That would have been nice. Who was he? Your date, I mean."

"It wasn't a date."

He swiped at his hair. "Sure looked like one."

"He lives down the hall from me, that's all."

"And you had to bring him, of all people? You understand when I asked you, I meant—" But he wouldn't say what he'd meant.

"It wasn't like that. It was an accident." That word. It just happened. It was no one's fault. "And then my aunt insisted we go together."

He moved closer. "You could have said no."

Lena felt the warmth coming off his body. There was that lemony-soap scent. Her knees went watery. "You haven't met my aunt. She's like a tram without a driver. Once she's on the tracks there's no stopping her."

Somehow his hands found their way to her face, and they were large, and warm, and he tilted her chin up and kissed her gently on the lips. It was something she had imagined many times—her first kiss—but she was unprepared for the rush of sensations that came with it. Not only the softness of his lips, but also the way every bone in her body had decided it was no longer needed. The way every connection in her brain lit up. It was Erich Honecker's lamp shop up there—the Palace of the Republic and its thousands of lights.

Max pulled away and smiled. She wanted him to kiss her again. *How do you ask for the second kiss?* And if the first kiss had lit a thousand lights, what would the second one do?

He wrapped his arms around her and held her. "There's something about you," he said softly. "You're brave. And I like the way your mind works."

She leaned into him, and her whole body relaxed. And then the spell was broken by footsteps and voices.

"The others are coming." Max let go of her. "We have to rehearse."

Lena waited for him to say something about the play, its awfulness, the sheer boredom of rehearsing it—but he didn't. "When will I see you again?" she asked.

Max pulled a play ticket out of his pocket. "This time, I'm only giving you one."

Lena laughed. *Thank God.* Nothing between them had been damaged. "I mean really see you."

"I could come visit you at your place tomorrow before rehearsal."

In the afternoon. "My aunt will be at work. She's a teacher."

"Is it all right," Max said, "to visit while she's not home?"

Lena hesitated. The voices and laughter drew closer. "Sure. It will be fine." *Auntie will lock you inside for a month if she finds out you had a boy over, alone, without permission. You better make sure she takes her headache medication to school.*

– 17 –

BLAH, BLAH, RUDOLPH GYPNER

Lena decided to surprise Sausage Auntie by waking up on time to line up for meat. Meat seemed like a good way to keep her happy.

Max's looming visit had been flashing a bright red warning light through Lena's dreams all night. Auntie might have been happy about one boyfriend—and somehow she was convinced Peter was Lena's One True Love. But Two True Loves was something else. Two meant you probably worked at a textile factory and wore lipstick and bleached your hair.

With any luck, Max would show up while Peter was busy with his radio. Peter worked a later shift on Mondays and would still be home when Max came over.

Lena lined up with all the other rumpled and tired citizens, bought some ham, and brought it home. She stopped at the mailbox before going upstairs. Not that she expected Herr Schulmann to have dropped off anything so soon—but sure enough, there was an unmarked envelope, something bulky. Lucky she'd gone to the butcher's that morning, or Auntie would have found it. There was no way she would open the package in the foyer. Instead, she tucked it inside her coat and went upstairs.

Auntie made such a fuss about the ham it was as if Lena had won another prize for Enthusiasm in Handicrafts. While she was preparing breakfast, Lena slipped into her bedroom and hid the package under her pillow. When she returned to the table there was sliced ham, along with an egg and some Western coffee, a gift from the bricklayer, maybe.

As soon as Auntie left for work, Lena went into her room and opened the package. Inside was a camera so small it fit into her palm. There was also a note:

I arranged for a friend to deliver this. Take it with you to work. There is film in it. Photograph anything you find. Contact me when you're ready to send it back.

There were also instructions about which radio frequency to use, and Herr Schulmann's call sign, whatever that meant. The phrase that would let him know Lena needed to meet with him again was a familiar Party slogan: "Work together, plan together, govern together." No problem. Peter wouldn't be the least bit suspicious. *He won't be, if you can keep him interested in you. Otherwise, see you in the prison cell next to Erich's.*

She didn't want to do that to Peter. Never mind that he was scabby and a bit goofy, she hated the idea of hurting his feelings. *Then what? Forget you ever had an uncle, live your life the way they want? You didn't see anything. You don't know anything. You don't say anything*. But she did know. She was well into the middle section between the Walls now—the death strip. She could see all the hazards: the lights and observation towers, the tank trap, the fences, the Stasi-trained dogs. *Yes, Mausi, there are dogs*: German shepherds and rottweilers, with big teeth. She could see the far Wall too, the one blocking the West.

But she had an idea. If she were to show an interest in radio, rather than in Peter, it might be less hurtful, and it would delight him. He didn't have to know why. She tucked the camera into her sweater pocket so there was no chance of it being found—by Auntie or anyone else.

*

By the time Lena arrived to help beautify the courtyard, Hans was sitting on one of his crying-shame benches with an already empty mug. Danika was talking about a photo session she'd done with a real fashion photographer from *Pramo*, one of her favorite magazines. Even Auntie approved of *Pramo*, because it included patterns so you could make the clothes yourself if you liked them.

"I was wearing a pantsuit, and high heels." Danika's voice went higher. "They took, like, ten thousand photographs. This way, then that way, then another way."

Her excitement was contagious. "What color was the pantsuit?" Lena asked. "Did you wear lipstick?"

"Obviously I wore lipstick. Red," she said, with a mischievous gleam in her eye, because red was one of those colors—reserved for flags and Pioneer neckerchiefs. It was not to be squandered on trifles. "The pantsuit was white. I had to be careful not to stain it."

Lena wished she had the magazine photograph of Marilyn Monroe to show Danika. "It sounds very glamorous."

"My friend has promised more paving tiles," Hans said. "But then there's the problem of sand." He tipped the cup back until his head faced the sky, as if maybe there was one more drop.

"What are we working on today?" Lena asked.

"Who cares?" Danika said. "Why are we even here?"

Peter appeared in the courtyard with an armful of shovels. "We're here because we live in this housing development, and the plywood path is sinking, and we want to make the place prettier." He turned to Lena for confirmation.

"That's right," she said. Somehow the way Peter had expressed it gave it meaning. She couldn't have cared less about Auntie's stupid Golden House Number plaque, but she did care about where she lived, and how the muddy courtyard made the whole complex look like a construction zone. A shithole, Erich would have called it. The housing developments were supposed to be a step forward for society: more housing for the People. It was part of what everyone needed to believe—that this Germany was the better one. But the muddy courtyard was a reminder that the entire city of Berlin was built on a swamp. It would be a tough battle to win.

"My father is bringing some shrubs," Peter said. "They'll help with the moisture. We have to dig six big holes, a meter apart, along this side." He pointed.

"I'm not digging," Danika said. "It will ruin my nails. The stylist said my hands are my best feature."

Lena tried to work out if that was really a compliment. Hans laughed.

"Shut up," Danika said to him. "What do you know? You with your *Trunksucht.*" His constant drinking. Hans put down the mug and ran his hand along one of the benches.

"The benches are beautiful," Lena said. "They're the nicest in the whole neighborhood." She took a shovel from Peter and began digging where he'd instructed so she didn't have to see Hans's face. He had pouches beneath his eyes, as if they were weighted with lead, which gave his face an air of sadness even though he was often smiling. The graying hair that curled at the collar of his pretend-leather jacket made him seem like the father of someone who owned a motorcycle. He lived alone; his wife had divorced him years ago and taken the children with her to Leipzig to live with her parents.

By the time Military Papa arrived with a truck full of shrubs, Peter and Lena had three of the six holes dug, Hans had refilled his mug, and Danika was examining her fingernails.

"I told you to be ready," Military Papa said. He was broad and muscular, though with a bit of belly that suggested he wasn't in the shape he should have been, even if he was retired from active service. His hair was cut short, his eyes small and squinting, and he had a long straight nose and a mouth that seemed designed for frowning. Lena dug harder and deeper. The thought of displeasing him terrified her.

He glared at Danika. "Why aren't you working? Did my son not bring enough shovels?"

Lena wondered if Danika would have the courage to tell him her hands were her best feature. She stepped in front of Danika and said, "Peter brought exactly the right number."

Military Papa turned toward Hans. "And you, the adult, what

kind of example are you setting?" Hans stood up unsteadily and Peter rushed over with a shovel for him, possibly suspecting he would need it for balance.

Danika took a shovel and stood in the mud with her elegant lace-up shoes. "Where are we supposed to do this?" she asked Peter.

"Watch your tone, young lady," Military Papa said. "We keep a good attitude on this team."

Peter indicated the spot for the next hole, but when Danika started digging, it looked as if she had never used a shovel in her life. Military Papa just shook his head. As he unloaded the truck, Lena's mood brightened. The shrubs were beautiful, thick and green.

"They'll need to be pruned for winter," Military Papa said. "They'll flower in the spring."

"*Beziehungen*," Hans murmured. Connections—it helped to have them. Unlike the friend with the two paving tiles and the sand he'd probably stolen from a playground.

They had just finished digging when a voice from the edge of the courtyard called, "Lena!"

It was Max. Not Max the cook, in his big hat, big stomach, and fake beard, but beautiful Max with the hair that wouldn't behave, and the dimple, wearing his green coat and walking in that precise way of his. Everyone turned to look at him.

"Who's that?" Danika held up her index finger—the One True Love sign.

Max must have sensed Military Papa was in charge. "Sir," he said to him. "Sorry to disturb. I came to visit Lena, but if she's busy—"

Military Papa gave him an up-and-down look. Conscription haircut: check. Military posture: check. Confident eye contact: check. "Did you just finish service, son?"

"Yes, sir. Eighteen months. The motor-rifle division in Potsdam."

"Very nice. Which regiment?"

"Artillery, sir."

"Ah. One of Rudolf Gypner's boys. You see, Peter?"

Peter hadn't looked up once since Max had arrived, but he had no choice now. Lena wondered what Military Papa wanted him to see. Everything, probably. The lack of slouching. No scabs. The easy conversation. The dimple.

"Did you enjoy your service?" Military Papa asked, and then he started nodding. It was like a machine had been turned on.

"Very much so, sir," said Max. "I'm considering a career in the military. I'm in the process of deciding with my parents."

"Fine, just fine. You let me know if you'd like me to put a word in for you. I'd be happy to do it." He gave Max's hand a hearty shake.

"You need some help here?" Max asked.

"They're almost done," Military Papa said. "Go ahead and steal Lena for a few minutes. Lena!" he shouted, as if Lena wasn't right there. Danika smiled and tilted her head, but Max barely noticed her.

Lena's face burned—she couldn't keep track of all the reasons why—as she stepped away from the shrubs and walked unsteadily along the plywood path with Max until they were out of the courtyard.

"That wasn't your aunt's husband, was it?" Max said.

"No, he died a long time ago. That's the father of the boy I came to the play with." Great. *Already we're wading into the bog.* Peter had seen him. There was little chance he'd recognize Max, but still. "You're considering a career in the military?"

"Are you kidding? I told him what he wanted to hear, so he'd let you come out."

Smart. *Also dishonest.* Should it ring an alarm bell? She wasn't sure. Didn't she do the same with Auntie? Didn't everyone do it, just to survive? People wore two faces: the public one that did what the children's magazine said—"be happy and sing"—and the private one that wanted to curse *Scheiss Osten* every five minutes.

Max put his arm around her. Lena craned her neck, but he laughed low in his throat and said, "Don't worry, they can't see. I was hoping to spend more than a few minutes with you."

"Monday isn't the best. That's usually when we work in the courtyard." She should have thought of it yesterday, but that kiss had turned all the days of the week into Sundays. In the background she heard the machine-gun bursts of Military Papa's loud voice.

"When can we spend more time together?" Max asked. "Like an evening?"

"I work nights. I'm free most other afternoons—if I don't sleep."

He looked up, and left, where a solution had to be waiting. "I rehearse in the afternoons, but I could come early, like today. If you don't mind missing some sleep."

He turned Lena to face him and she lost herself in his dark brown eyes. She wanted to touch his face, his hair. What were the rules? Why hadn't anyone told her? She reached up with one hand, using her fingertips. His skin was stubbly. And then his lips were on hers—soft, impossible. On the second kiss, his mouth opened and the lamp shop in Lena's brain lit up. The voices in her head went quiet, listening.

"Yes," Lena said finally. "I would like it if you came to visit." This was worth losing sleep over.

"How about tomorrow?"

"Tomorrow." She couldn't think. Her mouth barely worked. They stood in each other's arms, Lena absorbing every wonderful smell of him. His clothes. His skin. His soap.

"You should get back," Max said, "and I have to go to the theater. I'll see you tomorrow." One last gentle kiss, and then somehow Lena had to regain the ability to walk.

The moment she entered the courtyard a weight settled on her shoulders. Military Papa was still talking about the value of service and how great the artillery regiment was and blah, blah, Rudolf Gypner and, "Did you see that boy, son? Did you see the way he carried himself? That's what service does for a young man. There's a fellow with a career ahead of him. Just wait till you get called up."

Four of the shrubs were planted. Hans had made his way back onto the bench and was reminiscing about his time in service and how he used to have flawless aim. He started singing a song Lena had learned in kindergarten: "When I'm Grown Up I Will Be Joining the People's Army." Peter was patting down the soil and wouldn't look at Lena. Danika wouldn't stop looking at her. She sidled over to Lena and, right near Peter, said, "Who was *that*?"

"A friend." Lena's voice came out in a squeak.

"Is he ever cute. Could you introduce me?" She set her hands out in front of her as if her fingernails were drying.

Danika wanted to linger, but Lena put her head down and helped plant the last shrubs. "I have to get back upstairs," she said. "My aunt will be home soon." As if that mattered. Lena just wanted to get away from Peter. She couldn't bear for him to look at her. She tried to keep her face neutral, to keep the kisses from showing, but it felt like every part of her glowed. As soon as she had finished the job, she abandoned her shovel in the dirt and ran upstairs.

– 18 –

TIMING IS EVERYTHING

As Lena got ready for work, she took the miniature camera out of her pocket and held it in one hand: a tiny eye that hoped to capture giant secrets. "I'm just practicing an acceptable creative outlet," she rehearsed. As if anyone would believe that.

How would she carry it? Where would she keep it? It couldn't be in a place where Herr Dreck might touch it by accident. She tried tucking it into her kneesock, but it cut into her leg. *The coveralls.* They were practically made of pockets. She would slip it into one of the side pockets, along with something bigger that stuck out— like a hairbrush. Next to that, the camera would go undetected.

On the way to work, Lena hid both camera and hairbrush in her coat. The closer she got to headquarters, the heavier they felt. If anyone found out about this—and what did Herr Schulmann expect her to do? Poke around in the Comrade General's private files?

Auntie said each person was born with a talent. Lena had seen the Comrade General give speeches on television; he was not a talented speaker. Jutta claimed he couldn't sing or play a sport. He wasn't even a good shot. But he was better at hunting people than animals. He had a hunter's sense for prey, and he noticed—everything. That was one thing.

Two was that Lena didn't know what she was searching for. *Something with Erich's name on it.* Among the ten million or so documents in that building, there was sure to be one that explained everything.

Three was Jutta, who was maybe maybe-not keeping an eye on Lena at all times.

Four was the key. Mielke's drawers and cupboards were locked, like everyone else's. Unlike everyone else, however, he did not hide his key in one of the obvious places. Lena had never come upon it, but there were parts of his rooms she never cleaned. The key might be hidden on Jutta's side. But how would she search there without Jutta noticing?

And wouldn't Mielke know if someone had been snooping in his cupboards? That was why Jutta and Lena were required to clean his rooms together. They were supposed to monitor each other. "Trust is good," Lenin used to say, "but control is better." It was the Stasi's unofficial motto. And now Lena was going to do the unthinkable. She was going to spy on the man who spied on the Better Germany.

As she walked in the cool evening air, she listened to her breath, and to her feet clipping the edges of puddles. She passed the lit rectangles of ordinary upright socialist life—people making dinner, resting after their busy day at work, getting ready for the Black

Channel to come on television so they could shut it off. Who would be in charge of a problem like her uncle? She ran through the list of offices she cleaned, one miniature Lenin bust at a time, thinking, thinking. But she'd never opened any drawers or cabinets in those offices. She didn't know what any of the Stasi agents did.

And there were all the men who worked in the offices Jutta cleaned. She doubted Jutta would talk about them, not even if Lena tried to fool her. Jutta seemed dull, but she wasn't. It was a trick, *like being simple. When everyone thinks you're simple, they don't watch what they say around you.* Who would suspect Lena of the kind of subversion she was planning?

"Are you feeling better tonight?" Jutta asked when Lena walked into the ashtray room. *Sibylle* was on the table, turned to a different page today—a woman walking along a narrow white line on the road, as if balancing on a tightrope. Lena thought of Danika posing for the camera with pouty red lips, doing something impressive with her hands.

When will you transfer the camera to your coveralls? Lena put a hand into her coat pocket, pressing it against the end of the hairbrush.

"I feel much better," she said. For now. Herr Dreck would be waiting for her. It would be different—now that she'd done the last thing, the thing she couldn't bear to think about. He might make her do it again. She couldn't keep throwing up every night and going home early, or she'd lose her job.

"Good." Jutta planted her elbows on the magazine to hold it in place. "My neighbor made stew. I've brought some for us to share during our break. I don't want to have to tell her you've thrown it up all over our Comrade General's daybed."

"Thank you." *Now?* No, Mausi, not yet.

"Was it a stomach bug?" Jutta asked.

What would happen if she told Jutta the truth about Herr Dreck? Who was listening? Would they care? If it got back to him that she'd told—then what? He knew about the telephone call to the West. He had the power to send her to a place she might never come back from.

Jutta watched her, waiting for an answer.

"Must have been something I ate." Lena went to put on her coveralls. *There, the larger pocket down the leg.* Jutta was smoking and staring into space. *Do it now.* Lena took both camera and hairbrush and stuffed them into the pocket.

"What's that?" Jutta said.

Lena forced herself to look at Jutta. "What?"

"You plan to style your hair while you're vacuuming? Put it away. That's more than enough silliness for one night."

"My friend Danika says I have to be prepared at all times in case I meet my One True Love."

"*Mein Gott,*" Jutta muttered. "They don't pay me enough."

Lena held in her sigh of relief.

They gathered their supplies, crossed the compound under a sky full of stars, and entered House 1. Hello, three red flags. Hello, silent communist statues. And there was that smell: Lena couldn't put her finger on what it was. Hair tonic? Yes, but. Cigars? Yes, but. It was more like the corner of a cupboard that didn't get enough air.

Maybe if she didn't turn on her Purimix he wouldn't know she was there.

No. He'll wait.

Lena could wait longer. He had to go home to his pretty pink wife eventually.

He'll tell his wife he had to work late. Important men always work late.

He couldn't stay here all night. She could do his office last.

Jutta will be mad that you did things out of order.

What did Jutta care, anyway? She worked on different floors. The only time it mattered was when they met to do Mielke's rooms. Then and there, Lena decided. She dragged the Purimix and her other supplies to the office at the far end of the hall, as far away from Herr Dreck's office as possible. She entered, shut the door, and began with quiet things—wiping, dusting, lifting paper-weights and gently, so gently, setting them down again. She was the fairy she sometimes imagined herself to be, setting the room right with a wave of her magic wand. No one would know she was there.

The key to this agent's cupboards was hidden behind a family photograph. Her hand trembled as she reached for it. Her whole body knew she shouldn't be doing this. Silently she fit the key into the lock, and turned. The cupboard opened with a loud *click*. When she pulled the large door open there was the dry smell of paper. So much of it—thousands of pages. The wasps in her head opened their eyes and wiggled their antennae, and Lena felt small, and smaller.

"The cupboard was left open," she practiced saying, in case someone walked in. "I thought the agent meant for me to dust it." *Really? That's what you're going to say? If you get caught with the key in this lock, you will win that one-way ticket to smartening up.* She'd be placed in solitary confinement: no sleep, no proper toilet, no egg in its eggcup ever again.

Close the cupboard. Lock it. Put the key back where you found it. Just as she was setting it down behind the photograph, the office door opened. There, in the doorway, stood Herr Dreck. Lena was so startled she dropped the duster she'd been holding in her other hand.

"What do you think you're doing?" His voice was low. Jutta wouldn't hear it. No one would.

Think quickly. You are innocent, so act innocent. Think like an actor. "Cleaning." Lena settled the tremble in her voice.

Did he hear the cupboard lock click open? What is he doing here? Lena's heart raced. She couldn't ask him; it wasn't her place. There were prescribed areas where she was allowed, or not allowed, to go. Herr Dreck could go wherever he pleased.

"Fräulein, I was expecting you." His cheeks were pink.

"I needed to start here first," Lena said.

"Is that so? You didn't start here because you figured I would eventually have to go home?" A smile played on his face. "I'll be waiting for you. Finish up here, please, and come down the hall."

She had no choice. She finished up. She went down the hall. What if he noticed the hairbrush in her pocket? What if he put his hand in and fished out the camera? *Oho, what have we here?*

But Herr Dreck wasn't interested in the hairbrush. He stood behind his desk, hands flat against the wood. "Do you remember what I did for you last week? Do you remember how I covered for you with the Comrade General?"

Lena nodded. So much for acting. She didn't trust her voice.

"Close the door." He moved toward her and unzipped his pants.

It was big in her mouth. She had to breathe through her nose, which meant taking in the smell of him, a sharp sweaty odor that disgusted her. Her stomach roiled. He pushed himself in harder, and that was all it took. She gagged. Up came dinner, all over his crotch. All over his underwear, and his pants. He let out a cry: "You little *Sau!*" and backed away. "What am I supposed to do now?"

"I'm sorry." Lena's voice was smaller than small. *You did it! Your timing was spot-on.* But even though there was something satisfying in that, she did not feel anything resembling happiness.

"Get me some of your rags, or toilet paper, or some goddamned thing." He was wiping himself with tissue, but it only made things worse, the tissue sticking to the vomit and coming apart in pieces.

Lena stood up unsteadily. "I can't go into the toilets, sir. They're for men." Lena and Jutta only cleaned them when they were sure there was no one left in the building.

"I stink! Son of a bitch. How am I supposed to go home like this?"

There was a knock at the office door.

"Lena?" It was Jutta's voice. "Lena, are you in there?"

"Yes." Her voice sounded choked.

Trousers still around his ankles, Herr Dreck scrambled behind his desk. The door burst open and, one second too late, he thunked into his desk chair. Lena steadied herself against the wall. Her eyes were watery, her face bright red. The room reeked of vomit.

Lena wanted Jutta to yell at Herr Dreck, to call him names and say she would report him. But that was the sort of thing that happened in other worlds—like in Narnia, where a lion was in charge. In House 1, Jutta was the cleaning woman, and it didn't matter what she saw, or thought, or wanted to say. What mattered was that Lena was in a high-ranking Stasi agent's office while he was still there, and she was not doing her job. Not even pretending to do her job.

"Forgive me, Comrade Lieutenant General," Jutta said, "but I'm in charge of this girl, and she is tardy tonight. Lena, you must come with me immediately. We'll never finish the building at this rate, and it will be my job at stake, and all because you're work-shy. I won't tolerate it."

Lena caught Jutta's eye. Jutta knew.

"That's fine," Herr Dreck said, looking fully dressed but not quite normal. "She's finished here."

Jutta hooked Lena by the arm and pulled her out, shutting the door behind her with more force than she should have. She rushed Lena to the coffee room, where they were not allowed to be unless they were cleaning, but hardly anyone was left in the building now.

"Is this what happened last time?" She dipped a handkerchief in warm water and wiped at Lena's eyes.

Lena nodded.

Jutta filled a glass with water and handed it to her. "Why didn't you tell me?"

"I was afraid." Lena took small sips. Her jaw was sore.

"Of what, child?"

Everything. You. Him. The World.

Jutta held her face with both hands. "I don't think he'll bother you anymore. He knows I saw. And he'll have to go home tonight, somehow, and explain it to his wife." Jutta's smile was wry. "I'd love to be around to hear that one, wouldn't you?"

Lena tried to smile back. She wanted to believe everything would be that easy.

*

At midnight they met to do the Comrade General's rooms. Lena wiped down his prized red telephone and the photograph of his beloved Yorkshire terrier, Airen. She dusted the pictures of Stalin, Mielke's hero, even though Stalin wasn't supposed to be anyone's hero anymore. She dusted the photographs of Mielke shaking hands with various dignitaries. He was a small man, smaller than everyone. *He knows what it means to be small.* And yet—he was huge. How had he made that transformation? There must be a trick to it. Lena wished she could sit him down and ask him.

Jutta was talking about the South Korean airplane that had been shot down in September. There were a lot of stories going around about who had shot it down and why, and Jutta went through all of them. It was a regular scheduled flight full of innocent people that had gone off course by accident. Don't be ridiculous, it was an undercover spy plane. The Soviets shot it down. No, the Americans did it. Obviously. They were responsible for everything bad that happened, with their washed-up actor of a president and his crazy outer-space defense plans.

On and on she went, while Lena dusted and did her best to poke around for Mielke's key. Under vases, behind photographs. She managed to check her entire side of the office without finding anything other than cobwebs. It was hard not to be discouraged. *The key is hidden on Jutta's side. It must be.* Not necessarily. It might be in the Comrade General's briefcase. *Wouldn't he keep a spare?* Lena could only hope.

Carefully, while Jutta was cleaning his secretary's desk, Lena tucked her duster behind a chair. She would have to come back later, alone. It would be dangerous, but at least if she'd left something behind she would have a legitimate reason to return. They finished up, took a break, then did the men's toilets—which was Lena's suggestion, *good thinking*, because toilets did not require dusters.

Time passed.

Lena wished she could put it off. If anyone found out she was in the Comrade General's rooms alone—if anyone caught her with her hand in an open drawer, or worse, taking photographs. *Stop it.* Jutta was busy doing the fifth floor. It was now or never.

Lena climbed the stairs to Mielke's floor, walked through the conference room and into his office, where she turned on a small desk lamp. *Find that key.* Under. Behind. Inside. It was always the ugliest creatures that lived on the underside of things.

Under the radio. Behind the shredder. Inside planters. She was running out of places to look. Finally she lifted a pair of boots sitting on a mat, and there it was: a small silver key. A world of secrets, under his boot. Blood rushed to Lena's head as she pressed the key's sharp end into her palm.

She went straight to Mielke's desk—his personal desk, top secret, *my goodness, what are you doing?*—and fitted the key into one of his locked drawers. One turn, a *click*—and slowly, slowly, she pulled it open. *Remember. Herr Schulmann told you to remember.* She had to put things back exactly as she'd found them.

There were pens, a bottle of hair tonic, a stack of documents— which she pulled out and went through one by one. Her hands trembled so much that the pages sounded like the wings of a large moth. Mostly they involved things she didn't understand— permits and maps, reports about Such-and-Such or So-and-So.

There were lists, diagrams. The names were unfamiliar.

By the time she'd made it halfway through the pile, she still hadn't seen anything that seemed relevant. *It's only the beginning. You didn't expect to find answers right away, did you?* The truth was she'd wanted it to be in the first drawer she opened, right on top. She'd wanted it to be easy. Snap a photograph, send a message on Peter's radio, and Erich would be home the next day, moving out Friedrich So-and-So and his collection of undershirts and his cat—if he'd ever managed to catch it.

She finished with the first stack of papers and replaced them exactly as she'd found them. A second drawer. A third. *You're taking too long. You'll never get your work done at this rate and Jutta will be suspicious.* But she couldn't afford to look too quickly. If she missed something—she didn't want to have to backtrack.

She opened one of the tall cupboards, and her stomach felt like broken eggs: the cupboard was full of files. She was about to thumb through them when she heard a noise in the hallway. It was the rumble of the elevator, which meant Jutta was on her way. Lena shut the cupboard, made sure to lock it, and returned the key to its place beneath the boot. *Was it the left one? No, it was the right, I'm sure. Almost sure.* Lamp off. Duster in one hand. Take the stairs down. Down, fast. Into an office, any office, and dust.

Was it the left one?

Calm yourself, Mausi. Dust.

"Please don't tell me this is all you've done." Jutta stood in the doorway.

Lena wiped the sweat from her nose before turning around. "This was my last office. I'm going downstairs to do the foyer in a minute."

"Some of the windows need cleaning. You'll have to make time."

The eyes. Thank goodness they couldn't talk.

*

Lena had never been to the secret ward in the mental institution. She only knew about it because she'd overheard the nurses talking. They thought she was simple, meaning stupid, meaning deaf. They assumed they could say anything in front of her.

"Two more brought in yesterday," one whispered. "The forms weren't even signed by a doctor. It was a Major General So-and-So."

"From the Stasi."

The first nodded. "They've recommended electric shock."

"Is there anything even wrong with those patients?" asked the second. She was younger, with rosy cheeks, and chewed GDR gum, even though by then you could buy Western gum. If you chewed GDR gum for too long, it crumbled into pieces. She was forever complaining about the bits that got stuck in her teeth.

"Wrong opinions," said the first, an older woman with a boxy face. She was one of the nurses who checked Lena's mouth with her finger after giving her a handful of pills, to make sure she'd swallowed them. Holding wrong opinions was like not swallowing your pills—it was against the rules.

"Be careful what you say," Erich used to warn her. "Don't get in arguments with the other patients." Even Auntie used a hospital voice when she came to visit, extra cheery and socks pulled up and do you know another song—as if the doctors were watching her too.

– 19 –

A YOUNG MAN AND SOME MONIKA

There was nothing in the post when Lena checked the next morning. She hadn't taken a single photograph that night, though she wished she could have taken one of Herr Dreck covered in vomit and bits of tissue.

On the way upstairs she met Peter coming down, heading to work. *You have to say something.* "About yesterday—" she began. But there were so many things wrong with what had happened in the courtyard yesterday she didn't know where to start.

Peter stood there waiting, his back hunched.

"I'm sorry," she said at last.

"For what? Your friend came by. It's allowed."

Had he realized Max was in the play? Lena couldn't read Peter's face. She glanced up the stairwell to make sure no one would overhear. "Your father wasn't nice to you."

The way Peter shrugged made it seem as if the bag he was

carrying was full of cement. "I'm used to it. I'm not the son he wanted. Once I'm in service we'll be able to write to each other about guns and tanks, and he won't have to sit through dinner with me anymore." He tried to laugh.

No wonder he had eczema. He must have wanted to climb right out of his skin and be someone else.

"Would you still like to show me your radio?" she asked. *Right. Pretend to be nice.* She wasn't pretending. *Oh, so your motives are pure?*

Peter brightened. "Absolutely. Tonight? No, you're working. Tomorrow is youth group, and we're having that talk about Republic Day. Our schedules are so different, aren't they? I'm days, you're nights, except on Mondays—but then we work in the courtyard."

Lena wondered how long he would continue this conversation with himself. She thought about her egg getting cold while Peter counted days on his fingers.

"How about later this afternoon, after you get home from work?" she suggested. Max was supposed to be coming over, but he'd be gone long before Peter (or Auntie) got home.

"Sure, yes. All right, then. Well." He stood there, arms at his sides, looking as if he couldn't remember whether he was supposed to go up the stairs or down.

"My aunt is waiting. I have to go."

"Right." Peter bumbled down the stairs, nearly falling at the bottom and catching himself just in time. Was that what she looked like with Max? Why did Peter have to like her? Why couldn't things be the way they'd always been? He could go back to being the boy down the hall, the one she collected recyclables with.

She entered the apartment and took off her coat to the egg-getting-cold song and dance, which went like this: Where have you been? Your egg has been sitting, it's no good when it's cold (even though Lena had never minded a cold egg). Why are you so late? Would you like a roll with butter? I have cream for our coffee.

Butter! Cream!

Lena sipped the coffee slowly, forcing her mind to concentrate on the taste, which was as rich and deep as a sunset. Don't think about Herr Dreck and what might be waiting for you at work tonight—if you even have a job anymore. *Don't think about the uranium mines, or the textile factories, or the doctors with soft voices. Don't think about Erich.* Would they punish him for her misbehavior? They might. She'd heard the stories. It happened most often when someone fled the Republic—by sneaking out, or even with a legitimate visa. The consequence was called *Sippenhaft*, kin liability, and it meant that whoever had been left behind—parents, children, or siblings—would pay. But it didn't have to be because of flight. Collective punishment could be applied to any crime. And while it didn't always happen—there was no predictability to the system—the threat of it was enough to keep most people in line.

What if Herr Dreck told about the phone call Lena had made and they punished Erich for it? She should have—what? Erich wouldn't have wanted her to do what Herr Dreck wanted. No, he would have congratulated her for throwing up at the right time. *Think it through.* If Herr Dreck was angry enough, he wouldn't punish Erich. She was the one. Jutta thought it was over, but Dreck would punish Lena. Now her egg actually was cold, and she had trouble swallowing it—*see? you've ruined your breakfast, and all because you had to start thinking.*

". . . to the parade on Friday? My goodness, Lena, you're a million miles away."

"I'm sorry. Yes, the parade."

"Will you come with us then, or were you planning to go with the youth group?"

Us? Who?

". . . old friends. It's a great honor to be invited to attend with them. You might even learn something about being an upright citizen if you pay attention." Auntie puffed herself up. If she wasn't careful she'd pop the buttons on her dress.

"Sure. Yes." All Lena could think about was that if she didn't get to sleep soon, her eyes would be swollen and red when Max came over, and she would look hideous. "How is your head today, Auntie?"

"Fine. But it would be better if some people started listening to me."

Lena got ready for bed while Auntie crashed around in the kitchen. She set an alarm for one o'clock so Max wouldn't catch her in her ugly gray nightdress and flattened bed hair. *Good night, Mama and Papa.* What had Erich found? Was there really another story behind their deaths, a humming-underneath sound? *Good night, blank wall that used to have the important Erich's photographs on it.* Lena fell asleep remembering the times he'd come to visit in Magdeburg. Waiting for him at the train station had been like waiting for her birthday: watching the train doors, watching faces, waiting for the special one—that moment when he appeared, and caught her eye, and called her name.

*

Either the alarm hadn't gone off or Max had come earlier than Lena had expected. It didn't matter—the intercom was ringing, and Lena's head was full of wool, and there were her skinny bare feet poking out of the dishwater nightdress, and pillow creases pressed into her cheek. *No, no, no.* "Yes?" she answered.

"It's me." Max. "Can I come up?"

Her heart raced. "Yes, but—can you give me a minute?"

"I'll walk slowly."

Five things happened at once. Nightdress off, toothbrush with crumbly toothpaste, somewhere a sock, warm-water splash on the face, oh God the hair, what to do about her hair? Another sock. Where was her hairbrush? Still in her coat pocket. How long before the creases on her face went away? How had her nose gotten so big? No, a matching sock. *Take those hard things out of the corners of your eyes.* Maybe put the hair in a—there was a knock.

Lena checked to make sure she was wearing clothes and went to answer the door. A breathless hello, and then she peered up and down the building's corridor. No one was there to tell Auntie later. Max came in with the chill of outside still on his coat. It was cold against Lena's arms, but in the nicest way. He smelled of fresh air and lemon soap. Where had he gotten lemon soap? Did his mother shop at *Exquisit*? Danika talked nonstop about the fashions and cosmetics sold at *Exquisit*, but it was too expensive for Lena to shop there.

"I woke you," he said.

Great. That meant she looked like she'd just gotten out of bed. "It's fine."

There was an awkward moment in the hallway. Lena had never had a boyfriend before. "Can I take your coat?" She sounded like one of those people in a restaurant, the posh kind she'd gone to once to celebrate when Auntie had won a medal for beautifying the school grounds.

Max took off his coat, and Lena stared at his tanned arms. She held the coat as if she'd forgotten why she had asked for it. She wanted to bury her face in it. *Get hold of yourself.* The hook on the wall. *Hang it up.*

Now what? Should they sit in the kitchen? Not her bedroom. The sitting room, yes. She led him into the small room with its flowery orange wallpaper. There was the photograph of Auntie when she'd become a Party member. Soon Lena would have a similar photograph—*maybe. If you don't end up in prison.* There were knickknacks and Party paraphernalia on the shelves, an entire pet store of porcelain dogs. And there was Helmut's shrine. *Don't tell on me, Helmut.*

They sat next to each other on the couch and Max put his arm around her. "When will you come to the play again?"

"I'm not sure. I'll have to think up an excuse for my aunt if I'm going to go alone."

"I promise this time I won't forget what goes into the borscht. Dieter let me have it for that. He saw you in the audience. He knew it was why I'd messed up." He stroked Lena's hair so gently her eyes fell shut. "Your family name is Keller? I saw it on the buzzer."

"No." Lena drifted into another world where the only thing that existed was the feeling of Max's fingers through her hair. "That's my aunt's married name. My family name is Altmann."

"Like the writer."

Her eyes opened. "What?"

"Erich Altmann. What's the matter? Haven't you heard of him?"

Lena stiffened and drew herself away. "I've heard of him."

Max laughed. "Maybe you just don't like his books."

"I love them. I've read every one of them." *That's not smart.* "I mean, they're okay."

"Well, I love them. I lent my copy of *Castles Underground* to someone while I was in service and never got it back. I should really buy another."

"Good luck with that," Lena said before she could stop herself.

"Why?" Max's hands were now in his lap.

"Nothing. I'm wishing you luck, that's all."

He turned to look at her. "You're acting strange. What's going on?"

She wanted to tell him—right now, everything. He might be able to help. At the very least, it would make her feel better. Someone who had read the books, who knew Erich existed. You were supposed to tell your One True Love everything, weren't you? *Not everything. Does he need to know this? Really?* Herr Schulmann had said not to tell anyone, but he couldn't have meant Max.

"We need to go outside," she said. "Maybe take a walk."

He gave her an odd look. "All right." They got their coats and made their way to the street without talking. Max wasn't touching her anymore. *Well done. You've blown it by being weird.* It would be friends only from now on. But having Max as a friend wasn't such a terrible thing.

When Lena was certain no one was around she said, "If I tell you, you must promise—"

"Lena, you can trust me. You can tell me anything."

How can you be sure? She stared at him as if a black mark might appear on his forehead. If only it were that easy to spot an informer.

"I hid you in the pub," he said. "Remember?"

She remembered crouching beneath his legs under the table, before he'd even known her. But—"You were in service."

"Yes, like every other male between the ages of eighteen and twenty-six. So what?"

"My uncle didn't serve. I mean, he didn't carry a weapon. He served as a construction soldier."

Max stopped walking. "You told me you didn't have an uncle."

"I don't," Lena said. "But also I do." For the next half hour she told him about Erich and how he had been erased. She did not tell him about the munitions factory, or Herr Schulmann, or the camera. Max didn't need to know about those things.

After she was finished, they didn't speak for a long time. They walked, hands in their pockets, with no destination. The roads were long and wide and relatively quiet in the middle of the afternoon. The October sun played hide-and-seek among the clouds, turning the air warm, then cool, then warm again.

"So," Max finally said, "you're telling me if I go to a bookstore or a library or anywhere and ask for *Castles Underground*—"

"They'll tell you there's no such book. Erich Altmann? No such person. Never existed."

"But I've read the book," Max said.

Lena shrugged. "Not anymore you haven't."

Max lowered his voice. "Have you heard from him? Has he been arrested?"

"You don't understand. When I ask people about him, it's as if he'd never been born. I went to the state registry office to see his birth record and they said they didn't have it. Yes, I think he's been arrested, but no one's telling me anything. They just want me to go away. Keep quiet. Move on."

"But you're not going to do that. You can't."

Lena didn't answer.

"You won't tell me what you're doing." Max stared at his feet. "You don't trust me."

"What would you do? I've already said more than I should."

Max pulled her under a tree, brushing the branches above them and sending a shower of freezing water onto their heads. He kissed her hard on the mouth, his hands cupping her face. Then his lips were at her ear. "We're getting out. The three of us—me, Dieter, and Bem. You should come with us."

"To the West?"

"You see? I'm trusting you. I'm telling you my biggest secret."

He's more of a fool than you realized. A secret like that should never be told. "You put on quite an act for Peter's father. A career in the military and all."

"Now you see why. We don't want anyone to suspect. That's why we're doing that terrible play, and going to all our youth group meetings, and to the parade on Friday. We're going to live in the West, where people don't get erased—ever. Come with us."

Lena looked into his brown eyes, then at the dimple, the faint stubble on his cheek. "What about the people you're leaving behind? Don't you have parents here? Or siblings?"

"My parents have given me their blessing." He stroked her cheek. His fingertips were cold. "They want me to have a better life. I don't have any brothers or sisters."

"I can't. I couldn't. My aunt. And if I'm on the other side I can't help Erich." Herr Schulmann needed her here, at her job, gathering evidence.

"What if your aunt wanted you to go? Like my parents."

Lena chuckled. "Auntie is a Party member. She doesn't understand why anyone would want to leave the Republic. Anyway, I don't want to live in a place where there's crime, and people are unemployed, and the State doesn't care if you don't have a place to live. I don't want to leave." But was that true? She remembered the giant tree she'd imagined planting in the courtyard, how she would climb to the top and take flight. Flight! The thought of it created a breeze on her cheek.

He kissed her softly, his tongue exploring hers. Then he whispered close to her ear: "Maybe I'll help you change your mind."

Time shrank and expanded at once. Everything was this moment, but this moment was huge. They kissed for minutes on end, oblivious to the people passing them on the street. Lena had never understood before how a kiss could contain a whole world, how lips and tongue could be everything a person needed. How a kiss could possess her entire body.

"How long before you leave?" she whispered.

"Soon. Two weeks, maybe. There's a new tunnel near Bernauer Strasse. The soil is good there, and the tunnel entrance is hidden in the basement of a house. The people who've organized it have a system. They've already gotten two groups out that way."

She touched his face. "It sounds dangerous. Won't the border guards know about it by now?" People didn't use tunnels to escape much anymore; the guards had caught on to that trick. They'd installed metal bars and sensors in the sewers, fitted train tunnels with alarms. According to Erich, the guards had even placed a chain-link fence across the canal to block underwater escape routes.

"That's why we're waiting," Max said. "Our contacts have promised not to use the tunnel again until it's our turn. We won't go unless it's safe. I don't want to do prison time, thank you. In the meantime, we'll perform stunning renditions of *Factory: A Love Story* to full houses and standing ovations." His smile created the dimple on his cheek, and Lena kissed it.

They headed back toward her building holding hands. Such an ordinary thing, two human hands entwined—and yet, Lena had never felt a man's strong calloused hand hold hers, and with such gentleness. Erich and Papa didn't count. And now Max would leave, to the West, and she would never see him again. All the men in her life seemed to disappear—except for the one she wanted to disappear.

"Will you really go?" she asked.

"If it's safe. If we can—then yes. And maybe you'll come."

Lena shook her head. "I won't." The thought of being stuffed in a tunnel, like an elevator, like the principal's small office at school— It meant she'd have to savor every moment with Max, *or not start anything in the first place.* He squeezed her hand and she imagined letting go, walking away. No, it was too late for that.

When they reached the building entrance, he leaned in to kiss her.

"Not here. Someone will see, and tell Auntie, and then I'll be in trouble."

"Where, then?"

She opened the door and they stepped inside. The foyer was dark and empty. "Quickly."

They tucked themselves into an alcove and he leaned against her, pressing her back to the wall, pressing himself against her so that his chest, his legs, his shoulders were touching hers. As soon as he began to kiss her, the thought of *quickly* melted onto the floor. Nothing mattered. If someone should walk in, even if it was Auntie, Lena didn't care. The weight of him against her was strong but not heavy, powerful but not forceful. She could have kissed him like that all afternoon.

Lena heard the door open and shut a few times, but vaguely, as if in a dream. She had no idea how long she and Max had been kissing until the sound of the front door buzzer made him pull away. Max stroked her cheek. "It's getting late. I'd better go. I'll see you soon."

She stood where he had left her, unable to move. Her lips felt swollen. But it was nothing compared to her heart, which felt as disheveled as an unmade bed. Danika walked in as Max walked out, turning to look at him as he passed. The door shut behind her. Then she spied Lena.

"*Mein Gott*, that was him. I forgot my stupid key; thank goodness my brother is home. Did he kiss you? *Mein Gott*, he did, I can see it on your face. He's so cute. Is he nice? Do you like him?"

Lena was bursting—she had to talk about him to someone. She had to say his name out loud. Linking arms with Danika, she told her about Max's dimple, and the way he smiled. As they climbed the stairs, she talked about the lemony scent of his soap, and what it felt like to hold his hand.

"Please don't tell anyone," Lena said. "If it gets back to my aunt, I'll be in for it."

Danika hugged her. "I won't tell. I think it's wonderful."

She watched Danika climb the stairs to her floor, not thinking about how late it must be if she was already coming home from work. Not expecting, when she unlocked the door to her apartment, that the door had already been unlocked once before. There stood Auntie, still in the rubber galoshes she wore over her shoes to protect them from puddles. Meaning she'd walked in not long ago. Meaning she'd seen Max and Lena in the foyer.

"Where have you been?"

Think fast. It was difficult to control the rush of heat that came to Lena's face, so she busied herself with taking off her coat and hanging it up with extra care. "I went to check on the swimming pool. I thought maybe our petition—"

Auntie tsked. "It's too soon for results. We haven't even received a letter back yet. You should have gotten some sleep instead of wasting your time with such nonsense. Well, you're up now. You can help me prepare a banner for Republic Day."

Carrying banners on Republic Day was encouraged. But you couldn't just make up a banner and bring it to the parade. You had to choose from one of the Party's pre-approved slogans. "Protect peace by making socialism stronger" was the one Auntie had decided on.

Peter was supposed to show Lena his radio that afternoon. She was trying to work out when she might go over to his apartment while Auntie bent down awkwardly to remove her galoshes.

"I'll have to write to the building manager about the young people in our foyer, carrying on as if they were in a bedroom."

Lena stifled a cough. "Oh? Who was that?" *Take off your shoes, Mausi. Slowly. Concentrate on the laces, the pattern of the linoleum.* Peter and his radio would have to wait for another day.

"I don't know, do I? A young man and some Monika. In our building, of all things. I couldn't see the girl, but my goodness, some people have no shame."

I'm not some Monika, Lena wanted to say. The Monikas hung around the train station at Friedrichstrasse and rented rooms by the hour, even though everyone knew there was no prostitution in the Better Germany. *And anyway, how about you and your naked bricklayer?*

Another part of her savored the secret. *It was me, Auntie. Me!* Next time, though, they'd better be more careful—or that would be the end of Lena's freedom. Chain-link fence across the canal, nothing. The border guards hadn't met Sausage Auntie. Lena boiled water for Auntie's tea and concentrated on the banner spread across the kitchen table, biting her lip as the memory of Max washed over her again and again.

– 20 –

HOOLIGANS AND POETS

Lena wished there were some way not to go to work that night, but Auntie wouldn't hear of work-shy behavior and Lena had already been sick last week. She had to go, so she put on her coat, tucked the camera into her pocket along with the hairbrush, and set off. The dark sky above her felt heavy. The sound of car tires on the road flattened her into nothing.

Herr Dreck would be there, and he'd be furious. He would have a document bearing the address of the Wismut uranium mines. Or worse: a signed form admitting Lena to the hospital, where there were no sharp edges, no way to remind herself she was still alive. This time, she might be classified as someone who had wrong opinions. She'd have to go to the basement for electric shocks, or get the operation that would make her calm and put her in diapers for the rest of her life.

She wished Jutta could protect her, but there was nothing Jutta could do. Lena entered the ashtray room. She couldn't bear to hear one more word about Jutta's Slavic ears, or her Slavic jaw, or her Slavic fingernails, if there was such a thing—Jutta said there was. Words and more words: it was all empty noise filling the smoky room and crowding Lena's head.

She pulled on her coveralls, slipping brush and camera into the side pocket. Fear tugged at her stomach as she trudged behind Jutta to House 1 and entered the foyer. There was the wide stairway, going up. *Might as well get it over with.* She couldn't. The Purimix had become impossibly heavy. Jutta waited for the elevator, watching Lena struggle with her equipment. When Lena reached the second floor, the elevator opened and Jutta stepped out.

"What are you doing?" Lena asked. "This isn't your floor."

Jutta had a determined expression on her face. "We're going to clean this one together. I've noticed this floor has become particularly challenging and it's too much for one person. You stay on this end. I'll take the other." Where Herr Dreck worked. The light from his office puddled onto the red hallway carpeting.

Tears came to Lena's eyes and she wiped them away. "Thank you," she said quietly. They set to work with both Purimixes going at once.

"Good evening, Comrade Lieutenant General," Jutta sang into the lit office. "You're working late this evening."

What had happened to being invisible? Lena would never have dared to speak to the important Stasi men like that. But you could get away with things when you were older, and Jutta had always seemed slightly crazy—Lena was pretty sure she wasn't the only one who thought so.

She listened, but she couldn't hear Herr Dreck's response over the noise of her machine.

"I hope you get home soon," Jutta said. "Your wife and children will be waiting for you."

Nice one. Lena slipped into a darkened office to make sure she would be busy cleaning it when Herr Dreck left to go home—which he would surely do now that Jutta had spoiled the party. As she waited, her dust rag quivered across family photographs and another bust of Lenin. Maybe the agents used the sharp end of his beard to punch holes in paper. Was Dreck gone yet? *Don't look; don't dare.* Instead she listened.

Eventually she heard a man's heavy footsteps—muted on the carpeting, *clip-clip* on the floor toward the stairs, and then, blessedly, mercifully, down and away. He was gone. One night of freedom, finally. She found Jutta in Herr Dreck's office and hugged her.

"Enough of that, child. You get busy. I might need your help on one of my floors later."

"Anything, Jutta. I'll do a whole floor for you so you can look out the window and smoke, I don't mind."

Later, while Jutta was busy cleaning one of the higher floors, Lena slipped back into Comrade General Mielke's office and found the key under the right boot (*see?*). She returned to where she'd left off her search. The files in the tall cupboards were organized alphabetically. *At last, something easy.* She went straight to *A* for Altmann. There was nothing—not on Erich, or herself, or her parents. She looked up Friedrich So-and-So. He wasn't there. She looked up Auntie, and Max, and even Jutta. Whatever was in this cupboard, it wouldn't help her.

Don't be disappointed. You've eliminated one. And Mielke was a good one to eliminate. Lena didn't fancy being caught photographing documents in his office. That was the sort of thing you didn't come back from. She worked through the other offices on her floors, unlocking drawers, checking in cupboards. Everything was organized, but none of it was what she was looking for.

Was it possible no one had this information? Or maybe it was being kept somewhere else. What if it was so secret that the Comrade General kept it at his house? If that was the case, the game was over and they had won—as they always did. It was football against the Stasi team all over again. Not even the referees would help you.

She hurried upstairs to vacuum one of Jutta's hallways for her. The night passed pleasantly, and afterward Lena visited the *schrullig* world to buy a pretend-orange that tasted remarkably real—*stop it, Mausi, it is real and you know it.* Turkish delight: she could sit there and eat oranges all day, and buy any books she wanted (except Erich's), and pretend that this, right here, was the Better Germany. It was the Best Germany Ever.

*

Three days later it was Friday, the Republic's birthday—a national holiday. It was a day of parades and banners and singing. Lots of red. Anyone who had a balcony decorated it with a flag, that of the Better Germany, or the Party flag. You decorated, or someone made a note of it and you got in trouble later. Lena wore her nicest outfit, a polyester dress with zigzags, and accompanied Auntie to the parade. They marched past the stands filled with dignitaries on Karl-Marx-Allee, alongside children dressed in their Pioneer uniforms waving small flags and carrying balloons or flowers. They held up the banner they had worked on, despite the wind threatening to carry it away.

"The Party, the Party is always right," Lena sang with Auntie, and, *"Our Homeland has smartened itself up!"* and the song from the Pioneers that always made her feel a little silly, *"Got any waste-paper?"*

Auntie had arranged to meet some friends from Helmut's time after the speeches: a small round man named Rainer Koch and his small round wife. They shook Lena's hand vigorously and Herr Koch—Comrade Rainer—called her Comrade Lena. His wife patted Lena's cheeks and told her she was pretty, and that Auntie had spoken highly of her—how hard she worked, and how much of a turnaround she'd made now that she was living with Adelheid.

Lena was surprised to find herself enjoying the couple, who polished off one *Ketwurst* and beer after the next at the beer garden. They laughed and smoked cigarillos and talked about their summer vacations at the Baltic Sea. They insisted on buying Lena a Vita Cola, even though Auntie tried to object.

The four of them walked through the park, past a fountain and a playground, past strolling couples who held hands. Lena imagined what it would be like to stroll here with Max. *Until he goes through that tunnel and you never see him again.* Maybe he wouldn't go. Maybe she would change his mind. *You saw his face.* She knew that expression from Auntie: the mind-made-up face. No new ideas were getting past that locked door.

Soon it was time to talk business. That was what Comrade Rainer wanted to do with Auntie, because they were both active

Party members. As people passed, flags and banners tucked under their arms, Lena and Auntie sat with the Kochs on a wooden bench that was nowhere near as nice as Hans's benches. They talked about the petition to repair the swimming pool, and the lack of cloakroom space at Auntie's school, and the younger teachers with wrong opinions who wouldn't listen when Auntie tried to re-educate them.

One day, Lena would be inducted into this club. The process would start when she turned eighteen—the application form, the references, a detailed explanation of why she wanted to join. A yearlong probation period would prove whether she was worthy. It meant she'd have to start caring about the sorts of things Auntie and the Kochs were talking about. What would it feel like, to be buried in sawdust every Wednesday night? Youth group was fun, most of the time. But Lena remembered her father's face every time he'd come home from Party school—wooden, sleepy. One more Wednesday night wasted.

Lena's attention drifted to the people in the park: how they walked, who they were with. She noticed especially the older women, who scowled as they dragged their little dogs behind them. *They don't kiss anymore.* That was surely it. A good kiss could change a person forever. It had changed her, like in the best fairy tales.

"I'll bet your problematic teachers are from Prenzlauer Berg," Comrade Rainer said. Lena kept her eyes on the passersby, but her ears perked up at the mention of Erich's neighborhood. "That place, it's given the police nothing but trouble. Hooligans. Poets." He said the last word with the face of someone who'd just stepped in dog poop.

Maybe if Erich had lived somewhere else, none of this would have happened. One of the concrete prefabs in Marzahn, for example. But you had to know someone to get an apartment in one of those big new housing developments. Auntie would never have agreed to stand for him. Anyway, he would have hated living there. He called the new developments concrete wastelands, or stone honeycombs. All his friends lived in Prenzlauer Berg.

"What is being done about the area?" Auntie asked Herr Koch. "Who's in charge?"

"Ah, we have an excellent fellow at the helm; he's really been cracking down. Lieutenant General Bruno Drechsler, top-notch, works in the compound."

Lena nearly choked on her second Vita Cola. Yes, Lieutenant General Drechsler worked in the compound. Lena knew which floor he was on. She even knew which office was his. Lena knew many things about Bruno Drechsler that she shouldn't know at all, because Lieutenant General Bruno Drechsler was Herr Dreck.

That was why she hadn't found anything in the other offices she cleaned. All week Jutta had been cleaning Herr Dreck's office for her so he would stop bothering her. Lena had been so relieved she'd even quit biting her nails. An entire week had passed without him pawing at her or making her touch him. Lena had slept better, eaten better, and the noises in her head had calmed down.

But the proof she was looking for would be in his office. It had to be, if he was in charge of that neighborhood. Yes, he'd cracked down, right over Erich's head. At last she knew where to look. But how would she get in?

"Lena." Auntie looked extra pinched in her brown rayon pantsuit. "Comrade Rainer has asked you a question."

It was about the courtyard, the beautification project, did she think they had a chance at winning the Golden House Number plaque this year?

"Oh, yes," Lena said. *With our two paving tiles and ten grains of sand?* Not even Military Papa's shrubbery would win them that plaque.

Blah, blah about courtyards and rain, petitions and paving tiles. *Think.* She couldn't ask Jutta to let her clean Herr Dreck's office again. He still stayed late every night. Jutta would know something was up. And it would mean the *Dreck*, the filth, would start again. After she'd vomited all over him it would be worse. He would be angry, and rougher with her. Lena couldn't. She wouldn't.

If only Herr Dreck would give up waiting for her and go home when everyone else did, then Lena could go back to cleaning that floor the way she used to. Although he didn't seem like the type to give up. Papa had gone hunting once and he'd described to Lena how they'd crouched for hours in a treestand, even though it was raining and they were hungry and tired. A good hunter never got sick of waiting—like the man in the Lada. Maybe all the men who worked at the Stasi were like that. Maybe it was the only job requirement.

Well, then. What if Lena snuck into his office after Jutta had cleaned it? It was risky. But if she was quick about it—

The afternoon came to an end, and she and Auntie took their leave of the Kochs. On their way back to the housing development, Auntie gave Lena a complete rundown of the day's events, pinning them in place like dead butterflies, as though Lena hadn't been there.

There was still a weekend to get through before she could search Herr Dreck's office. The thought of going in there made her feel queasy, but there would be answers—at last. It would be hard to wait until Monday. Like Mielke's men, she would have to learn patience.

– 21 –

RIT. MEM.

On Saturday, after they'd dropped the recyclables at the collection point, Peter invited Lena back to his apartment. When they walked in, Military Papa was seated at the kitchen table. In front of him was a plate, a cup, a variety of bills and receipts probably in alphabetical order, and a copy of that day's *Neues Deutschland*. All of it was lined up and in its place, including Military Papa, who sat straight-backed with his arms bent at right angles.

Frau Military Papa bustled in the kitchen. She was a thin woman with lips that looked as if they'd been pulled too tightly with thread. Lena took off her shoes and straightened them at the door. She didn't have to be told. The row of shoes already there had issued the command.

Frau Military Papa asked if Lena wanted a cup of tea, but the way she asked it told Lena the answer had better be *no*, so Lena said *no* and followed Peter toward his bedroom.

"I'm showing her the radio," Peter called from the hallway. "We'll leave the door open."

His mother appeared. "You're shouting," she said. "Your father is reading the newspaper. You'd better keep the volume on the radio down."

"We'll be quiet, I promise." Peter shrank down, and Lena felt so sad for him she wanted to step on his mother's toe. But his mother wasn't the problem. What Lena really felt like doing was running over to the kitchen table and messing up Military Papa's receipts—throwing them in the air, poking him in the eye.

Your father is reading the newspaper. The newspaper was ridiculous. Important Party speeches were printed there, complete with the amount of applause each statement had elicited. Lena and her friends used to struggle through them at school. *Comrades! (applause) Dear guests! (lively applause) The Socialist Unity Party (long applause) has delivered good results (prolonged applause) with the development of socialism (intense applause) in the (intense long applause) German Democratic Republic (prolonged strong applause)* . . . Was Military Papa that enthralled with his newspaper, or was it just one more rule for Peter to follow?

Peter's bedroom was small but tidy. One glance and Lena knew this room was his sanctuary. Everything that mattered to him was set up in the far corner: a desk covered in machinery and wires, with maps and diagrams and lists pinned to the wall. Peter must spend all his spare time in here, she thought. The alternative was a silent dinner table, that look of disappointment, his mother tiptoeing around as if the floor were set with land mines. At least Auntie liked listening to music, chatting over sandwiches, and thinking up new projects.

Lena was eager to see the radio. But as soon as she did, panic closed in. She had expected an on/off button, and a dial for finding the station you wanted, like on a regular radio. This? There were dials and buttons everywhere, and notes stuck here and there that were supposed to explain what they were. M1. M2. RIT. MEM.

Don't worry. He'll show you how it works. Peter would be right there when she needed to contact Herr Schulmann. She'd find a way to do it without him suspecting anything.

He pulled up an extra chair and patted it for Lena to sit. Then he positioned himself in front of the radio, unplugged the headphones so that they could both hear what was happening, and adjusted the microphone. His hands moved so smoothly from one button to the next; he made it seem easy. All the while he was talking. RIT was receiver incremental tuning. MEM was for memory input.

Lena loved watching anyone who was an expert at something, it didn't matter what. An expert had a secret life. How many hundreds of hours had Peter spent in front of this machine? It wasn't as if he'd never mentioned it. He talked about it all the time while they went door-to-door picking up cans and glassware. But Lena hadn't put it together—how the talk translated into time, devotion, and practice. It reminded her of Erich and his armfuls of notebooks.

When she studied Peter now, he seemed different—not quite so gangly and awkward. He wasn't attractive, *let's not get carried away,* but he was interesting. And while he was engaged with the radio, he seemed to forget all about hand-holding and cow eyes. Lena was drawn into the things he was telling her, about Q signals and offsets and channel spacings. It was a new language, an unfamiliar one, but Peter spoke it and that was all she needed.

"What would you like to do?" he asked. "You want to listen to someone in Canada? How about Hawaii?"

Hawaii was one of those places that belonged on a cake, something she'd seen on Western television at Danika's house: pretend palm trees and icing-sugar sand, blue water so clear you could see right to the sugar bottom. How often had she imagined strolling into a travel office and saying, "I'll have one ticket to Hawaii please, first class, leaving tomorrow."

"Sure," she said. "Let's talk to someone in Hawaii."

"No, we can't make contact," Peter said. "Hawaii is West. We can only monitor." Slowly he turned the big dial, and the radio made static and a spooky radio-wave sound that brought Frau Military Papa rushing to the bedroom door with a large frown and one thumb down.

Peter turned down the volume. More adjustments, and then—there it was, faint, but someone was definitely speaking English, and ukulele music played in the background.

"Did you hear that?" Peter asked. "KH6WZ. That's a Hawaiian call sign."

They were listening to someone halfway around the world. Suddenly the notion of sending a message across the Wall seemed doable, even easy.

Peter pressed the MEM button. "There. It's in memory now, in case we want to go back to it."

An hour passed in five minutes. Frau Military Papa had begun preparing dinner (intense applause), and was making the kind of kitchen noises that were code for *it's time for Lena to go home.*

Peter shut off the radio reluctantly and they made their way down the hall.

"Did you like it?" he asked, sidling close to her for the first time that afternoon. He had the face of a small child who'd brought home his first finger painting.

"I loved it," she said.

His shoulders sagged with relief. "Want me to teach you Morse code next time?"

Lena slipped on her shoes. "Sure." *Careful. Don't encourage him too much.*

"Does Lena have clearance to learn Morse code?" Military Papa called from the table.

"We'll get permission through the youth group," Peter said. "I'll arrange it."

"She shouldn't be operating that radio at all," Military Papa said in his deep voice. "I'm not sure I approve of this arrangement. You should have come to me first."

Peter gave Lena a strained smile and she left, feeling as if she were making an escape. It was amazing how much you could understand about a person by spending an hour at their house. She needed fresh air so she went downstairs and stood in the courtyard near the formation of shrubs.

"Fall in," she whispered to them. "Groups of six."

They'd come from Military Papa. They knew how to follow orders.

*

It was midnight, and Lena was wide awake. Auntie didn't like it when she stayed up late and wandered around the apartment. "Like a thief in the silverware," as she put it, though who would want to steal a bunch of crooked forks? It was difficult for Lena to turn her nights back to sleeping after a week of staying up for work. There was no point tossing around in bed. She switched on her lamp and unpinned the photograph of her parents.

Her mother had been a good swimmer; an Olympic hopeful. She'd gone to a special school where she trained in the pool twice a day and was given vitamins to make her stronger. Well, Mama had called the pills vitamins, but Lena had overheard her once talking to a nurse about the headaches and skin problems they were causing. And there had been the miscarriages—several before Lena had been born, and several afterward. Mama said Lena was her miracle baby.

The photograph of her parents had been taken before her father had gotten sad. Papa was making his silly face, the one with his eyes wide open as if everything in the world was shockingly funny. When Lena was little he'd made up stories for her, using a different voice for each character and making sure every story ended with the Sandman coming to put her to sleep. But that had stopped when he'd gotten sad, which had happened around the time he and Mama had started working in the freight car factory, the one Herr Schulmann claimed had not produced a single freight car.

Lena hadn't put together the timing until that moment. But it made sense—if her parents had been troubled by their job, and especially troubled that they couldn't tell anyone about it. When they went to work, they made ammunition. When they came home, they talked about trains. All of it had been a lie.

And yet—this was secret ammunition. Why?

If only Erich had confided in her. Had he not trusted her enough? *No, Mausi, he didn't want to get you in trouble. The more you know, the more trouble you'll be in.*

She probably knew too much already. But if she wanted to save her uncle, she'd have to know everything.

– 22 –

THE BEGINNING OF A PATH

At last it was Monday, which was supposed to mean the best cuts of meat at the butcher shop, but there was only rump roast. The unused theater ticket was still in Lena's coat pocket, jumping with impatience to take her there. Lena didn't know when she would see Max again. She was tempted to skip her photography class that afternoon and go to the theater instead, to check if he was rehearsing, but Auntie had already pounced on the day.

"There are more paving tiles coming," she announced before she left for work. And maybe wood, if Hans's connections came through. They were going to make a garden in one corner of the courtyard. "It should be ready in time for spring planting," Auntie said. It made Lena think of Mama's allotment garden.

In Magdeburg Lena and her family had lived in an old building with no hot water. She used to trudge down to the basement with

Papa for charcoal to heat the stove. But, like many people, they also rented garden space outside the city. Mama had loved their garden, even with all the rules about how high to grow the hedge and how often to mow the grass. The garden had been the main source of their fresh vegetables when they couldn't count on carrots and cucumbers being available in the shops.

Auntie had never seemed like the gardening type, but she was so excited by the prospect of fresh vegetables she had made a drawing of the perfect courtyard, with arrows and measurements indicating the garden in the corner and fully grown trees that hadn't been planted yet.

"Where will we get soil?" Lena hadn't meant to ask the question out loud. She didn't want to damage Auntie's morale.

"One thing at a time," Auntie said. "Peter and Danika are busy today. Hans will be counting on you, so make sure you get right down there this morning."

Hans had also lived in Magdeburg before coming to Berlin. He hadn't known Lena's parents, but he knew the city—its choking brown-coal air, its factories, its cathedral with the stone virgins that stood at the northern gate. Sometimes Lena liked to hear him talk about the city; at other times, it produced a sadness in her so deep she feared she might drown in it.

But sadness was also their connection. Hans knew what it was like to lose important people. Lena could see where his eyes were pinched by loneliness. He didn't even have a cat. Once he'd told Lena he liked to leave the television on so he could hear someone in the next room talking.

"You watch Karl-Eduard von Schnitzler?" Lena had asked. The Black Channel.

Hans had laughed. "No. Even in my apartment, his name is Karl-Eduard von Schni."

After Auntie left, Lena took her time getting ready. She knew Hans wouldn't get an early start, no matter how many paving tiles his friend was bringing.

Three, as it turned out. Three tiles, in the wrong color, and another child-size box of sand. Lena spread the sand with a shovel while Hans and his friend carried the tiles over from the truck.

"Do you think your aunt wants them set in a straight line," Hans asked, "or should we do something more artistic?" He threw out his hand and did a pirouette that Auntie would have called homosexual.

Lena would have loved to put Hans in charge of designing the courtyard, but Auntie had drawn her perfect courtyard with a ruler. "I think you'd better lay them straight."

Five tiles were better than two. It now looked more like the beginning of a path than the end of an idea. Hans raised his mug: coffee, with a dash of "blue strangler" vodka. He'd offered to fetch some for Lena but she had declined. "Here's to the Yellow Brick Road, Lena. We're off to see the wizard."

The wizard of the German Democratic Republic. The small man behind the big machine. It had to be one of the Erichs.

Hans's friend had also brought a spindly willow sapling. "One day," the friend said, "in about fifteen to twenty years, this will be a grand tree. A real beauty."

This was the tree Lena had imagined climbing—standing at the very top, taking flight. She held the sapling in both hands like a sacred object, imagining birds in its branches, cool shade beneath, the way the leaves would sound in a breeze: like the ruffling of thousands of feathers. "Let's plant it in the center of the courtyard," she said.

Hans narrowed his eyes. "Will it survive in all this muck?"

His friend seemed anxious to leave. "Plant it, Hansy. You'll find out."

Lena spent a long time determining where the exact center of the courtyard was. Then she dug a hole and planted the tree. Grandeur had seemed possible when she'd held the sapling in her hands. Planted, it was dwarfed by everything around it—not just the buildings, but also Military Papa's shrubs, and the benches, and the lack of sunlight.

"It's so small," she said. "How will it survive?"

"We'll need to put markers around it or someone might step on it," Hans said. They gathered sticks and rocks and made a fence.

Fifteen to twenty years: it sounded like a prison sentence.

They sat down on one of the benches he'd built and Hans stroked its smooth wood as if it were a favorite horse.

"Where did you work in Magdeburg?" she asked him.

"I was in construction." He held up thick, calloused fingers. "Factories, mostly. Making sure the damn things didn't fall down."

It didn't seem like he worked much anymore, but that wasn't Lena's business, and anyway there was no unemployment in the Better Germany so he must have a job.

"Did you know about the freight car factory?"

He put down his cup. "The place that blew up. Where your parents worked."

Lena nodded. She had spoken to him about her parents before. Hans was a good person to talk to when she was sad. He knew how to listen without trying to fix her.

"It wasn't really a freight car factory, was it?" she asked.

He looked at her. "How old are you now, Lena?"

"Seventeen."

"Old enough, then. I knew about that factory, yes. I'd been inside it many times, probably walked right past your parents. How was I to know I would one day be such good friends with their daughter?"

A shiver went up Lena's arms. How strange life was.

He put a hand on her shoulder. "You're right; it wasn't a freight car factory. The people who worked there were sworn to absolute secrecy by the State. So was I. But if you don't mind my saying, fuck the State. You deserve to know." He took a long drink from his mug.

So—Herr Schulmann hadn't been mistaken, and Erich *had* been onto something.

"We all signed forms that came from the big mucky-mucks in Berlin. You had to be approved to go into that building, even to fix a pipe or work in the canteen." He let out a laugh. "Me. They trusted me. Well."

"They were making ammunition," Lena said. "Right?"

"You have heard. Good. I didn't like working in that place even for the short time I did. It was exceptionally dangerous and the conditions in that factory were—well, they were not top-notch. The lighting was substandard, the machinery kept breaking down. The whole thing was an accident waiting to happen. Naturally there were Stasi agents working there as well, making sure nothing ever went public, but still. For a country that was planning a big takeover, all I can say is, they should have equipped their factories with better machines."

"A big takeover? Of what?"

Hans stared into his mug.

"They were my parents. I deserve to know."

"I'm not the right person to tell you. I only heard rumors, and I could be wrong. Not even the people who worked in that factory knew why they were making so much ammunition. There was talk of many things, but there was only one thing that made sense."

Lena perched so close to the edge of the bench she was in danger of falling off. "Please."

"A takeover of West Berlin—the island of Western decadence, as they call it. The last corner of class-enemy territory in the GDR. The authorities have always hated West Berlin. Its existence is an insult to them. Ever since the end of the war, the Soviets have believed they should have control of the whole city. But that's only my opinion. I don't have proof."

"What if someone had found proof?" Lena asked. "What if they planned to write about it for a Western publication?"

"Proof that the GDR was preparing its army to take over West Berlin? *Mein Gott*, Lena. We wouldn't have a Cold War anymore; we'd have a hot one. The Americans would get involved, and the Soviets. It could turn into a disaster you wouldn't even want to think about. In the last war they didn't have nuclear weapons." Hans took a long drink. "You don't know of someone who's planning to do that, do you? Write about that factory?"

Lena chewed on her bottom lip, gazing at the mismatched paving tiles, the unfinished path that led to mud, the tiny tree that could not possibly grow into a grand willow, no matter how many years it was sentenced to. Didn't Erich realize how much trouble he'd get into? But maybe his manuscript was intended to stop the conflict before it got started. *Remember the way he closed the curtains that afternoon—the last time you saw him?* He'd understood the danger. He must have thought it was worth the risk.

"That boy who came to see you," Hans said. "It's him, isn't it? The one with the military haircut."

Lena laughed. "No, not him." *He's just planning to escape through a tunnel.* Lena didn't want to think about that. Would he really go, and so soon? *You could go with him.* No, she couldn't.

"I'm serious. If you have a friend who's thinking about taking this on, you must discourage them in the strongest possible way. If the Stasi ever got wind of that, they'd come down hard. As hard as they can."

"They'd make the person disappear," Lena said—more to herself than to Hans.

But he must have heard. "Oh yes. They would."

There was another thing, though. "What did you hear about that accident?"

Hans shrugged. "Nothing. The place blew up. It was full of ammunition. It wouldn't have taken much for that to happen. As I said, the State should have taken better care. Whenever I had to work there, I got in and out as fast as I could. Pitied anyone who had to show up there every day. It's a damned shame, and I'm sorry for what happened to your parents. And to you."

"Thank you." Lena stood. "Are you sure it was an accident?"

Hans tilted his head and studied Lena. "Accidents happen. What else could it have been?"

Yes, that was what accidents were best at: happening. Except when they weren't accidents.

*

In the mental hospital, they took away her belt, her shoelaces. She ate with a plastic spoon. The artwork was all soft pastel landscapes—no glass in the frames. The cups were plastic, every corner rounded. Even the pencils were blunt.

One day a boy down the hall had an outburst and had to be placed in the quiet room. Quiet once the door was shut, because the room was padded. By then Lena had been to the quiet room several times, screaming until there was no scream left in her.

She refused to go to group therapy. She wouldn't take her medication unless she was forced to. She refused to play the noodle game, which involved sorting different-shaped noodles into piles. Sometimes the noodles were colored, and then there were arguments. Colors or shapes—which was more important? Lena sat to the side with her arms crossed. "You idiots," she said. "Who cares?"

When she finally got out, her friends had already made the important decisions about their lives. Thankfully Lena only had to endure a few awkward moments of silence over coffee with them, a few of their appraising looks (*is she all right?*), before Auntie had whisked her away to Berlin where she knew no one but Erich. No amount of begging to live with him had made any difference. Auntie was the one who'd gotten her out. She was filling out the progress reports. She was the one who would conquer Lena's inner pig-dog, one way or another.

– 23 –

EVERYTHING IN ITS PLACE

At last it was time for work. Lena had never looked forward to her walk to the compound so much. She didn't know how she would get into Herr Dreck's office to search for evidence about her uncle, but with any luck Bruno Drechsler would go home before all his squeaky children were in bed.

But Erich was one thing; clearly there was more. An attack on West Berlin had to be bigger than Bruno Drechsler and his little fiefdom of Prenzlauer Berg. The plans for that attack had to be in the Comrade General's office. Lena must have missed them, but she hadn't known what she was looking for. There was no choice but to risk searching his office again.

Jutta was in the ashtray room, smoking and staring at her beloved copy of *Sibylle*. The room smelled of garlic and onions, probably from her supper. "What are you so happy about?" she said through a stream of smoke. "It's Monday, for God's sake."

You see? That's why you're no good at card games. "I'm not, really," Lena said. It was always best to deny such things. "Though we did get more paving tiles for our courtyard."

"There's a reason to dance a polka. I once waited a year for paving tiles from the building store, and when they finally came they were the wrong color."

Lena sat at the table. "These were the wrong color too, but I don't think anyone cares." She leaned forward and smiled. *You might as well tell her one thing.* "I met a boy."

Jutta's face broke into a genuine grin. "Well, well. What's his name?"

"Max. He's an actor. He has a dimple." It was exciting to talk about him.

"I've always been a sucker for a good dimple. They're Slavic, you know, dimples."

"No, they're not."

"What do you know? You're just a pipsqueak. I've been around dimples longer than you've been alive."

They got dressed and set out for House 1. Lena made her two trips up the stairs to the second floor while Jutta took the elevator. Light from one office shone into the corridor as usual. He didn't give up easily, Herr Drechsler. Jutta began vacuuming the hallway while Lena hid in another office. She couldn't bear to see him, even in passing.

Crash went Jutta's Purimix into every possible wall. Was she vacuuming with her eyes closed? She didn't do this on her floors; Lena would have heard it. Maybe this was her plan: if she bothered Herr Dreck enough, he would leave on time. They wouldn't fire Jutta; she'd been a member of the club for too long.

"Good evening, Comrade Lieutenant General," she sang. Lena couldn't hear his response. She held her breath as she wiped down the bust of Lenin, the clock on the wall, the flag stand with the Party flag in it. Waited. *Smash. Bang.* "Are you going home already, sir?" Extra-loud-and-cheery Jutta was even worse than everything-is-miserable Jutta. "Your wife will be pleased."

No response.

Footsteps sounded in the corridor, then *clip-clip* down the stairs. Lena peeked out into the hall. Jutta was laughing so hard she was bent over double. She switched off her Purimix. "I've outplayed him. He couldn't stand it anymore." She wagged a finger at Lena. "My work here is done. The floor's all yours."

All yours. Explore at your leisure.

"Make sure you do the windows. Mr. Can't Keep It in His Pants leaves a lot of smudges."

Those big sweaty hands, no wonder. "I'll do them," Lena said.

"And when you're done, come find me so we can do the Comrade General's floor."

Jutta gathered her things, and the elevator clunked as it took her up to the higher floors. Lena entered the office and her stomach turned over. The scent of him was still in the room. Pulling the curtains open, she dabbed a piece of newsprint with vinegar and scrubbed. The thousand eyes that watched everything—*great idea, clean them so they can see even more.* The newsprint made squeaking noises on the glass, and the tang of vinegar made Lena think of Mama's *solyanka.* This was a waste of precious time; she wanted to start snooping. *Patience.* Let Jutta settle into her rhythm.

All Lena could think about was that she would finally find

something helpful, something significant enough to save her uncle. She would send whatever she discovered to Herr Schulmann. There would be an international outcry. Maybe the Other Berlin would send spies to rescue him, or there would be official negotiations. Something would happen.

Get him out? Right, out to the West. *But if you went with Max*— No, it was a tunnel, remember? And she couldn't do that to Auntie. She wouldn't. *But if Erich gets out.*

Lena set down the newsprint. Jutta would be busy by now. Let Herr Dreck deal with his own smudges. She found his key, which she'd seen him tuck beneath the telephone countless times when he'd thought she wasn't paying attention, and went straight to one of the large cupboards. It was filled with an intimidating number of boxes, each of which was packed with files. Some were organized by number, others by name. *Trust him to have his own filing system.*

But wait, these weren't just numbers. They were addresses. Lena wasn't sure where to look first. The streets weren't in any order, and there were names thrown in seemingly at random. One name caught her eye: the People's Theater of Prenzlauer Berg.

With great care she pulled out the file—*remember, remember exactly where it goes*—and opened it. The theater troupe had an extensive file. There were notes on all the actors, including Max: his age, where he'd been to school, details on his time in service, the books he'd taken out of the library recently, the girlfriend he'd had—before Lena? Now? The file didn't specify. It only said her name was Rita and she was a figure skater: *A little on the pudgy side* was added in cramped handwriting.

But Rita wasn't the important part. *What?* Yes, she was.

No, Mausi. Look. At the bottom of Max's page were two words: *flight risk.* They knew.

She flipped through the other pages. Some of the actors' names she didn't recognize, but then she found Dieter's page. *He likes to paint portraits and once considered a career in flower arranging.* They suspected him of homosexuality. He, too, had *flight risk* written at the bottom of the page.

Who was the third one? Bem, with the big nose. She read right through to the end of the file but didn't find any mention of him. Maybe that wasn't his real name—it sounded more like a nickname. She went through the pages a second time. The nickname would surely be in there. It would be So-and-So, also known as Bem, wouldn't it? But there wasn't any mention of Bem anywhere. *Because he's the one doing the telling.*

Was that how it worked?

In the file there was a handwritten declaration of willingness to work for the Stasi. It had been signed, but the signature had been blocked out and replaced by the word *Kingfisher.* That must have been a code name. Another letter recommended the launching of a surveillance operation to monitor *certain people* who were *negatively inclined toward the State.*

Who was Rita? Should Lena ask Max? She would have to tell him about this file, at least. If they knew he was planning to leave, if they were using a reliable source, she'd have to tell him. And maybe casually mention figure skating, or pretend she had a cousin named Rita and gauge his reaction.

Why had she told Jutta about Max? Herr Schulmann had warned her about friends with dangerous leanings. What if she'd gotten him in trouble? Suddenly Jutta came crashing down the hall calling Lena's name. She slammed the file shut, its contents in disarray, and threw it into the cupboard, then closed the doors and grabbed her balled-up piece of newsprint. *Squeak, squeak,* it went on the windows.

"Where are you, child?" Jutta's voice was louder now.

"In here." *Calm down.* But the wasps were going wild. There was Rita, and flight risk, and the possibility that Bem was an informer. There was also *if you get caught doing this you will go to prison.* Or the uranium mines. Or who knew where—*really? You don't know?* She knew. Pastel landscapes, padded rooms—hush, hush.

Jutta opened the door. "I trust you've done the other offices already. This isn't going to be one of those molasses nights, is it?"

"I've done some of them," Lena said. *What if she checks?* But she wouldn't. She only pretended to care because she liked giving the orders.

"You'd better pick up the pace or we'll be sweeping around the agents' shiny shoes tomorrow morning, and they won't thank us for that. We'll meet on the third floor at midnight."

Lena had poked around enough in Herr Dreck's office. After Jutta left, she returned the file to its proper place, straightening the papers and resisting the urge to reread Max's page. She would do more tomorrow. In the meantime, she got down to work.

*

At midnight she met Jutta in the Comrade General's rooms. *Maybe tonight is not the best night for this.* No, Lena couldn't delay. Time might be running out for Erich, and who knew what tomorrow would bring for her? A change in the work order, a transfer to another building. She had to do it tonight.

Lena could hardly stand the waiting—*be thorough, be normal, sing something.* She sprayed disinfectant onto Mielke's special red telephone, not the solution that smelled like turpentine because Comrade General Mielke didn't want his office to smell like a railcar. Again she left her duster behind. Again she suggested doing the bathrooms. They did the bathrooms. They took a break. Then Jutta stepped into the elevator to go upstairs and told Lena to do the main floor.

Lena had never mopped the foyer faster in her life. Hello, red flags. Hello, Herr Marx, Herr Dzerzhinsky, soapy water splashing the bases of their pedestals. And then—*you seem to have misplaced your duster.* She climbed the stairs as quickly as she dared and entered Comrade General Mielke's office. The key was under the right boot. *Steady your hand.* Go back to those desk drawers. There was his hair tonic, pencils, notes for this and that. *Careful. Put everything back in its place.* Another drawer: in it were stacks of paper that had nothing to do with the West.

And then—yes, she remembered having seen this one. It was a list of places in West Berlin, together with a map: bridges, airports, train stations. Radio and television stations. They were all places that might be the first targets during an invasion. Was it possible? The heading on the page said *Day X.* There were suggestions for new street names, and medals being made in anticipation of bravery. Lena took out the camera, positioned it over the sheet, and snapped a photograph.

In the next document was a diagram filled with arrows. Code name: THRUST. There were notes and more notes, which became clearer as she skimmed them. The Eastern forces would comprise 32,000 men, made up of members of the People's Army, Soviet forces, and People's Police Alert Units. They planned to invade West Berlin over three days, overpowering its government and military defenses. They had tanks, a fighter-bomber squadron, helicopters, guns, and mortars. Lena found lists of regiments and battalions, different types of aircraft, and routes for the ground forces to follow. The Stasi's job would be to occupy police stations, intelligence offices, and research centers, and arrest any trouble-makers. They seemed to know already who the troublemakers would be: senior police officers, important politicians, unsympa-thetic journalists, intelligence officers, people with scientific or technological secrets, anti-communist leaders, and others. It was a long list.

Could they take over an entire city in three days? *They put up the barbed wire for the Wall overnight.* They could do it.

None of these documents had carried meaning the first time Lena had seen them, but this time it was different. *Thank you, Hans.* She felt like opening the bottle of hair tonic and pouring it all over Mielke's chair so his pants would be soaked with it the next time he sat down. Plans and diagrams—it was so easy when you did it from a desk. Arrows, lists, place names—it was merely a puzzle, an arrangement of *X*'s and *Y*'s that had nothing to do with the people who would be affected by it.

"Protect peace by making socialism stronger": that was the slogan on the banner she and Auntie had carried in the parade on Republic Day. All the vows they'd made in youth group to love peace—it was a puppet show, and they were the puppets.

Lena took pictures of everything, and then carefully put the sheets back. She replaced the key beneath the boot, gathered her duster, and went downstairs, the camera in her pocket beside her hairbrush. The sight of Jutta on the second floor startled her so badly she dropped the duster and it clattered to the floor.

"Where were you?" Jutta demanded.

Think fast. "Looking for you. I thought you needed help."

"You don't have enough to do, Pippi Langstrumpf?"

"I was trying to do a kindness for you." Her voice cracked.

"Oh." Jutta's face softened and Lena felt guilty for lying. "My floors are under control. I'm going for a smoke break. Get back to the main floor and keep those feet moving."

Lena did her best not to fall down the stairs on her shaking legs. When she got to the foyer she steadied herself against the statue of Marx. She'd done it. Some of it. *Not the most important part.* She hadn't found Erich, but at least now things made sense.

Her mind wandered as she vacuumed the hallway. Should she contact Herr Schulmann about West Berlin now? *Wait until you know for sure what happened to Erich.* Who knew how many times she'd be able to fool Peter with the radio? Once, yes. Twice, maybe not. It wasn't worth the risk.

*

That afternoon, the front door of the People's Theater of Prenzlauer Berg was locked, so Lena went around to the back. When she knocked, it was Bem who answered. He said "Hi" and "You're the girl from under the table"—*God, he knows that too. What has he said to them about you?*

So many words crowded into Lena's mouth she didn't dare

speak. She wasn't sure which ones would edge out first. She studied his face for signs of betrayal. Surely it would show somewhere: a shift in the eyes, a crease at the mouth. But there was nothing, only his giant nose, and his small eyes crowded against it.

"Are you all right?" Bem asked. "You're here for Max, huh?"

All you have to say is yes. So—"Yes."

"I'll fetch him for you. But you can't keep him long. We're rehearsing a new play."

He shut the door and Lena waited alone outside, wishing things hadn't gotten so complicated. Someone yelled from a nearby window for a child to hurry up. A crow cawed; a breeze picked up. Real life never stopped. All she wanted to do was disappear into Max's strong arms, lose herself in the lemon scent of his soap, shrink the world down to lips and skin.

The door creaked open and there he was, with his misbehaving hair and his not-Slavic dimple. "Hi," he said in a rush of breath, taking her in his arms. He hadn't bothered to wear a coat.

Lena wanted the kiss to last forever, but they didn't have much time. "We need to talk."

Max held her away from him. "What's the matter?"

She shook her head. "Do you have time to walk? Bem said—"

"Don't listen to Bem. He's way too keen on all this acting stuff."

Don't listen to Bem. Someone was listening to him. Kingfisher. *You don't know that for sure.* She walked down the alley, leaving Max no choice but to follow. "Tell me," she said when they were far enough away from the theater, "who are all the people in your troupe? How many actors?"

Parked cars were everywhere. The ones nearest them were empty, but Lena kept her eyes open. A man sitting in a Lada, pretending to read the newspaper—he had to be here somewhere.

Max listed off the actors on his fingers. "There's Margitta—"

"Right," said Lena. "The girl who failed math in *Oberschule* and may or may not have a boyfriend she's corresponding with in Portugal."

"Do you know her?" Max asked.

"Sort of."

"All right. There's Dieter. He was at the pub that day we first met. You remember him?"

"Possible homosexual," Lena said.

"Hmm, I never thought of that. He does wear a lot of flowery shirts. There's Petra."

"The girl with relatives in Munich who send her knitting magazines."

"Do they?" Max stopped walking. "Wait, how do you know all this? What's going on?"

Lena looked around, as if the trees might be listening. It was ridiculous to be this paranoid, and yet maybe that had been her big mistake. She hadn't been paranoid enough. "There's a file on all the members in your troupe. I found it in one of the offices I clean. You're in there too."

"Me?" The color drained from Max's face. "This is a joke. You're kidding."

"Do you want to tell me about the figure skater? Rita, right?"

"*Mein Gott.*"

"Are you still going out with her?" The rage came out of nowhere. Lena's face grew warm and she wriggled away from his arm.

"Is that what this is about?"

Yes. "No. Not only that. At the bottom of your page it said you were a flight risk."

Max started laughing. "Sure it did. I'm an actor in Prenzlauer Berg. It probably said that at the bottom of every page."

Think back. "No, it didn't. Only you and Dieter."

"And Bem," Max said. "That must have been on Bem's page too. He's coming with us."

"Bem doesn't have a page in the file."

She could see Max's shoulders tense through his T-shirt. "What are you saying?"

"I'm not saying anything. I'm just telling you what I saw. I went through the whole file twice. All the actors were in it except Bem. Someone named Kingfisher signed a declaration of willingness to work for the Stasi."

"Kingfisher. That could be anyone." Max was walking as if his legs had turned into wood. "Maybe Bem's page had been taken out for some reason. To update it or whatnot. Maybe it was on someone's desk or in another office."

Lena's mouth went dry. Bruno Drechsler's desk had locked drawers which were probably full of files. She hadn't had time to look through them.

But Max wasn't finished. "Whatever it is those important men do in that wonderful place where you work."

Ah, now comes the truth. It always came down to Stasi headquarters sooner or later. "I risked my job for you. If I had gotten caught—"

"Have you considered working somewhere that doesn't make you dirty?"

"I only clean the building, Max. I don't work there in that way."

"Right. Only now you're telling me one of my friends, someone I've trusted with the most important secret of my life, is an informant. Bem's the one planning the whole thing. He knows the people at the tunnel. How could he—how could he be—how could—" But the question wouldn't come out no matter how many times he tried to ask it. "I have to get back."

He walked toward the theater, but Lena didn't follow him. "I'm trying to help you. Don't you understand that? I'm trying to warn you. If you go—"

He marched back to her and spoke through clenched teeth. "I am going. We're going, the three of us. I know I asked you to come, but now—"

"Now you don't trust me." Lena wanted to punch him, and she might have, except for one small thing. *What if he's right? You didn't check Drechsler's desk.* Even so: "It said you were a flight risk."

"Nearly everyone's a flight risk, except maybe you. True believer—you'll never leave."

That was how quickly it happened. Just when she thought she'd found her One True Love, he stormed away.

– 24 –

BEING NORMAL IS OVERRATED

Dear Herr Honecker, Mr. General Secretary,

I believe my pig is whistling. Didn't you know about the freight car factory in Magdeburg that was not making freight cars, or anything even close to freight cars? Didn't you know about the plan to take over West Berlin? My parents were in that factory when it exploded, Mr. General Secretary. And now my uncle is—

Lena ripped the letter into tiny pieces and sprinkled them into the trash. It made her feel better to think about sending something like this, but it was pointless. *Takeover of West Berlin, Lena?* the doctors would say. *Hush, now. You're getting over-heated.*

It was all true, and all lies—just like Erich had explained about writing a novel.

Auntie was calling for supper, but Lena had no appetite. Had she been wrong about Bem? Had she made a mistake in warning Max? Maybe he would go back to Rita, whoever she was. A figure skater. Even if she was overweight, Lena couldn't compete with that. She was agile, but only when it involved shoes and solid ground. Gliding on ice in a tiny skirt, with extravagant makeup on? How could she eat supper after thinking about that?

She would need Danika's pinking shears to cut Max out of her life—only she didn't even have any photographs of the two of them. Maybe they hadn't been together long enough for him to qualify as a One True Love. But he was the first boy she'd ever kissed. It mattered. He mattered. And now they'd never kiss again, and she'd grow up to be one of those angry women who owned a small yapping dog that never wanted to walk in the right direction.

Someone was parading up and down the fourth-floor hallway in big boots. It took a minute for Lena to recognize Military Papa's commanding voice. *Doorways at attention!* She entered the kitchen, where Auntie was preparing sandwiches.

"What's going on out there?" Lena asked. Maybe Military Papa would order the baby next door to stop crying.

Auntie was always careful when she spoke about Military Papa. He was loud, and a bully, but he'd also been a very important man in the military, and you didn't make jokes about very important men unless you badly wanted a job in mining. "They've had news. Peter has received his conscription notice."

Conscription. Peter would be gone for at least eighteen months.

Lena hadn't liked the turn things had taken with the purple shirt, but she was fond of Peter as a friend. She would miss him. What would the army be like for him? How would he cope with the marching and machine guns? Maybe there would be radio. Peter could be in charge of Morse code—which he wouldn't have time to teach her now.

The radio. "When does he leave?" Without thinking, Lena reached for a slice of salami with her fingers, and Auntie tapped her hand with the sharp end of a fork.

"Two weeks. His father has expedited the process to get him into a special regiment."

Of course he has. That meant Lena had two weeks to gather as much evidence as she could and then contact Günter Schulmann on the radio. She would not be able to do that without Peter's help.

On her way to work she stopped in the courtyard to check on the willow sapling. It hadn't gotten any bigger. In fact, it was droopy. Maybe the ground in the courtyard was too wet even for willow trees. She patted its thin branches and whispered, "Don't be afraid of those shrubs over there. You won't be small for long. One day you'll be telling them what to do."

When she looked at the sad little tree, she felt a pang of despair.

*

That night, for the first time in Lena's memory, Herr Dreck did not stay late. By the time she and Jutta reached the second floor, every office was dark.

"The cheerful Slav triumphs again," Jutta said.

"His wife will think he got fired," Lena said.

"Maybe she'll realize she needs to do more than keep his feet warm."

Lena thought of Auntie with the naked bricklayer and took an extra-long time to plug in her Purimix. "I'll go back to my regular duties here, then."

"Yes, you will, and not a moment too soon. Working poor Jutta like a mule." She dragged her supplies back to the elevator and thumped them all in. It creaked and rumbled and took her away.

Lena started with Herr Dreck's office. If there was a document that labeled Bem as a flight risk she was determined to find it—before Max and Dieter headed into an escape plan that would land them in side-by-side prison cells. And she still hadn't come across a single thing with Erich's name on it. She had to find something—everything—before Peter left for his military service.

She didn't even pretend to clean Herr Dreck's office. He could choke on the dust for all she cared. She went straight to his desk, unlocked the drawers, and riffled through the papers. The office smelled of something spicy, maybe what he'd had for lunch. Lena felt prickly at the thought of him sitting there, presiding over people's lives with a frown on his face. Picking up the telephone, giving an order. Ruining a life and then checking it off his list.

Be careful. If he had even the slightest inkling she'd been through his desk, who knew what he would do? But he wasn't here. Jutta had scared him away. Herr Dreck would no longer be part of Lena's life. The thought settled her, like a pond where the wind has finally died.

Quickly, quietly, she opened drawers and cabinets, flipped through files. There was nothing on Bem—*if that's his real name.* But if it wasn't, then she had no idea what to look for. Kingfisher—but there was nothing about that person either. She flipped through the People's Theater file one more time, in case Bem's page had been returned. Nothing.

Then she remembered—*the files on Erich's street will be in this office.* Lena searched the documents methodically. She found street names, then building numbers. Addresses. There it was, Erich's address. Her hands shook as she pulled out the file and opened it.

There was something gratifying about seeing it all in print. She wasn't crazy, even though everyone had tried to make her think she was. Her body filled with so much rage she felt she could have glowed in the dark. Someone had written it all out as if it meant nothing. Someone had sat at a typewriter, *clack clack clack*, just like the sound of Erich's typewriter on the table by the window— but instead of creating a world, they had destroyed one.

There was the letter transferring the apartment from Erich to Friedrich So-and-So. Lena took out her camera and snapped a photograph of it. There was the order to remove all writing-related items from the apartment. *Snap.* There was the requisition for the flower-delivery van, the one Lena had seen parked outside the building. *Snap.* Orders to libraries and bookstores to remove all his books.

It was exactly as she'd feared. Her uncle was in the blank space on the map. The hole people fell into if they weren't careful—and sometimes, even if they were. The place where it took ten days to break a person, often less. And if they weren't broken in ten days? Then what? No one ever talked about that.

Bruno Drechsler was cracking down, was he? Lena glanced

around the office, wishing there was something she could break. She tucked the camera away, gave the shelves a perfunctory dusting, and left. She had proof, of certain things anyway. She would have liked to know if Erich was still alive, and if the explosion at the factory had been an accident. But she knew enough now to contact Günter Schulmann. She couldn't afford to wait much longer or she might miss her chance.

The night passed more quickly than usual. There was something about cleaning that made a person feel better. You could work things out on stains and dirty floors. Whatever it was, it could be the floor's fault, and then you could scrub and scrub until it was clean again.

But tonight there was more. Lena's body relished the feeling of not having been touched or forced to do anything—of not even worrying about it. This was what it felt like to be normal. No wonder the doctors made such a big deal of it. It was pleasant. A normal person could gaze into the night sky and enjoy the stars without hearing a distant buzzing, an approaching swarm— without feeling the need to run and hide.

Lena enjoyed being normal so much that when she went to the *schrullig* world she decided to go into the travel agency and ask about Hawaii.

The man behind the counter eyed her as if she wasn't normal at all. "You want to go to Hawaii, do you?"

"Not really." She backed away from the idea as if it had grown teeth. "I've seen photographs, though. It doesn't really look like that, does it?"

"How else do you think they got the pictures?" he said.

The usual way. By making them up.

On the way home Lena lost herself in thoughts of Hawaii and being normal. What about Hawaii with Max? *Don't get carried away*—that would mean escaping, which was not going to happen, and anyway things with Max were done. She walked straight up the stairs and into the apartment, plunking herself at the kitchen table in front of an egg that was still warm.

She chatted to Auntie about the willow tree in the courtyard, and about the plans for the vegetable garden, and she yawned and realized she was exhausted. Like a normal person. "Auntie, I'm tired," she said, as if this were the most exciting thing.

Auntie shook her head. "I don't know. I just don't know."

Eight hours later, Auntie knew. She woke Lena up by waving an envelope back and forth. It had been opened. "What's this about?"

It was from Günter Schulmann. *Scheisse.* Lena thought back to the morning, how happy she'd been—so happy she had forgotten to check the mailbox. She took the envelope from Auntie and removed the note that was inside.

Use frequency 14.285 MHz
What's going on? Are you okay?

"So?" Auntie said.

Lena's thoughts still wore their winter boots. "It's a message," she said.

"That much I could deduce for myself, thank you. What is frequency 14.285? Who is this from?" Auntie had painted her nails orange. Her hands were her best feature too. Lena decided not to say this out loud.

"It's about the radio," she said. Boots off. Wool socks out of her head. "It's from Peter. He's teaching me."

"Is that so?" Auntie tilted her head as if she was listening for the pig. "Why is he asking if you're okay?"

"All the things he showed me the last time. He was worried. Because I'm simple." *Ha! Mausi, one. Auntie, zero.*

"And he has to leave you a note in the mailbox? Like a thief in the silverware?"

Lena turned to her pillow. "I think he intended it to be romantic." *What are you doing? You'll make things worse.*

"I'm not sure I like that."

It's better than being naked in the bedroom with that bricklayer. Don't mention bricks. "It's fine, Auntie. His parents are home when we're there. And anyway—he's leaving soon."

"I'll be investigating that." Auntie stormed out of the room.

Lena would have to arrange to use the radio with Peter right away. She mentioned it to him as they walked to youth group.

Peter was delighted. But then he said, "It will have to wait till the weekend. With everything that's happening, my parents are keeping me very busy."

Lena tried to hide her disappointment. "The weekend, then. All right." It would give her a few more days to poke around, but she couldn't delay any longer than that.

Behind him, Danika's eyebrows joined in a fierce *What?* Lena shook her head, mouthing, *Just friends.*

"He doesn't think so," Danika said when they had a moment alone. "He's in love with you. You're leading him on."

"He's leaving in two weeks," Lena said. "He's teaching me how to use his radio."

Danika studied her nails. "Why on earth? Talk about Dullsville."

"It's actually pretty interesting." Lena wanted to tell Danika that she and Max had had a fight, but if she didn't say it out loud, maybe it would fade, like a bruise. In a few days she'd never even know it had been there.

*

It turned out being normal was overrated. It had made Lena careless, and that was one thing she could not afford. On the way to work that evening she decided to be less normal. The days were growing shorter, and it was dark and cool now when she walked to the compound. It made her want to walk faster, but she resisted the urge.

Night had fallen, and if she slowed down and listened she could hear the sound it made as it landed. Not a *thump*, like Auntie sitting down at the dinner table. It was more like water running slowly down a wall; inky water, darkening the sky as it slid down. If she listened, she could hear leaves deciding to let go of tree branches.

And she could hear footsteps. *Behind you.* Lena sped up. The footsteps sped up. *Don't turn around.* Lena turned around. It was Max. "You frightened me!"

"I'm sorry," Max said. "I needed to talk to you. I came to the building but I could see your aunt from the window. I decided I'd better not buzz up."

"Good thinking." She sighed. "I looked for Bem's page. I didn't find anything, but maybe Bem's not his real—"

Max took her gently by both hands. "You didn't find anything because there was nothing to find. You were right about him. I didn't want you to be, but I followed him yesterday before rehearsal. He told me he was going to visit his parents, but that wasn't where he went. It was some apartment in a strange neighborhood."

"A girlfriend?"

He shook his head. "When he came out, he was with two men. The way they were standing, the way they checked up and down the street—" He stared at the ground. "When he got to rehearsal, I asked. Oh yes, his parents were fine, he'd just come from seeing them, spent the whole afternoon there, had coffee and cake."

The pain of Bem's betrayal was written so sharply on his face it made Lena wince. "I'm sorry. Maybe they threatened him." Who knew what they'd said to make Bem do it? *Maybe nothing.* Some people chose to be informers—to advance their careers, or because they were true believers, like Auntie.

"It changes everything," Max said. "Now they'll be watching us. We'll never get out."

Lena thought of the tiny tree in her courtyard, how hard it was when everything around you was bigger and stronger than you were. "Well . . . maybe it's still possible. But you'll have to be careful what you say to Bem from now on."

Max cupped her face with his cold hands and kissed her. "Come with us. Please."

"I'm scared." Besides the obvious risk of getting caught, it was a tunnel: small, dark, not enough air. And besides even that, the thought of running away with a man carried certain questions in its backpack. Would they live together in the West? One bedroom? Two? What if they didn't get along? And what would she do about Auntie?

"We're scared too," he said.

Max rested his lips on Lena's forehead and her eyes fell shut on a terrible realization. She had imagined photographing the incriminating evidence in the House 1 offices. She had imagined handing the camera over to Günter Schulmann. But not once in all of this had she imagined what she might do when the news got out, if anyone traced it back to her.

Flight had always been a dream, and not necessarily a good one. It was for birds and desperate people. Lena had never seriously considered leaving the Better Germany, but now she might not have a choice.

– 25 –

NATURAL CAUSES

It was Friday, the fourteenth of October—Erich's birthday. Lena was embroidering a blue bird next to the orange flowers on her decorative tablecloth. She'd already poked herself six times with the needle. The bird looked more like a blob with wings, but she wasn't sure how to fix that without pulling out all the thread and starting over.

Normally she would have been mulling over what to buy for her uncle as a gift. She would have set money aside. Auntie would have used her connections to get her brother something special from the pricey shop, *Delikat*—a good bottle of vodka, real coffee. They would have all gone out for lunch together on Sunday. Auntie's entire body would be pulled tight, but she would be polite and pay for lunch, and Lena would stay longer so that she and her uncle could go for ice cream together and walk in the park.

Republikflucht. Flight from the Republic. She'd been turning the word over in her mouth like a pill that was too big to swallow. Would it really be necessary? Would anyone suspect the secret documents had been photographed by her, of all people? It was more likely the bigwigs would point fingers at one another. All the bitter grudges and suspicions they'd been harboring for years would come out.

You take too long in the toilet. You must be doing something subversive in there.

I saw you talking to a man on the street corner.

What about all those telephone calls to the West?

Maybe even Lieutenant General Bruno Drechsler would be a suspect. Lena could fade into the background where she belonged, dusting and mopping each night, the invisible fairy that arrived to set things straight in the messy world of important men.

Auntie bustled into the sitting room with her arms full of bags. She was so excited she had forgotten to take off her outside shoes. "You'll never guess! I've gotten hold of some seeds. We're going to have a winter garden—collards and turnips, even garlic. We'll plant the seeds indoors to give them a good start, and then we'll transfer them outside. We've got soil coming tomorrow, and Hans has found wood. He's going to build an enclosure. Imagine that. It will be a raised garden." Also a crying shame, but that would come later, once Auntie's excitement had died down.

"That's wonderful," Lena said. A month ago she would have put down her embroidery. She would have asked to see the seeds and the little pots they would plant them in. She would have wanted to help. Now there was a boot poised over her life, waiting to stomp on it. What was the point of planting anything?

As soon as she gave Günter Schulmann the camera and told him what she'd learned, everything would change. If she stayed in the Better Germany, she would risk being caught and thrown into prison. If she fled, she would risk being caught and thrown into prison. And if she escaped and wasn't caught, there was a good chance she would ruin the life of the woman standing in front of her getting so excited about turnip seeds. Was she ready for any of that?

There was another choice. *You could lose that camera in the Spree, or tell Günter Schulmann you couldn't find anything.* But Erich had been prepared to risk everything. Hadn't he known what would happen if he got caught? Hadn't he understood the sacrifices he'd be facing once the news became public? He must have had these exact thoughts and decided it was worth it. But it didn't feel worth it right now.

Lena put down her embroidery and made herself smile. Auntie deserved that, at least. "I'll help you plant them." *Before I go and make both our lives a misery.* Tomorrow was Saturday. She and Peter would collect recyclables and work in the courtyard, then spend the afternoon on some radio instruction. Auntie had only agreed after making sure Peter's parents would be home. *Let's use frequency 14.285, Peter. Can I say something? Just one thing: I promise it won't be subversive.* She was despicable.

Tomorrow was the day her life would change forever. She could at least pretend for twenty-four hours more that everything was all right.

That night Lena took the camera to work with her just in case. There were still some important unanswered questions, and she hoped to give Günter Schulmann as full a picture as she could.

As a student, she had never left a question blank on an exam. She didn't want to start now.

Jutta was smoking in the ashtray room as usual, a mug of bitter coffee beside her. "Did I ever tell you about my mother? I mean my impostor mother, not my real one. I don't know my real one."

Lena let her talk. The sound of her voice was soothing, in a way. And it was immensely satisfying to think of the person on the other end having to listen to and take notes on the most boring conversation ever. Lena was tempted to say hello to him, the way people sometimes did on the telephone. *Whoever's listening, please let us know if you need us to repeat anything.*

Instead she said, "My mother was a swimmer."

Jutta studied her, evaluating this new fact. She tapped one of Lena's shoulders, then the other. "I can see it. Your bone structure. I bet you swim too."

"When the pool is open, yes." She talked about pool repairs, and the petition they'd sent to the authorities. And so it went: a conversation about nothing. They gathered their supplies and crossed the compound to House 1. Lena took the stairs; Jutta took the elevator.

When Lena reached the second floor, every room lining the hallway was dark. She loosened her grip on the bucket. It seemed Herr Dreck was well and truly gone from her life. She switched on the Purimix and vacuumed the corridor, humming the Sandman tune, letting Jutta know she was hard at work. One last search through his office, and then she'd be done.

Lena went into the room next to Herr Dreck's and flicked on the light. She brought in her Purimix and started it. If Jutta happened to pop down to the second floor, she would see light and hear the machine. Meanwhile—

She slipped into Herr Drechsler's dark office and switched on the small desk lamp. It wasn't the best lighting, but it would have to do. The last thing she wanted was to get caught at this late stage. She was reaching for the key when . . . What was this? He had left papers on his desk. This was carelessness of the highest degree. If only there was a spot security check that night, he would be dragged into Mielke's office and forced to think on his feet again.

She flipped through the documents—boring, boring, boring— and then felt guilty. These were real lives she was dismissing, decisions with consequences not just for those directly concerned, but also for their parents, their children, their spouses. Who knew the power contained in a *no*? A line crossed through something important, a notation in the margin to send Herr So-and-So an invitation to lunch with a few Stasi agents and an offer he couldn't refuse. *We'll take your children away. You'll lose your job.*

She began going through another pile—then tumbled backward, right into Herr Dreck's big chair, nearly toppling it. Her hand shook so badly she could barely read the page it held, no matter how hard she tried to steady it. Near her head, a sound was coming closer. Fast, and faster. A swarm of wasps so loud it sounded like an approaching plane.

It was a preliminary death report—for Erich Altmann. *Occupation: writer. Date of death: October 12, 1983.* Two days ago, *of natural causes.* The man who'd never been born was dead.

Lena took out the camera, placed the death certificate beneath the circle of light made by the desk lamp, and pressed the shutter button so hard it hurt her finger.

Snap. Did he suffer? Of course he did: a plank bed, isolation, constant questioning, no sleep. They would have fed him under-cooked potatoes and meat fit only for dogs, though the food was hardly the worst thing at Hohenschönhausen.

Snap. Would the authorities even bother to send Auntie a letter? *We regret to inform you . . .* Lena stared at the official document until her eyes burned, then folded it and stuck it in her pocket. Herr Dreck would think he'd lost it. Maybe he'd get in trouble, but she doubted it. They could fill out another one. What difference did it make to them?

Günter Schulmann would get these photographs; Lena would make sure of it. Even though they wouldn't bring Erich back, they would mean something. She switched on the overhead light and picked up her broom. *Smash something, Mausi. Just one thing. It will make you feel better.*

But she didn't get the chance. She sensed, before she saw—maybe because of the warmth, or maybe it was the scent. He was there. He'd been there all along.

The breath left her body.

"Fräulein, is that you?"

The door was already shut. He locked it and shut off the main light. Only the desk lamp remained lit, one small bright circle in the darkness.

"I was right to suspect you. Always follow your gut, you know? Others would have said, 'Her? That cleaning girl, little Lena Altmann? She doesn't have it in her.' But I knew you did."

He knows your name. There'd been some irrational part of Lena that had imagined she would be safe as long as he only knew her as Fräulein.

"You killed my uncle." Hatred was not just something you felt. It had its own body, its own beating heart, and it could consume you from the inside until there was nothing left of you. If she'd had a weapon, she would have stabbed Bruno Drechsler with it right then.

"Your uncle had lung cancer, in the advanced stages. It was only a matter of time."

The worst thing was that Lena couldn't completely disbelieve it. All those years in the mines, the cough that had been getting worse: it was possible.

"Give me the camera," Herr Dreck said.

Lena slipped it into her pocket. "What camera?"

In two steps he was in front of her, shoving his hand into her pocket. "Don't play games with me. You have no idea what you're dealing with."

Though she didn't want to touch him, she grabbed his wrist, but he twisted away easily and emptied the contents of her side pocket: hairbrush, camera, death certificate. He tossed the brush onto the floor, but tucked the camera and the document into his jacket.

What does it matter? You've seen the truth. Herr Dreck couldn't take that from her. "I know about the invasion of West Berlin."

She might as well have dumped her bucket of mop water on him. He stood absolutely still and stared at her for a long time. *You shouldn't have said that.*

"I don't know what the hell you're talking about," he said.

"Yes, you do." *Stop. For your own good.* But the conversation was a wild horse and Lena was on its back. Hang on or fall off; those were the choices, and it was a long way to fall. "The freight car factory in Magdeburg, where my parents worked. It was a munitions factory, you know it was. The State was planning to take over West Berlin, but the factory exploded. They called it an accident, but it wasn't."

His big square face deflated. "Actually, it was. No one was supposed to have died in that explosion."

No one was supposed to have died? "It was planned?"

"Don't pin that on me, you *Sau.* I wasn't involved in the incident."

Incident. That word. Something terrible, smothered in a blanket.

"A different department handled it," he added. "And it never should have happened anyway. We had eyes and ears on that site. One of the workers was planning to talk to the West. We had no choice but to destroy the factory. But it was supposed to happen at night, when no one was there."

No one was supposed to have died. Everyone had died. Lena should have figured it out on her own. The State had planned the explosion, and the result had been the exact opposite of what had been intended. *Scheiss Osten.* This had been the story of the Better Germany from the beginning.

"I've told you what you wanted to know. And now—" Herr Dreck unbuckled his belt.

Not this time.

Lena ran for the door, but her fingers struggled with the lock. Too slow. Herr Dreck raced up behind her and yanked her hands away.

"I'll scream," Lena said. "Jutta will hear me."

"Try it." He clamped a hand across her mouth. With the other, he tried to push her to her knees, but she kicked him in the shins. He winced, even though the blow was not that hard. *Aim higher.* But she couldn't; he was using all his weight to force her to the floor. He was so much bigger and stronger than she was. Her legs buckled, and then she was where he wanted her.

When he took his hands away to pull down his trousers, Lena cried out as loudly as she could, but then she remembered: she'd left the Purimix on in the next room. Jutta wouldn't hear her. She'd hear the Purimix and assume everything was fine on the second floor. Lena reached out to strike Herr Dreck between the legs, but he caught her hand. Then he squeezed her jaw so that she had no choice but to open her mouth. He held her head back, pulling her hair so hard it made tears come to her eyes.

It was an accident. At a freight car factory.

There was no planned takeover.

Your uncle died of natural causes.

You don't have an uncle.

Which was true. She didn't have one anymore.

He thrust so forcefully she was choking. Her eyes watered and snot ran from her nose. She gagged and coughed, and still he pushed it in.

At last it was over. If only she could throw up like last time. She spat his semen onto the carpet.

Herr Dreck shrugged. "More for you to clean later."

I don't think so. She would let it dry and harden. "What happened here, Comrade Lieutenant General?" someone important would ask, stepping around the stain in the carpet. Let Bruno Drechsler think up something clever.

He fastened his trousers, a smug expression on his face. "Enjoy your last night of work in House 1, Fräulein. Effective Monday your employment here will be terminated. Security risk; it was to be expected."

Terminated.

The events of the night fell on Lena like an anvil. It was too much. Erich was dead. And now—her job. She didn't want to cry in front of this man, and she certainly wouldn't beg for anything. *Let him fire you. On Monday.* That gave her two days to make sure Günter Schulmann, and the world, would know the truth. She'd seen it. She'd remember.

"By the way," he said as he buttoned his coat, "in case you get any ideas about telling someone about this?" He held up the camera. "I have a copy of your admission forms to the asylum. With your history of mental illness, no one will believe a word you say. Especially without proof." He walked out, clicking the door shut behind him.

Lena needed to sit down, but not in Herr Dreck's leather armchair, with the patches worn away by his body. She sat on the carpet in the dark, rested her face in her hands, and wept.

Where was the Wall, the one in her mind that could make everything feel okay? *Too late for that. You're deep in the middle part now.* Was it the trip wire that had gotten her? Or the lights? *Please don't say it was the dogs.* What did it matter? Once you were stuck in the middle part, it was over.

There was no way to pretend this hadn't happened. So she got up, fetched the Purimix from the office next door, and went back to work.

The minutes passed like soldiers on parade: methodical, mechanical. They knew where they were going, and so did she.

Someone would telephone Auntie. Arrangements would be made. "There wasn't enough progress, Frau Keller, it's not your fault. You were the Guardian of a Difficult Child." Lena would be allowed to pack a small bag: nothing subversive, nothing sharp.

In the morning, when her shift was over, she lingered in the ashtray room. Jutta was putting on her coat, and Lena wrapped her arms around her. Jutta's coat smelled like cigarette smoke and fried onions.

"What is it, child? What's gotten into you?"

"You're still a great beauty," Lena said to her. "Thank you for helping me."

"It's only the weekend, you silly goat, not the end of your life." Then Jutta stepped back and took Lena by the shoulders. "Was he here tonight? Did something happen?"

Lena's face grew hot. "It's okay."

"It most definitely is not okay. I'll put in a request to change the work order. We'll switch floors permanently, see how he likes that. I'll do it first thing Monday, don't you worry. Now go, have a good weekend."

First thing Monday. Too late.

Lena walked over to House 18 and entered the *schrullig* world, probably for the last time. In the entire year that the special grocery store had been open, she had never once bought anything to take home. She'd seen others leave with grocery bags, but somehow she'd never believed she was allowed.

"I'll have three oranges, please, and three bananas." Lena paid for the fruit and packed it into her bag.

Ernst was not on duty at the compound gate. It was the other man, the one who kept a firm grip on his rifle and made sure not to smile. Lena walked home in the quiet of Saturday morning. The air was damp, the sky misty with indecision—to rain or not to rain. By the time she arrived at the housing development, she was still not sure how to break the news to Auntie that she had lost her job.

Before mounting the stairs, she checked the mail—nothing. Then she went into the courtyard to check on the tiny tree. It was still standing, maybe less droopy than before. She patted the ground around it. "Hang on," she whispered.

– 26 –

HOW ABOUT 14.285?

When Lena arrived at the apartment, her egg was still warm. The eggcup stared at her with its happy-chicken face. Everything in its world was fine. Sausage Auntie asked, "How was work?" Lena's jaw was sore, and her scalp still hurt where Herr Dreck had pulled her hair.

Tell her. But she couldn't. Instead, she took a banana from her bag and set it on the table.

Auntie stared at it as if it had dropped from the ceiling. "Where did you get this?"

Lena said nothing. It felt grand to bring home something special. She wished she'd done it sooner.

Auntie wanted to cut the banana in half, but Lena said, "No. You take the whole thing."

She hugged Lena and tucked it into her bag before leaving for school.

That afternoon Lena overslept, and Peter had to collect the recyclables without her. When she woke up, she went down to the courtyard and passed nails to Hans as he built the enclosure for their raised garden, the one where turnips would grow. Turnips she'd never get to eat.

She brought him an orange and a banana. "I lost my job," she said to him. "Please don't tell my aunt."

Hans put down his hammer. "There are other jobs. And working at Stasi headquarters? Not such a loss." Though the fresh fruit at his side had a different opinion.

Lena pressed the sharp end of a nail against her fingertip. "I think something very bad is going to happen to me." *I have a copy of your admission forms.*

"It's never as bad as you think," he said. "Whatever it is."

But that wasn't true; sometimes it was worse. Erich was dead. Lena knew too much. And the men who sat under the orange space helmets would get to decide what happened to her. This time, they knew exactly which buttons to press to send her into a black hole.

In the center of the courtyard stood the willow tree, protected by its wall of sticks so no one would step on it by mistake. "Will you take care of it for me?"

"You'll take care of it," Hans said. "You're not going anywhere."

When she came back upstairs Auntie was home, dusting her porcelain dogs with a green rag.

"You don't have a German shepherd in your collection," Lena said. German shepherds were one of the big dogs that the border police used; the ones with the *woof* as deep as a cave.

"I'm missing many breeds." Auntie said this with great sadness.

"Helmut had planned to get me some first-rate porcelain from his brother in the West, but we had to break off contact with him."

If I go to the West, I'll find a store that sells the best porcelain and I'll send you some dogs. One per month, maybe. Not in the mail, because the workers in Department M would either smash them or steal them. She'd send them through Günter Schulmann: Western editor and smuggler of porcelain dogs.

If she went. Would she? How would she endure the tunnel? And what would they do to Auntie? Tell everyone she was a lesbian? Or maybe a prostitute, or a raging alcoholic. She would lose her membership in the Party, all her special relationships. This apartment. Her job as a teacher.

Lena couldn't bear to think about it any longer. It was time to go to Peter's. She wasn't sure she could stomach Military Papa that afternoon, but she was also feeling reckless. There was no longer anything to lose. Erich was dead, and Lena had no future. The worst had happened—or was about to. She could do whatever she wanted.

Lena knocked on their door harder than necessary. When Frau Military Papa answered, Lena said, "Hi. I don't want tea, so you don't have to pretend you want to make me some." She took off her shoes and left them in a crooked heap next to the line of straight ones.

"My goodness, did you leave your manners at home?" Frau Military Papa said.

Military Papa stared at her, straight-backed at his straight table, with all his receipts in straight rows (prolonged applause). "I've a good mind to march right over and tell your aunt how you're behaving."

"Go ahead," Lena said. "She won't be surprised. She is the Guardian of a Difficult Child." (*Standing ovation, Mausi.*) Then she remembered that Military Papa could send her home before she had the chance to transmit her message to Günter Schulmann, so she said "Sorry" and "Where's Peter?" and went back and lined up her shoes.

Peter was in his sanctuary, headphones on, hunched over buttons. He hadn't heard anything. Lena touched his shoulder and he turned around, startled.

"Who are you listening to?" she asked.

He took off the headphones and hung them around his neck. When he unplugged them, the room filled with foreign words. "Peru, I think. Or Argentina. It's Spanish, anyway."

He'd already set up a chair for her, as close to his as possible. Lena sat down, moving it slightly away. Without saying a word, she passed him an orange and his eyes widened. He slipped it into one of his desk drawers.

"What would you like to listen to?" he said.

"Can you get a specific frequency?" Lena asked in her most innocent voice.

"Sure." He moved the dial and static crackled through the room. Frau Military Papa bustled in and said, "Peter, Peter," in a stage whisper, both thumbs vehemently down.

He adjusted the volume. "What should we try?"

"How about—oh, I don't know—14.285?" Lena said, as if she'd pulled the number out of nowhere.

"Wait, what?" Peter stared at her. "What's going on?"

Lena wished he would adjust the dial, but he sat motionless.

"I can't—" she began. "You'd be in trouble just for knowing."

"I won't help you unless I know what you're doing. You have to trust me." His face was solemn.

If he tells his father. But Peter was leaving soon—and Lena had the feeling he wouldn't tell. She drew a deep breath and said, "I need to make contact with someone in West Berlin. It's about my Uncle Erich." She told him Erich was dead, that he'd paid the ultimate price for information that now might never be known. What information? No, Peter didn't need to hear about that. "I have to meet with this man, and your radio is the only way I can get hold of him."

Peter gazed into the corner of his room. Whatever was hovering there must have given him a sign, because he adjusted the dial. They listened.

"It doesn't sound like anyone's there," Lena said.

"You can't tell. Someone could be monitoring."

"Can I say something?" Lena asked. "We have a code."

Peter's disapproving expression made Lena think of his mother's do-you-actually-want-tea face. "You don't have your license. And Father—"

Father: one word that carried the weight of a tank.

"It's a Party slogan," she said. "Even if he overheard, how could he object to that?"

"All right. Quietly," Peter said. "Or you'll get me in trouble." But he didn't seem that worried that he might get into trouble. He sat taller now, as if he had a mission.

Lena picked up the microphone. "How do I start?"

"Use my call," Peter said. "It's Y38XG."

"I'm just supposed to say that?"

"Not exactly." Peter took the mic from her and spoke

quietly. "CQ, CQ, CQ, this is Yankee-three-eight-X-Ray-Golf, Yankee-three-eight-X-Ray-Golf, Yankee-three-eight-X-Ray-Golf, standing by."

For a long time there was only static. Lena could hardly control her impatience. "Try again."

Peter repeated the whole thing. More static, and then, "Yankee-three-eight-X-Ray-Golf, this is Delta-Mike-three-Lima-Tango-Foxtrot, Delta-Mike-three-Lima-Tango-Foxtrot, do you read me? Over."

A wide smile broke out on Peter's face. "Loud and clear, old man. Over."

"He's not actually an old man," Lena said.

"All men are called old on the radio. Is he the one you want to speak to?"

Lena nodded, and Peter handed her the mic. There was a look of admiration on his face, and for once Lena didn't feel small. Even though the game was over, and she'd lost, in that moment she felt as if she were doing something important. She held the microphone, looked at Peter, and said, "Work together, plan together, govern together." As soon as she put the mic down, he adjusted the dial to another frequency.

"I did it," she whispered. "Was that all right?"

"It was brilliant."

She glanced back at the partially open bedroom door, waiting for the silhouette of Military Papa to appear. It didn't.

"Thank you. I hope you don't get into trouble with your father."

He stared straight ahead at the notes he'd tacked onto the radio. "So what if I do? I don't care anymore. I'll be gone in a week."

Me too. Sooner than a week. Monday.

In one corner of the room Peter had piled books, a hairbrush, a small stack of folded clothes. Lena should probably start a pile of her own. Bland things—slippers, porridge, scratchy gray nightgowns.

"I don't want to go," he said.

Neither do I. "It's only for a year and a half." Though it would be longer if Military Papa insisted that Peter extend his service—which he would. *It's not the rest of your life.*

The rest of her life meant arranging colored noodles alongside that boy with the unfocused eyes, and enduring the girl who screamed if you touched her blanket or mentioned the color orange. The nurses would rush in with the strong man whose job it was to pin the girl's arms to her sides and take her to the quiet room so she could have her outburst in private. Of all the colors for her to be afraid of, it had to be orange. Half the decor in the Better Germany was orange.

It had been a long time since Lena had thought about the people she'd left behind in the hospital. She hadn't planned to see them again. They were probably still there, their lives stuck on the same page. That was what it meant to be crazy. You got stuck—on orange, or wasps—and then the people around you started speaking as if every word was wearing socks.

"You can write to me," Lena said. How many lies had been told to her to make her feel better? *Your parents died in an accident. We can get your uncle out. It's all going to be fine.*

"Can I?" The way Peter's brown eyes brightened in his narrow face, as if writing to Lena was the one thing that would make military service endurable, Lena knew the lie was necessary. Sometimes honesty was too cruel.

There was a commotion in the other room; Military Papa was going out. That meant all life stopped so that he could get ready. When the front door finally shut, Peter turned up the volume on the radio and he and Lena listened to people talking in South Africa, and Tokyo. Soon Frau Military Papa stood in the doorway, which meant Lena had stayed long enough.

"Thank you," she said to Peter. Should she hug him? *You might never see him again.* But it was too soon to believe that, and she didn't want to alarm him. She left his bedroom, passing the kitchen table, where Military Papa's receipts were still sitting in perfect rows. When no one was watching, Lena brushed a hand across the table and messed them up. Probably Frau Military Papa would notice before he got home, and would straighten them herself, which was less satisfying than imagining him coming home to the mess. But still—she had done it.

*

There was a note in Lena's mailbox the next morning. She was to meet Günter Schulmann in the pub in Prenzlauer Berg at two o'clock. Auntie and a friend were going out for a walk that afternoon after their Sunday roast. Lena laced up her Zehas, *because you never know when you might have to be fast,* and wondered if this would be her last day of freedom.

Günter Schulmann's face was so earnest. He should have been a scholar, or a scientist working to discover the cure for a dangerous disease. There was something foreign about him that Lena couldn't put her finger on. Maybe it was the cut of his clothes, or the way he smelled like chocolate—*Milka* chocolate, not the lentil-colored *Fetzer* bars she knew. When he spotted Lena walking toward him, he stood up and held the table with both hands. Lena wished she had something to offer that was worthy of his excitement. If only she hadn't been greedy for that last bit of evidence. If she hadn't taken the camera with her that last evening, she'd still have it. Proof: validation of Erich's life, and an explanation for his death. Instead she had nothing.

It must have been all over her face, because Herr Schulmann's hopeful expression popped like a balloon and he sat back down. "What happened? You didn't find anything?"

Lena sat down across from him. There was a plate of meat and cheese on the table, and a small glass of beer that she didn't want. "No: I did. I found everything. That ammunitions factory—they were planning a takeover of West Berlin. Day X: it was all organized—a three-day plan. They blew up the factory on purpose because someone was going to talk. No one was supposed to have—" She couldn't say it. "That part actually was an accident."

"And Erich?" He was still perched forward, as if surely Lena had some good news.

"He's dead." She'd wanted to be matter-of-fact about it, but the word caught in her throat like a bone. She took a gulp of beer after all, and another.

Herr Schulmann put a hand on her arm. "Are you sure?"

"I saw the preliminary death report."

"Then you're not sure. It might have been a sham. It might have been—"

"Don't." Hope could be something sturdy, a life raft. But false hope was a life raft with a hole in the bottom. "I am sure." Herr Dreck's face—*you can't fake that kind of smugness.*

"Didn't you take photographs?" he asked.

Lena nodded. "He—they—they've got the camera. So—great. I know what happened. You know what happened. But the rest of the world will never know."

"I'll get you another one."

"Don't you understand?" Lena's voice rose, and Herr Schulmann gave her a look that told her to tone it down. "I've lost my job. They're going to send me somewhere terrible, probably the mental hospital where I was before."

"Lena, they can't do that. They need a reason to commit you."

"Maybe on your side of the Wall they do. Here they just need a pen."

Herr Schulmann looked away. He took a long sip of beer and set the glass on the table with care, so that it didn't make any noise. No sudden movements. See? *Already he's putting hats and mittens on everything.*

"I'm getting you out of this place," he said.

"Forget it. They're watching me. They've been watching all along. You want to get someone out? Help my friend. He was supposed to go through a tunnel with two other boys, but it turns out one of them has been telling the Stasi everything."

"I'll get you both out. I know people who can make up false documents. You'll go through Romania. I'll organize a plan."

Lena laughed. "Between now and tomorrow morning? Good luck."

Herr Schulmann took a notepad and pencil from his briefcase. "What's his name? Your friend. Where do I find him?"

Lena wrote down Max's name and the name of the theater. "They're watching him too. I saw his file. He's a flight risk."

"We'll make new identities for both of you. All I need are photographs. My people are wizards with travel documents."

Do they have magic wands? Can they make Herr Dreck disappear? That was the only solution that would work for Lena. But she promised to leave a photograph in the mailbox. Let Herr Schulmann think his plan would work.

She took a few bites of meat and cheese, drank some more of the beer, and agreed to meet one of his contacts on Tuesday—if she was still walking the streets freely by then. But when their meeting was over, she wasn't ready to go home. What, then? She couldn't bear to face Max and tell him about the mental hospital. No one treated you the same way once they knew you'd been locked up, even if both your parents had been killed in an explosion.

Lena went to the park where she and Erich used to go together. She sat on one of the benches and imagined her hands getting sticky with every vanilla ice cream she'd ever eaten. Though it was cool and windy outside, she felt all the past suns warm her back, and saw all the children learning to walk, and the lovers holding hands, and the old men doddering on their canes, and the single women pulling their misbehaving dogs home. Turns out this had been the *schrullig* world: all the time she'd spent with her uncle on Sundays. It was quirky, outlandish, impossible. And it was gone.

The thought that this had been taken from her made her so incredibly angry she marched over to Erich's building, went up the stairs, and leaned on Friedrich So-and-So's bell. "Yes?" came his irritated voice, like she'd interrupted him spilling something else on his undershirt. By the time he opened the door, she had already crept down the stairs.

She waited half a minute, enough time for him to sit back down, then ran up and pressed the bell again.

"Yes? Who's there?" he called.

It's Sunday, she wanted to scream, *and I'm supposed to be visiting my uncle, and he's supposed to live here, and he's supposed to be alive, and you have no right to be answering this door.* But she hid on the second floor and said nothing.

She let half a minute pass, then rang again.

"Listen, you little shit, I'm going to call the police," came the voice from behind the door.

"Flower delivery, sir," Lena said.

"Oh. Forgive me."

Before the door opened, Lena took off. She needed to go home. She needed to have the talk with Auntie. But when she got home, it turned out Auntie had bought her some pretty hair barrettes from a vendor at the S-Bahn. There didn't seem to be any way to slip *I lost my job and your brother is dead* into casual conversation. So she said nothing.

– 27 –

THE TRUTH SHALL SET YOU FREE

For the first Sunday night in the history of Sunday nights, Lena slept. Sleeping was easy. She didn't have to think. She didn't have to lie about what she was doing. There was no opportunity to wonder what would happen next. She woke up rested and ready to line up for Monday-morning ham and bring it home to Auntie, who included some in their breakfast along with a boiled egg and a cup of real coffee.

Auntie had planted the turnips and collards in boxes on the adjustable multifunction table by the window. "You'll be sure to water them this morning," she said.

Lena nodded.

"And you will do something useful with your time today. Help in the courtyard, take out the trash. Before your photography class."

Nod, nod, nod—Lena's head was a moving toy. *Photography* was another one of those words now.

What would she do when the time came to go to work? Well, they hadn't terminated her yet. If she hadn't heard anything, she would go. And face Herr Dreck? She'd bring Jutta. Jutta would understand.

After Auntie left for work, Lena did everything that was expected of her—all the while watching the telephone as if it were a live animal. She waited for the knock at the door. How would they do it? What would they say? Would they take her directly to the hospital, or would she have a chance to say goodbye first?

By eleven o'clock nothing had happened.

At midday, Lena stopped peering out the window. She chose a novel from her shelf, sat on her bed, and was completely immersed in chapter one when the buzzer rang.

They're here. That was her first thought. Her second was *don't answer it*. Right. They would use their own key, and they'd stomp up the stairs and pound on Auntie's door, and the baby next door would start to cry, and anyone who was home would open their doors very slowly and peer into the corridor so that later, when others came home, they could say, "They came to Adelheid's this afternoon. It was the orphan, the difficult one. They took her away."

Lena got up, and with stiff legs and a heart so heavy she could barely carry it she went to the intercom and said, "Yes?"

"You're home, thank God. It's me. Can I come up?" It was Max.

Lena slumped in relief. "Yes, come up."

She waited at the door until he knocked, and let him in, and let him envelop her with his cold arms so that she could breathe and breathe until she'd taken the scent of him into every part of her body. He kissed her forehead, the tip of her nose, and then his lips found hers and she forgot about every bad thing that was going to happen, and thought only of how she wanted to stay here, this close to him, for the rest of her life.

He led her to the sitting room. She sat down. He switched on the television and turned the volume up as loud as it would go, then sat beside her. *Glück Muss Man Haben* was on. *One Must Have Luck.* If you were very lucky on the show, you could win a Trabi.

"Your friend came to see me yesterday," he said into her ear. "Günter Schulmann."

What did he tell you? But she already knew by the way he'd held her at the door and kissed her. Günter Schulmann had told him she was in trouble. Max took off his coat slowly, watching her the way a person would watch a bomb.

"You have to come to the West with me," Max said. Cheers erupted on the television show.

She tried to block out the sound. "I can't. I'll ruin my aunt's life." The porcelain dogs stared at her with their creepy eyes. *You've already ruined it,* they said.

He crossed his arms. "Then I'm not going."

"What are you talking about? Herr Schulmann can help you. He can get you out. You have to go." *Anyway, what if—* "What if we don't get along? On the other side."

Max took her hands in his. She still wasn't used to the sensation—the size of his fingers, their strength. "We'll be giving ourselves a chance at a better life. That's the point. If it turns out we don't stay together, then we don't stay together." He cupped her face in his hands. "But we'll be free. Otherwise—"

Otherwise, you get to go to a pastel landscape and eat bland food for the rest of your life, and he gets to act in moronic plays like Factory: A Love Story.

One of the teams on the television show had given a wrong answer. There was pandemonium on the screen. Max took his hands away. "Is it true what Günter said about them threatening to lock you up?"

Lena nodded. "It happened once before, after my parents died." They didn't just die. *They were killed. At last you have someone to blame.* But what did that matter? The people responsible were bigger than she was. They were hunters. They had all the guns, all the buttons to press, and all the forms to sign.

"And now? Günter said you'd found out something important."

Yes, Lena had found the truth. *The truth shall set you free.* Not in the Better Germany, it wouldn't. In the Better Germany, the truth got you locked up. To live in this world, you needed to be able to do three things: keep your head down, keep your mouth shut, and learn to like cabbage. Lena had only mastered the third thing, and now look.

"It doesn't matter," she said. The less he knew, the better—for his sake.

"It must matter to them. Come with me. Günter is getting false identities for both of us. You'll need to be ready. We're going to be part of an East German circus traveling to Romania."

Laughter came from the television. "A circus?" Lena said. "And who will I be—the tightrope walker?"

"Why not? There will be jugglers and flame-swallowers and a bearded lady."

"Well, then. We'll blend right in," Lena said. "What about the police at the train station?" They were always on the lookout for people they suspected were trying to flee the country.

"We'll be part of a group. That's why it's a good idea. The circus is leaving for Romania on Thursday, and we'll go with them. Once we get there, we'll make a magical transformation into West Germans, and then we'll get on a plane and fly home to Munich."

Thursday: that was three days from now. A lot could happen in three days, and even so—what about Auntie? "I don't know."

"But you'll think about it." Max shut off the television.

Sure. In the meantime, she curled herself into his body like a cat, tucking her head under his chin and pressing her ear to his chest, listening to the life flow through him. *At least you've had this.* It was something to be thankful for, even if it got taken away from her. He wove the fingers of one hand through hers, and stroked her hair with the other. They sat like this for a long time, an island of beating hearts in this brown and orange room.

Finally Max said, "I should go. They'll be waiting for me at the theater."

She lifted her head and kissed his warm neck. "I wish you could stay."

"So do I." He kissed her, then stood up and put on his coat. "Günter's friend will come see me with the details. I'll let you know as soon as I hear more."

The dogs' eyes were fixed on her. *Stop staring at me. I don't know if I'm going.* She said goodbye to Max, gave him another kiss at the door, and then he was gone, his footsteps echoing down the stairs. She went to the window, waiting to see him leave the building and cross the street.

Would she sit Auntie down and tell her she was leaving? Or would she simply disappear? *And then Auntie will worry about you and telephone the police.* Wouldn't it be better if she knew?

Wouldn't it be better if she didn't?

What if Auntie came too? *Are you kidding? Auntie, leave the Better Germany?* Mausi was right: Sausage Auntie would never leave.

There was Max, a walking contradiction—the military precision, and the hair that wouldn't behave. The lemony scent of his soap was still on Lena's skin. And there, parked on the street, was a Lada, with a man inside reading a newspaper.

Surprise.

Lena sat down. Picked up her book, then put it down. Stood up, looked out the window. The man was still there. Maybe he wasn't there for her. *Stop. You can't afford to play these games anymore. You know that's why he's there.*

Lena got her coat and put on her regular shoes. Not her Zehas: there was no point running from these men. She'd go for a walk, see what happened. If the man in the Lada had something to say to her, he could say it.

She turned the lock twice and went down the stairs, into the cold. It was windy, and the sky was darker than it should have been for mid-afternoon. Rain was coming. Lena thought immediately of the courtyard, and the willow tree. It hadn't had much time to set down roots. One big rain might wash it away.

The courtyard was not yet the refuge that Lena and Auntie had envisioned, but they had made progress. The trench gathered rainwater so the ground wasn't as muddy, the military bushes stood sentry against subversive winds, and the raised garden

Hans had built in the corner would soon be full of plants. Even the tile path to nowhere would one day lead to the other side of the housing development. Lena might never see that happen. The courtyard's unfinished state was suddenly painful to her. If only they'd worked harder, she might have had one game of *Skat* at a table outside with Peter and Danika.

She hunched herself against the wind, wishing for one of the winter coats in Jutta's magazine. Walked past the Lada without looking at it. Waited. Waited. *See?* There must have been other class enemies living on her street, and she'd had no idea.

And then—there were footsteps behind her. Someone tapped her on the shoulder. "Citizen Altmann?"

Lena turned around. It was a plump bald man in a brown suit. "Yes?"

"Come, please. A little chat. It will only take a moment."

He led her to the car and opened the door to the backseat. The man in the driver's seat was still reading his newspaper. His fingers were black with ink.

So—there'd been two of them. The plump bald one must have been waiting outside, hiding somewhere. Lena got in, wondering which side of the car she should sit on. She hadn't been in many cars in her life. The Lada smelled like mustard and bratwurst, and newsprint, and sweat. Should she put on the safety belt? Her hands were shaking so badly she wasn't sure she'd be able to fasten it.

She decided to sit right in the middle. She waited for the men to turn around and speak to her, but they stared straight ahead, as if the car were moving.

The bald man in the passenger seat held up a small camera that Lena recognized. "You're in a lot of trouble, Citizen Altmann."

Lena nodded. There was no denying it now.

"You understand that if this camera were to land in the wrong hands, you would be charged with treason."

Lena was quite sure it was in the wrong hands right now.

"Do you know what the punishment for treason is in this country?" he asked.

She nodded again. It was the death sentence: execution by one close shot to the back of the head.

"However, you have a friend in the ministry," he continued. "A special relationship with Lieutenant General Drechsler, isn't that so?"

Lena wanted to say *no*. She wanted to scream it. But *no* was the wrong answer, and in this case, the wrong answer might get her killed. So she said *yes* in a small voice, because she was small and Bruno Drechsler was huge.

"The Lieutenant General has argued for clemency. Do you know what clemency means?"

Lena was tempted to smack this man on the back of his round bald head. "Yes," she said politely. "My aunt taught me that word."

"He believes it would be an act of kindness on the part of the State to return you to the institution that took care of you after your parents died."

They didn't just die. They were killed. Lena's hands curled around the cold edge of the brown leather seat. An act of kindness—were they kidding?

"Would you like that? Would you like to go back to the hospital?"

"No!" The word leaped out of Lena's mouth. "Please, I'll work somewhere else. A textile factory. Anywhere. Please don't send me back there."

The inky man rattled his newspaper. "I don't see why not. A warm bed, three meals a day. It's better than a bullet to the head." He spoke in a flat voice.

But the plump bald man said, "Kurt, the girl doesn't want to go. We're reasonable people. Surely there's a job at a textile factory for a pretty young girl like Miss Lena, isn't there?"

The inky man shrugged.

"The thing is—" The bald man turned in his seat and smiled at Lena. His teeth were stained and his lips were chapped.

What is the thing? Do you even want to know? Lena knew three things: head down, mouth shut, eat cabbage. Was there a fourth?

"The thing is, you want something from us. But we're not in the charity business, you know? If you want something, you must give us something in exchange. That's fair, wouldn't you say?"

Lena realized she was supposed to nod, so she did, but she did not like where this conversation was going.

"You have a friend."

Lena waited.

"Max Baumann. He left your apartment a few minutes ago. You know Max Baumann, don't you?"

"Yes." Lena couldn't lie. They'd seen him.

"Max Baumann is planning on doing something very silly. He's going to try to escape from the Republic. Can you imagine?"

"That's not true," Lena said.

"Please." The inky man rustled the newspaper and it made a sound like dead leaves.

"We know about his plans to escape with his actor friends. And we suspect, given the present circumstances, that Citizen

Baumann has asked you to come. You're not thinking of joining them in that tunnel, are you?"

"No, I'm not." Lena had never thought the tunnel was a good idea.

"We've had some trouble finding out when your friends are planning on carrying out this adventure of theirs. But you seem to have a very special relationship with Citizen Baumann. Perhaps you might overhear something interesting. I can't make any promises. But it could go a long way toward keeping you out of the hospital."

"I don't see why she doesn't want to go there," the newspaper man said again. He didn't even look up.

"You've never been there," Lena said. *That's enough. Don't tell them things they don't need to know.*

"What do you think, Lena? Can you find out the details for us? You understand that failing to report a planned defection is a punishable offense."

Say you'll find out. Just say yes, and figure it out later. "I could try."

"Try hard," the inky man said.

The car fell silent. Lena could hear the wind outside.

"You know about Max, don't you?" the plump bald man said.

What does he mean? Lena said nothing.

"You know he still sees that figure skater. What's her name? Rhea? Ruta?"

"Rita." The inky man put down his paper. "She's a hot one."

The bald man went on. "My friend here has a thing for red hair. Me, not so much. But apparently Citizen Baumann likes them fiery."

"Hot." The newspaper man turned and winked at Lena.

"But Max would have told you he already has a girlfriend." The plump bald man set the camera on the dashboard. "Well, then. Shall we meet back here tomorrow? Around the same time? What do you say?"

Lena couldn't say anything. Her mouth was stuck shut. Her body felt heavier than it ever had in her life. "Can I go now?"

"Silly girl, you've always been free to go."

She slid to the passenger side of the Lada and fumbled with the door handle, pulling harder and harder until she realized the door was locked. As soon as she had unlocked it, she got out, and shut the door in such a rush she nearly caught her hand in it.

She ran across the street without turning around. When she arrived back in the apartment she went to the window. They hadn't moved.

– 28 –

THE USEFULNESS OF A BABY NEXT DOOR

Lena and Auntie were having supper. It was Monday night, Black Channel night, a work night for Lena. No one had telephoned or shown up to tell her that her employment at Stasi headquarters had been terminated. Maybe Bruno Drechsler had changed his mind. What that might mean for her tonight at work Lena didn't even want to consider.

Tell Auntie.

She struggled with her ham sandwich. She wasn't the least bit hungry.

"We've had a response to our swimming pool complaint," Auntie said between bites. Her appetite was more than making up for Lena's lack of one. "Our letter has been passed on to the proper authorities."

"That's wonderful." Someone in the neighborhood would get to go swimming. It wouldn't be Lena. *Tell her now. Get it over with.* Tell her what? Which part would she want to hear?

"The leaks will be repaired, and the roof. In the meantime, the whole building could use a proper cleaning. We could form a work brigade."

Not another one. After the turnips were planted outside, they wouldn't be able to work on the courtyard until spring came—therefore, *yes, let's clean the pool building while we're waiting.* Lena finished her sandwich and got ready for work.

As soon as she was outside, she took a long look up and down the street. The Lada was gone. Lena walked quickly at first, because of the cold, then more slowly as she drew closer to the compound. Nothing about this felt good. They had called what she'd done treason—and it was. She'd photographed documents, like an enemy spy out of some Western movie: James Bond, except without the clever weapons or exotic drinks.

Thank goodness it was Ernst at the gate. She spotted his long arms from half a block away as he stood sentry beneath the lights.

"Good morning," she called when she was near. At least she'd see one friendly face.

"Comrade Altmann." He stood with his legs planted like posts and wouldn't let her pass. "I'm sorry, you don't have clearance anymore."

It would be like that, would it? She shouldn't have been surprised. *Your arms are too long,* she wanted to yell at him, but it wasn't Ernst's fault. He was only doing what he'd been told.

Now what? Go home and explain everything to Auntie? Auntie would yell until it was time for the Black Channel. Then Lena would have to sit through Schnitzler's whole tirade, and afterward lie awake in bed for hours waiting for the ceiling to fall on her, piece by tiny piece.

Wait a minute. *Auntie doesn't know you've been fired.*

Lena felt around in her pocket. There was the single ticket to *Factory: A Love Story*, which was still playing, even though there couldn't have been many people in the audience anymore. *Rita.* A wave of heat rushed through Lena. *He already has a girlfriend.* Sure he did. Lena worked nights. She was probably his daytime girlfriend, and Rita was for later. She marched over to the U-Bahn station. The night was wide open ahead of her. It was time to settle this.

What will you do about the men in the Lada? The exchange they'd demanded. Was Max even planning to go with Lena and the circus troupe, or had that just been a story? Maybe their tunnel scheme was still going ahead.

She transferred onto the S-Bahn and sat very still, wishing she could trade lives with anyone else on the train. Like that man in the corner—she could be him, gripping his battered briefcase and staring straight ahead at nothing. She'd be the lady holding a mesh bag of potatoes and wishing people wouldn't stare at the giant red birthmark on her face. Everyone on the train was carrying something in their heart that weighed them down. *If we could all say one, two, three, drop it, the train would become so light it would lift off the tracks.* That was the trick, to stop carrying the heavy things; to learn how to put them down and walk away.

When she arrived at the People's Theater, she took a seat near the back. There were fifteen people in the audience, including her. *Factory: A Love Story* had been bad enough the first time. Seeing it again made Lena angry. There was a cast of eight: eight people wasting their lives memorizing the dumbest lines in the history of theater. For what?

This time Max knew all the ingredients for borscht. There was no way he could see Lena so far back in the dark. *Good. You'll surprise him.* Maybe Rita would be waiting for him, and Lena could run over and kick her in the shins.

But when the play was over and Lena went backstage, it was just the actors. Someone had brought beer, and they were drinking it, but it didn't seem like a celebration. No one was talking. It was more like *Factory: A Love Story* had inspired each of them to drink alone, in the same room.

Dieter saw her first. "Max, your girlfriend's here."

Lena glanced around to make sure Rita hadn't snuck up behind her, but no, *he meant you.*

Max took off his chef's hat and pulled the cushion out from beneath his apron. "Right, you're not working tonight. I'd forgotten." He led her away from the group, took in the expression on her face, and said, "I'll get my coat."

Outside, Max draped his arm around Lena, but she pulled away. "Tell me the truth about that girl Rita. You're still seeing her, aren't you?"

"What? No, I saw her once when I got back from service, but we both knew it was over. You and I have been through this. Why are you so worked up about—"

"There's no circus troupe, is there? You're still planning on going with Bem and Dieter."

"Who talked to you? What's happened?"

It began to drizzle, and they took cover beneath the awning of a restaurant with darkened windows. The paint was peeling off the building, and bits of molding had broken away. Across the street was a bakery with half its sign missing. Lena wondered if you'd only get half a bun in there, or half a loaf of bread. Everything in the city was dying.

"They told me. Everything. You're still planning on leaving through the tunnel." Lena's nose began to run and she wished she had a tissue. Wiping her face with the back of her hand seemed like the wrong thing to do in front of Max. She tried sniffling, but it made an awful sound and didn't solve the problem.

"That's what I've been telling Bem. He asks me nearly every day. He must be reporting it all to them."

Lena studied Max's wind-reddened cheeks, his dark eyes. She could smell the beer on his breath. "How do I know you're telling me the truth?"

"Günter's contact is bringing our documents tomorrow. Ask him. We're meeting with him to discuss everything around noon. Is that okay? Can you come? I was going to suggest meeting at your apartment, but—"

"No. They were sitting outside my building all afternoon. They saw you leave." Herr Schulmann wouldn't lie, that much Lena knew. "Why isn't he coming himself?"

"They've been following him, and he just did a day trip. He doesn't want to take any chances. How about we meet at the pub?"

"Sure." Lena sighed. "If they haven't arrested me by then. They want me to give them all the details. When you're planning to go, with whom."

Max picked at the crumbling building. "Then you'll tell them."

"What do you mean?"

"Tell them I'm going on Thursday night with Bem and Dieter. They'll be watching the tunnel at Bernauer Strasse. Meanwhile we'll be at the train station with the bearded lady, a lion tamer, and a bunch of tiny gymnasts, on our way to Bucharest." He cupped her face with his hands. "You are going to come, aren't you? You must."

It was happening too fast. Lena needed a moment, a week, a lifetime, to catch up. "I don't know. I can't decide. Please don't push me."

"I'm not pushing you, but time is running out and you don't exactly have options. You need to save yourself. Isn't that what your uncle would have wanted?"

Lena stared at the broken bakery sign. It said *kerei*. It was missing the *Bäc* at the beginning. It didn't make sense without it. Erich must have been in a position similar to hers right before they'd taken him. He'd had crucial information; he might even have had proof. But he hadn't been planning to run off to the West with it. Maybe because his life wouldn't have made sense over there. Maybe because it wouldn't have made sense without her. Was that too much to hope for?

What would he have wanted for Lena? For her to be happy, sure, but also for her to feel at home, to have a place that was as familiar as worn slippers or a favorite chipped mug. That place had been Magdeburg, with her parents, but it was gone. Erich had been home for her after that. And now—where was home? Was it with Max? She thought of her bedroom, with the subversive pictures, and the courtyard with its persistent willow tree, and Auntie in her home perm making the cold-egg face. Oma and Opa had passed away years ago. Auntie was the only family she had left. If Lena went to the West, she would never be able to come back again, not even as a tourist.

"I need to go home," she said.

Max held her for a long time. "Are you going to be all right?"

She nodded, though she wasn't sure it was true. They walked back to the theater and Max kissed her with the taste of beer in his mouth and said he would see her tomorrow at the pub. By then her mind would have to be made up.

*

She tried her best to enter the apartment quietly, but one, two turns of the lock, and there was Auntie standing in the hallway in her housecoat and slippers, a book in her hand as if she'd been waiting up.

"I had a telephone call," she said.

The phone had rung? Lena would have liked to be there to hear it. Had it been loud? Had it startled the baby next door?

"It was an agent from Stasi headquarters, telling me you were no longer employed there. Is this true?"

Lena took off her coat and hung it up. "Yes." There was no reason to pretend anymore. "I'm sorry, Auntie. I didn't mean for it to happen."

"Did you shirk your duties? I haven't raised you to be a shirker. The fellow wouldn't tell me what had happened."

"I looked at the papers." It was the most straightforward of explanations, and the truest.

"You looked at the papers."

"In the agents' drawers."

"In House 1, at Stasi headquarters, where the most important men in the country work."

Auntie took off her reading glasses and clutched them so tightly Lena was afraid she might crush them. "Didn't you know you weren't supposed to do that? Haven't I told you a thousand times?"

"Uncle Erich is dead."

Auntie's glasses fell to the floor. She ran a hand through her permed hair and blinked several times. Lena took two steps toward her and Auntie took her in her arms.

"Are you sure?" she said.

"I saw the preliminary death report," Lena said.

"How?"

"It was sitting on the—"

"No," Auntie said. "How did he die?"

Lena wiped her eyes on Auntie's housecoat. "The report said natural causes. The man—" How should she refer to him? Herr Drechsler? Comrade Dreck? The terrible man who'd made her do terrible things? She would not use his fancy military title. "He said Uncle had lung cancer."

Auntie frowned. "He'd never mentioned it. Did you know?"

Lena shook her head. "It isn't true."

"You don't know that." Auntie bent to pick up her glasses. The slow, awkward way she folded herself to the floor and back up again made her seem old and fragile. "All that time he'd spent in the mines—and his smoking. He might have wanted to spare us. He cared for you very much, you know."

"Mama and Papa didn't work in a freight car factory. They were making ammunition. The State was planning a takeover of West Berlin. The explosion wasn't an accident. It—"

Auntie's hand came flying out to cover Lena's mouth. "Hush." Her eyes were wide. "You're getting hysterical. I'll make you some warm milk and you'll feel better." She took her hand away.

"I don't want warm milk," Lena said.

"Yes, you do."

She led Lena to the kitchen, sat her down, and turned on the radio, her mouth pressed into a firm line. When she pointed at the walls, Lena knew what she meant. You could hear everything through those walls, and everything could hear you.

The radio played loud marching music. "You'll wake the baby next door," Lena said.

Auntie fixed Lena with a strange look. She took out a pot and a large spoon and banged away until three, two, one, there he was, screaming his head off. Then she sat close to Lena.

"You mustn't talk like that. No matter what you found out, and not even if it's true. They came here tonight. They want to send you back to the hospital. They asked me to sign some forms, but I refused. You must straighten up, Lena, please. For your own good. I don't know how long I'll be able to hold them off this time."

Lena held her aunt's formidable arm. It was like holding a sturdy tree branch. "I can't go back there," she said.

Auntie put a firm hand over Lena's. "Drink your milk, and go to bed."

Lena stood up, went to the table in the corner of the sitting room where Helmut lived, and lit the candle. She looked up. She looked left.

"Auntie? We need to talk."

- 29 -

A NEW COAT

Auntie invited the two men up for coffee, real West German coffee, which put them in a good mood, even the man with inky hands. It was late the following afternoon. They'd been sitting in the Lada all day.

"Lena has something to tell you," Auntie said.

Lena sat with her hands in her lap, twisting them as if they were soaked with water and she was trying to wring it all out. Earlier that afternoon she'd snuck away and met with Max and Günter Schulmann's friend in the pub. The barman had waved and smiled and asked how she was. That had been strange enough. But the strangest part of the meeting had been seeing her face on a Western passport. Günter had used the photograph she'd left in the mailbox for the false documents. He had connections to intelligence, which meant access to the printers that the government used for regular passports. The right ink. The right paper.

They would use forged East German papers to get to Romania, in case their names were on a watch list. In Bucharest, they would trade their documents for Western ones and board an airplane for Munich. Lena's were hidden beneath her mattress. She was terrified the papers would somehow reveal themselves that afternoon, give off a bad smell, or start beeping.

Don't think about the passports. "Max is planning to leave on Thursday," she said to the men.

"Tell them the plan." Auntie stirred her coffee vigorously. "Tell them everything."

And Lena did.

*

"That's good, Lena," the plump bald man said when she had finished. "You've done the right thing. We're arranging for a new place of employment for you. There are openings in the Clara Zetkin rayon factory in Elsterberg—"

"No!" Lena took a breath to settle herself. "I mean, I'd like to stay here in Berlin, with my aunt."

The two men glanced at each other. Auntie went into the kitchen and came out with the entire package of Western coffee, pressing it into the bald man's hands. His hands were small, like a woman's. They would probably be damp. He nodded and said, "We'll look into it, won't we, Kurt?"

The inky man shrugged, as though Lena's future was the thing he cared least about in the world.

"There must be other cleaning jobs in Berlin," Auntie said. "Ones that don't require security clearance."

"I imagine so." The plump bald man closed his notepad and tucked away his pen. "We'll be in touch."

Lena watched from the window as the men got into their Lada and drove away.

"I'm sorry you had to do that," Auntie said loudly. "It's a terrible thing to break a friend's confidence, but rules are rules and he should have known better."

Max wasn't just a friend. He was her boyfriend, maybe even her One True Love, though *it's better not to think that way.* Lena wanted to shout, *It was me in the foyer, kissing him. That girl you called a Monika, it was me.* But she needed Auntie on her side.

She and Auntie had supper together, and then Lena went to bed. She listened as the crashing started in the bathroom, and then stopped. She waited until she heard Auntie's bedroom door click shut. Then she slid the documents out from under her mattress.

Herr Schulmann's friend had done a top-notch job. There was Lena's face next to a different name, a different place of birth. It was odd to think of another life waiting for her, something she could slip into as if it were a new coat: *the winter coat you've always wanted from the magazine.*

"You are not to see each other between now and Thursday," Herr Schulmann's friend had advised Lena and Max that afternoon. "No matter how much you might like to. It's important, do you understand?"

Lena understood. But it didn't stop her from crying herself to sleep.

*

The next couple of days were busy. Arrangements were made for Lena to take a cleaning job at one of the train stations. She would start the following week. Peter was packing for military service, and kept showing up at her door at odd hours to make sure she had his address, and the recyclables box, and this, and that. Once he arrived with a small bag. In it was the swanky purple shirt.

"Will you take care of it for me? My mother—she'll clean while I'm away. She'll find it for sure, and she'll feel obliged to show it to Father. I'll never hear the end of it."

Of course Lena would take it. Peter leaned in to hug her, and she let him.

On Thursday afternoon, she went to the courtyard with Auntie to check on the tree. Auntie had gotten hold of some fertilizer, and she and Lena mixed it into the soil.

"I believe it's taken root," Auntie said. "It doesn't look quite so sad anymore."

Lena thought the tree was maybe the saddest thing she'd ever seen in her life. She touched its branches and whispered goodbye.

– 30 –

THE GREAT SLEEPING GIRL

It turned out palm trees were a real thing, not something that only appeared on cakes. Coconuts grew from them. Ukuleles were also real. People in Hawaii knew how to play them. Lena lay completely still, listening to the wind rustle the branches of the palm trees, listening to the surf, and the plink-plink *of the miniature guitars that sounded like toys.*

There would be drinks coming, with tiny paper umbrellas and slices of pineapple. There would be sand between her toes and in her hair and under her fingernails. There was no Herr Dreck in Hawaii.

Max lay beside her in the sun, holding her hand. By now she knew the shape of every one of his fingers. If ever she were to go blind, she would be able to identify him by his hands. His conscription haircut had grown out, but that section in the front still refused to behave. He would always have a bit of Prenzlauer Berg in him.

"Here we are, Lena. Here's a little something to settle you down."

Lena stuck out her hand for the pill. The little something calmed her nerves, but it also dulled every sharp edge in her mind and muffled her instincts.

"Here's your juice," said the nurse. In a plastic cup. So much of the Better Germany was made of plastic. All it would take was one really hot day and the entire country would melt.

"Where's the umbrella?" Lena asked.

"What do you need an umbrella for?"

"In the cup," Lena said. "With the pineapple."

"Honestly," the nurse said with a huff. "How do you expect to fit an umbrella into that cup?"

Silly girl, what are you thinking? This was the real world, where umbrellas were for rain, and orange was a wild animal, and you could play with colored noodles all afternoon if you wanted to.

Lena shared a room with a girl who saw people that weren't there. When they appeared, she screamed at them. *And you complained about the baby next door.* Twice a week Auntie came to visit. She tried numerous times to give Lena's roommate a talking to. Soon the girl hid under her covers whenever Auntie showed up.

On her first visit, Sausage Auntie had brought a postcard from Munich. Two words were written on the back: *Thank you.* Lena knew it was from Max. He'd made it; he was out. Her heart ached as she thought of the documents that were probably still hidden beneath her mattress. She could have gone with him. Those Stasi agents had been convinced she was telling them the truth when she'd given them the details about the escape through the

Bernauer Strasse tunnel. Even Auntie had said she should go with Max and the circus, that night when Lena had told her everything. But Lena couldn't do it. She had trusted Auntie with her biggest secrets, and Auntie hadn't betrayed her. Auntie had done such a good acting job, she could have been the star of *Factory: A Love Story.*

Thursday night on Bernauer Strasse, there must have been a pack of agents waiting to swoop down on the three boys. All they would have found was their informer, Bem, probably sweaty and confused—checking his watch, the moon, his shoelaces. "They said they were coming," he would have told the agents. But Max had warned Dieter not to go. That night he would have been doing his best to blend in with the circus troupe, possibly carrying the bearded lady's suitcase, or the lion tamer's chair.

Lena had spent a long time imagining Max's anxiety at the train station. Imagining him waiting for her, watching each train that arrived, hoping she would show up—while she sat on her bed, an overnight bag beside her, Auntie pacing in the kitchen. Auntie had marched over and opened Lena's door without knocking. "If you're going, you need to leave." The way she'd stood in the doorway not knowing what to do with her arms, then rushed in and hugged Lena harder than she ever had before—Lena knew it was her way of saying, "Go, you can go." But also, "Please don't, because my life is nothing without you in it."

Maybe Lena had been foolish not to take the opportunity to escape. At the meeting with Herr Schulmann's friend, she'd promised she would be at the station; she had to be sure Max would go. But in the end, she couldn't do it. Auntie was gruff sometimes, and stern, but she needed Lena, and it felt good to be needed.

Erich wouldn't have left. He didn't leave. And Lena didn't either. Even though when the clock chimed eight and she pictured Max's train pulling away from the station, the scaffolding that had been holding her up came crashing down.

When the men from the Stasi realized that Lena had lied and Max was gone, they'd been livid. The new job was off. As they stomped up the stairs to Auntie's floor, Auntie held Lena's hand and said she was proud to have a niece who was so brave. They stormed into the apartment and, despite Auntie's loud protests, took Lena away. Lucky she'd already packed her bag.

And now here she was, imagining Hawaii. Imagining hard, because it was the only way she could keep the wasps from flying into her ears and building a nest right in her head. No, that was not the clatter of a metal door. No, that was not the jingle of keys on a nurse's belt. Those weren't cries, and that wasn't music without words. Lena was in the place so pretty it belonged on top of a cake. The land of icing, where the maps were made of chocolate.

How had Erich survived his time in Hohenschönhausen? What picture in his mind had kept him going? Lena thought about the time she had spent with him every Sunday, the questions he would ask about her *schrullig* world, how he'd brighten whenever her answers made it grow. Those were the happiest times they'd shared.

What if she were to tell her story? Write it down. Not there, in the hospital, but one day, maybe—if she ever got out. She would sit by her window with a small table and a typewriter. She had a story the world needed to hear.

In the meantime, she slept.

*

She slept through 1984 and 1985, even when Mikhail Gorbachev became the General Secretary of the Soviet Communist Party and taught the world two new words: *glasnost* and *perestroika*.

She slept through the Chernobyl nuclear disaster of 1986. West Germans were told not to eat mushrooms and berries, or drink milk, in case of contamination, but the citizens of the Better Germany could eat whatever they liked.

In 1987, Berlin turned 750 years old, and an outdoor concert was held in the West to celebrate. Westerners turned the loudspeakers eastward so people in the Better Germany could hear David Bowie sing—but it didn't wake Lena. Protests occurred on the nights that followed, thousands of people shouting "Gorbi, Gorbi, down with the Wall!" And still, Lena slept.

She slept through the Bruce Springsteen concert in 1988. She slept through 29,000 letters of complaint that were sent to Erich Honecker. The State Council received tens of thousands more, but they didn't wake Lena either.

In June 1989, when the GDR sided with China during the protests in Tiananmen Square, Lena slept. In September, Hungary broke with protocol and allowed citizens of the Better Germany to cross into the West from Hungarian territory. On Republic Day, demonstrators expressing support for Gorbachev were subdued with force. There were anti-government rallies in Leipzig every Monday night. Lena dozed right through them.

Then came the day an East German Politburo member made a big mistake. It was November 9, 1989, and Lena was asleep. A new travel law had been passed. Günter Schabowski announced that

Easterners would henceforth be entitled to proper passports that would allow them to travel to the West whenever they wanted. "When does this take effect?" a journalist asked. Schabowski was unprepared for the question. He'd just come back from vacation. He stammered, glanced down at his notes, didn't know what to say, and answered, "Immediately."

That night Auntie burst into the hospital, shook Lena awake, and exclaimed, "The Wall! The Wall!"

"What?" said Lena. "What about it?"

Auntie took Lena's hands in hers. "The Wall has come down."

Lena's room had not changed in six years. Her roommate still saw strangers in the corners. The pastel landscape still hung above Lena's bed. She wanted to call the nurse to offer Auntie one of her pills. "Who's the crazy one now?"

"No, I'm not crazy." Although her home perm looked ready to spring off her head, and her eyes were huge. "There's no more East and West. No more Lenin and Marx." Karl-Eduard von Schnitzler and his Black Channel were gone. Erich Honecker and his big black glasses: gone. Erich Mielke and his hair tonic: gone. Herr Dreck with his hairy hands and hairy ears and pointed Lenin beard: gone.

The Better Germany had decided to stand on its head, and all the men in charge fell out of its pockets. Lena hoped it would stay upside down long enough for her to enjoy it.

"I'm getting you out of here," Auntie said. "They can't hold you anymore. There's nothing wrong with you, Lena. There has never been anything wrong with you, other than the trauma you suffered at the death of your parents. You're coming home."

That was when Lena started to cry.

from the information I found about the general security measures at headquarters.

Bruno Drechsler is a fictional character. Erich Mielke is not. After the Wall came down, Mielke was arrested and served time in prison for two murders that had occurred in the 1930s. He was never prosecuted for his actions as the head of the Stasi.

Some of the German proverbs in this novel come courtesy of Jack Schmidt's blog *Oh God, My Wife Is German*. The jokes about Erich Shitbucket, East German concrete, and the People's Police all come from Oliver Fritz's excellent memoir *The Iron Curtain Kid*. The excerpt from Erich Honecker's speech to the Eighth Communist Party Conference in April 1971 appeared in *Neues Deutschland* newspaper and was cited in *The Iron Curtain Kid*. Fritz's memoir was also the source for the Enthusiasm in Hand-icrafts award, October Club's song "Tell Me Your Standpoint," the rumor of lentils being used to turn East German chocolate brown, and the bee stamp on students' homework.

The expression "the mark of the Western devil" comes from Mary Fulbrook's nonfiction book *The People's State: East German Society from Hitler to Honecker*. The idea of a wall forming in one's mind originated with Peter Schneider's novel *The Wall Jumper*, although it is used in a different manner there—as a barrier rather than as a form of self-protection.

ACKNOWLEDGMENTS

There are many people I must thank, people without whom this novel would not have been written. Thanks to my two trusted readers and great friends Tanya Bellehumeur-Allatt and Nikki Vogel, who are patient, honest, and enthusiastic, and don't let me get away with anything. To Penny Croucher, author of the blog *Berlin Unwrapped* as well as the guidebooks *Berlin: An English Guide to Known and Unknown Treasures* and *Berlin Unwrapped: The Ultimate Guide to a Unique City.* Not only did she read the manuscript for factual accuracy, she verified the tiniest details and, while in Berlin, double-checked my description of the Stasi's headquarters. Any errors that remain are my own.

To my daughter, Madeleine, who endured long afternoons in Berlin museums while I took copious notes. To my cousin Fritz, who took time out of his busy schedule to draw the illustrations for this book. To my cousin Heide and her husband, Jürgen, for